THE KING OF THE MOUNTAINS
A Treasury of Latin American Folk Stories

THE KING

A Treasury

The Vanguard Press, Inc.

New York

OF THE MOUNTAINS

of Latin American Folk Stories

M. A. JAGENDORF *and* **R. S. BOGGS**

Illustrations by Carybé

Second Printing

Preface

We hope you will like these folk stories about the people living in Mexico, Central America, the lovely islands of the Caribbean, and over the great continent of South America. For this is a good way to come to understand and enjoy the friendship of our New World neighbors and to learn something about them as well. For the way of life of a people, its work and dreams, its hopes and desires, are all reflected in its stories and other folklore. And though history books may tell us about leaders and battles and conquests, it is folk tales and legends that tell us about the history and life of the people.

It was easy to find stories from the many lands of our neighbors to the South; it was difficult to select which ones to put in this book. The young countries of the Americas have stories without end. They have tales not only of the Indians who have lived there for thousands of years but also those of millions of people who, by their own choice and desire, went there in the past few hundred years from other lands, to make their homes in this great world. These people brought stories from their native countries and re-molded the tales to fit the scene of their new homeland.

We went through numberless tales in published collections, and we traveled through all the nations of the New World. We heard stories that have been known for countless years, both in the Latin American countries and from Latin Americans in New York and in Miami, where hundreds of students from these lands come to study. Then we selected those we thought were typical and that would give you an idea of the folk life of our Latin American neighbors.

It was a pleasure and an education for us to hear and read these tales, and we hope it will bring you as much pleasure to read them as it was for us to tell them.

In the notes given at the end of the book, you will find a few comments about the background of these legends and stories and their relations to similar tales from other lands. They show that people are basically the same all over the world and often have the same thoughts, the same desires, the same hopes, no matter what their race, religion, or government may be.

The glossary, which is also at the end of the book, explains how the Spanish, Indian, and Portuguese words are pronounced, and what they mean.

M.A.J. *and* R.S.B.

Contents

THE KING OF THE MOUNTAINS
A Treasury of Latin American Folk Stories

ARGENTINA

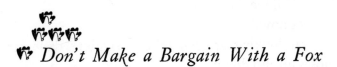

Don't Make a Bargain With a Fox

Sometime back, long ago, two *viscachas*—rodent animals, about the size of a hare—lived together in the brush of the Argentine pampas. They were good friends, and they were always together. One day they were scampering along over the stubble and the grass, smelling this and smelling that, and now and then stopping to do a little gnawing. It was pleasant for them to live on the great pampas of Argentina.

Suddenly they saw two red blotches. They ran up to them carefully—you never can tell what you'll meet on the pampas. They went up to those red blotches and sniffed. They were two pieces of a ragged red blanket someone had left, either forgotten or thrown away.

"This is a valuable treasure," said one.

15

"Some Indian must have forgotten it and left it here. Or maybe he didn't know he dropped it," said the other.

"In any case, we've found it and it's ours," said the first.

"Yes, it's ours. What shall we do with it?"

"Well, I know. Let's use it for a blanket. We can cover ourselves with it when it's cold."

"That's a good idea. But, look, I'm lying on one piece all stretched out, and it's too small."

"Yes, it is too small, but we can sew the two pieces together."

"Yes, we could do that, but where can we find a needle and some thread?"

"That's a thought. I haven't any, and you haven't either."

"What shall we do?"

"I don't know."

They sat looking at each other, wiggling their sharp little noses up and down.

Just then Señor Fox came along. He had a long nose and a long tail, and a keen brain in his head besides.

"*Buenos días*, good day, my good friends," he said. "You look worried. Is anything wrong?"

"Yes!" they both said at once. "We need a needle and some thread to sew together these two pieces of our fine new blanket."

"What will you do with it after you have sewed it?"

"We'll cover ourselves with it on cold nights," they both answered. "It will keep us warm."

"I'll give you a needle and some thread if you'll let me share your fine blanket."

"That we will, just give us the needle and thread."

Señor Fox gave them the needle and thread, and they

went to work. In a short time the two pieces were sewed together.

"You have done a fine piece of work," said Señor Fox. "Now give me back my needle. I'll see you tonight." Then he went away.

The little viscachas ran around and picked up bits of food here and there. Night came, and the cold wind began to blow all over the pampas.

"This is the time of year when our blanket will feel good," they said, and they were very pleased with themselves.

Señor Fox came loping along. "Good evening, my good little friends," he said.

"Good evening, *buenas noches*, Señor Fox."

"It's a cold night, *compadres*."

"Yes, it is a cold night, Señor Fox."

"But *we* won't be cold, *compadres*. You have that fine blanket for which I lent you my needle and thread. If it weren't for me, you wouldn't have a blanket at all, so I have as much right to it as you do."

"Yes, that's true, Señor Fox."

"Now, let's see," Señor Fox said, and scratched his head. "Let's see. I gave you the needle and I gave you the thread, and you used my thread to sew it down the middle, so the middle is really my part."

"That sounds right, Señor Fox."

"Then the right thing is for me to lie under the middle part, which is my part, and for you two to be on the sides, which are your parts."

"That sounds right, Señor Fox."

So Señor Fox lay down on the ground, and the two viscachas put the middle of the blanket over him. Then they lay down, one on each side of him.

Now, you know that Señor Fox is large and wide, so the blanket covered him, but there was little left to cover the two poor viscachas lying on either side. Each one had only one edge of the blanket, which barely reached halfway across his body, leaving the other half out in the cold wind. And that's the way they had to lie, shivering all night long.

So you see that you can never strike a bargain with a fox. He'll get the best of you every time.

The Eternal Wanderer of the Pampas

On the vast pampas of Argentina, the endless plains where it is always summer and the grass is always green, there are thousands, sometimes millions, of grazing cattle. The cattle are herded by Argentine cowboys called "gauchos," who are marvelous horsemen. Their most important tool is the *boleadora,** which they can throw with wonderful skill, just as the North American cowboy can throw his lariat.

These gauchos are fearless and free men, famous in the

---

* The *boleadoras* are three *bolas*, or balls, often of stone, worn smooth and round by the waters of a river, covered with rawhide. Three twisted rawhide thongs are tied together at one end, and at the other end of each thong is one of the balls. The gaucho holds one ball in his hand, swings the other two around and around, then lets them fly through the air, aiming them at an animal or a person, in whose legs they become tangled, hobbling and stopping the creature as effectively as a lariat.

songs and the tales of the land. Some of these stories tell of their strength, some of their adventures, and some of strange happenings among them.

Once there was a gaucho who was a great expert in weaving, for often, while out on the pampas watching his cattle, he would pass the lonely hours at this work. He was famed for the beautiful designs he made, which everyone admired.

But he was a vain fellow and always said that he was the best weaver in all the pampas—the greatest in all Argentina. One day he decided to weave a poncho. Now, you probably know that a poncho is a square or rectangular piece of cloth of varying designs and colors, with a slit in the middle. You put your head through the slit, and the garment covers your shoulders and your body, front and back, serving as a kind of coat.

The gaucho began to weave the poncho. He worked carefully and slowly and wove many colorful designs in it. He was determined to make it the finest in all the land.

The more he worked, the more ambitious he became. Soon he began to neglect his home, his family, and his work. He did not look at his children; he did not see his friends; he left his cattle to shift for themselves. Day and night he sat weaving and weaving that poncho. There was no food for his family; choosing the colors for his poncho was more important. The wind blew through the cracks in his house, but he didn't fix them; the designs of his poncho were much more important. He didn't even go to church or to any fiestas; he just sat weaving all the time and singing to himself. Nothing in life mattered for him except that poncho.

One day one of his friends came to see him.

"Ho there, *amigo!*" he cried, "there are other things in life besides weaving. Rich José is giving a big fiesta and he's 'throwing the doors out the windows.' Everybody is coming and there'll be enough food and drink for a whole army. You're coming, too, aren't you?"

"I'll go if my poncho is finished by then."

"I see there's still a great deal to be done."

"I'll show you that I can finish it in time."

"You're a vain fellow and you boast too much. You'll never finish that poncho for the fiesta. You have only three more days."

"Won't I? I'll show you! I'll be at that fiesta, and I'll be wearing my new poncho."

So he began to weave as fast as fire burns dry grass. He worked day and night. His eyes burned, his fingers were numb, but he kept on. His designs began to be uneven, he lost threads. It didn't matter; he kept on. That poncho would be done in time for the fiesta. It *had* to be!

His fingers worked faster and faster. The garment was almost finished, even though it was crooked and lopsided.

On the afternoon before the fiesta . . . the poncho was finished!

"Now I'll go to the fiesta with my new poncho," the gaucho said.

Without asking his wife or son or daughter to go with him, he got on his horse and set out alone for the fiesta, his new poncho over his shoulders. But it was not a poncho to be proud of. It was beautiful at one end, but ragged at the other.

His horse went like the wind, for the gaucho hadn't ridden it for a long time. It went through brush and grass, hardly touching the ground.

They were going at a great pace, and the gaucho was in high spirits. The poncho was over his shoulders, the finest in Argentina, he thought.

Suddenly a bird touched the horse's eyes and frightened it.

Suddenly a great night bird swooped down from the sky. Its wide wings brushed over the horse's eyes and frightened the animal. It reared up on its hind legs, threw its rider off into the brush, and ran away.

The gaucho lay on the ground stunned, for he had landed on his head. After a while he awoke and looked around him. The brush was full of *things!* Hands with long, crooked claws got hold of him and began tearing at him. The claws dug deep into his flesh. Thick fists pummeled him right and left. Big hands squeezed his body. They molded it into all kinds of shapes, as if he were dough. He hurt all over. The pain was more than a man could stand.

Heavy lead pressed on his shoulders. Down! Down! It was the poncho! He couldn't breathe. It was heavier than tons of rock. He shouted; he roared in pain and fright. But his tormentors kept right on. Now there seemed to be shouting and screaming all around him.

"You let your wife and children starve for that poncho! You neglected your cattle for that poncho! You say you have the finest poncho in Argentina! Look at it! A child could have finished it better than you did! You are vain and proud and conceited! You rushed your work, just so you could go to that fiesta and fill your belly with food and drink! See how it looks! It's ugly! Anybody could have done a better job than that! Because you neglected your wife and children, your friends and your work, to feed your vanity, you will be punished.

"Now you'll ride over the pampas forever, because you were mean and vain. You'll have no rest. You'll be riding and riding forever."

And since then the gaucho, who forgot his home, his wife, his children, his cattle, and his work because he was vain and mean, has remained a lonely figure, riding, always riding, in far-off, desolate places, over the pampas of Argentina.

🦚 *The Girl and the Puma*

This happened long ago, in the early days in Buenos Aires, in Argentina, when it wasn't a city at all but just a little colony. It was the days when the Indians were battling fiercely with the Spaniards to keep from being conquered—in the year 1535 or thereabouts.

When the Spaniards first began to come to South America, some of them started a little colony not far from the Indian villages where Buenos Aires is now. It did not take long before the Indians learned that the white settlers wanted to enslave them, and they rebelled fiercely and attacked the intruders. They wanted them out of the land.

So the Indians surrounded the Spanish settlement and assaulted it day and night. Soon there was no food among the newcomers, for they could not go out to hunt. Behind the tall grasses, behind bushes, behind trees—everywhere —Indians were hidden, armed with arrows and *boleadoras*, the stones covered with rawhide and tied to ropes, with which they could entangle men and animals.

The settlers were starving; they ate anything on which they could lay their hands—leather from their boots, rodents, roots—but soon even these gave out. There were fewer and fewer defenders, and the women had to do the hard work.

The captain of the colony had given orders that no one was to leave the settlement except to hunt for food, and then only with his permission. Anyone who disobeyed these orders would be hanged.

Among the Spanish women there was a lovely young girl, Señorita Maldonado. She was as fearless as she was lovely, and she was very hungry.

"If I stay here, I will die of hunger, as many have died already. If I go out against the captain's orders, I will be hanged, but at least I might find some food and have a good meal before I die. I will go out," she said.

In the afternoon, at siesta time when everyone was resting, she slipped quietly out into the wild land. The grass was high and the straggly trees were full of brush. Wild ostriches rushed by, and other animals and creeping creatures ran over the wild land.

When Maldonado came to a river she crawled along its bank, looking for something to eat—anything to still the gnawing pangs of hunger. Every so often she found bits of old fruit on the ground, and she ate them ravenously. Before she knew, it was twilight.

"Perhaps I'll find some meat left by an animal that I can take back. Then I won't be punished," she thought.

It was growing darker all the time, and she was very tired, tired from hunger and from worry. There were a thousand noises around her. Sometimes "things" ran past her and touched her. She was frightened, and when she came to an opening that seemed to lead into a cave, she crept in.

She hadn't gone far when she saw two green eyes,

gleaming like stars. Then she heard a deep, fierce growling!

"Beloved Mother Mary! It's a puma!" She stopped, frozen with fear.

Her eyes had become used to the darkness and she could see the large catlike puma, which had just given birth to cubs and seemed to be in great pain. Señorita Maldonado's fears were gone. She saw in the eyes of the creature that it was looking for help.

Without thinking, she crept up and began to clean the cubs with her dress. Then she helped the puma while one more cub was born. Animals understand kindness, and the wild creature let Maldonado help her.

From that moment on there was friendship and understanding between the mother puma and the Spanish girl.

Maldonado stayed in the cave with the animals. She played with the little cubs and shared the food the mother puma brought in. Sometimes she went out to look for berries and other fruits.

Once when she went out of the cave to drink some water from the river, a band of Querandí Indians happened to pass and saw her. They quickly captured her and took her to their village.

Maldonado was lovely to look at, and so kindly a person, that the Indians liked her and kept her as one of their own.

Maldonado was content in the Indian village. She had all the food she wanted, the Indians were friendly, and she liked living among them.

One day the Indians went out hunting and the women were left behind. Soon a band of Spaniards of Maldonado's settlement appeared. The Indian women and children fled, but Maldonado did not. The Spaniards were surprised to find her, and took her back to the colony. When the captain of the colony saw the girl, his face was black with anger.

"We thought you were dead. Where have you been?"

"I was hungry, and I went out to find food." Then she told them about the puma and how she had been captured by the Indians.

"You knew my orders," the captain said with a grim face. "That anyone leaving without my permission would be hanged."

"I knew them, but I was hungry. I was dying of hunger."

"You disobeyed orders."

"I was dying of hunger."

"Others were hungry, too, but did not leave. You shall hang for this."

"You are more cruel than the wild animals and the Indians, who were kind to me."

"You disobeyed the orders and you must hang!" the captain growled.

The people were angry and shouted their disapproval.

"I am captain here," the cruel fellow roared. "But I will show you that I, too, can be kind. I won't have her hanged; let her be tied to a tree outside the colony, and let the beasts devour her."

Maldonado was taken out to the wild woods and tied to a tree and left there. The captain's orders were that anyone who went near her or who helped her would be hanged —and the people knew he meant exactly what he said.

The colonists were deeply angered, but no one dared to go near Maldonado, although some wanted to. Days passed, and finally those who had courage said, "She must be dead by now; let us go and see."

So a few of them took heart and went. As they came

near the place where Maldonado had been tied, a large puma suddenly appeared and then quickly disappeared. When the people were close to the tree, they saw that Maldonado was still not only alive, but unharmed.

"You're not dead!" they said in surprise.

"No," she answered. "The puma I helped with her cubs let no animal come near me, and she brought me raw meat to eat."

They untied the girl and took her back to the colony. The people shouted and cried for the captain to be at least as kind to her as a beast had been. They begged so hard that he finally gave in, and Maldonado stayed in the colony for the rest of her life.

This story spread far and wide, through the centuries and down to our day. The people of Argentina like to tell it, even as I have told it to you.*

* The people of the colony soon left, went up the river, and founded the city of Asunción. Some settlers returned to the old colony and refounded Buenos Aires. Across the Río de la Plata (the Plata River in English), in Uruguay, a city was founded named Maldonado, in memory of the lovely señorita.

BAHAMAS

Jack Who Could Do Anything

'Twasn't my time,
'Twasn't your time,
'Twas old folks' time.

There was great trouble in the land. The trouble was a terrible snake that killed everything in its way. The king was dead, and there was nobody to fight that snake.

The queen didn't know what to do, so she called Jack, who was always gettin' folks outa trouble.

"Jack," she said, "kill that snake an' I'll give you lots and lots o' money."

"I want five hundred dollars right now. That'll give me just enough to have a little fun."

The queen quickly gave Jack five hundred dollars, and

Jack went and had a great spree. When it was over, he went to look for the snake.

He walked and walked, and finally, there was the snake. Jack had a big rope in his hand. He tied a slip noose in it.

"Bo' Snake," Jack said, "the foolish people of this island say you can't get in that slip noose."

"They sure is foolish folk," Br'er Snake said. "I kin get in that slip noose any time I want, even right now, this very minute."

Br'er Snake slithered right into the slip noose.

When Jack saw this, he slipped the rope tight, and Br'er Snake was dangling on each side. Br'er Snake couldn't move.

Jack called the soldiers, and they came mighty quick and finished that snake so it couldn't do any harm.

He walked and walked, and finally, there was the snake.

Jack came to the queen. "Queen," he said, "Ah've done mah deed. What's mah reward?"

"Before you get your reward, Jack, you gotta do one more thing."

"An' what's that?"

"You gotta go to the cornfield and kill all the rice birds that's eatin' my corn. If you do that, you kin marry my daughter."

"Sounds good to me," Jack said.

He went to the cornfield with a big, big basket in his hands. The field was full of rice birds eating corn.

"Bo' Rice Birds," said Jack, "just you listen to what these foolish people of this here island say. They say you rice birds can't fill this basket o' mine."

"Can't we? Can't we?" the rice birds screamed. "We'll show 'em!"

They fluttered down and plopped right into that basket tight as fish in a barrel, and Jack closed it so quick none could escape. Then he went to the queen.

"Queen," he said, "here's the rice birds from the cornfield. You do with 'em as you please."

That pleased the queen and she said, "You're a fine fellow. You marry my daughter."

> *E bo ban, my story's en'.*
> *If you don't believe my story's true,*
> *Hax my cap'n an' my crew.*

Smart Working Man, Foolish Boss Man

Once it was a time, a very good time.
De monkey chewed tobacco, an' 'e spit white lime.

There was a man in the Bahama Islands who was a very mean man. He was a farmer man, and he was always thinking of ways to make his laboring men work harder for less pay. If they took a minute's rest after their meals, he was on their back. If they spoke, he'd cry, "Speak less, work more."

Now, there was a very smart fellow in the village where that farmer man lived. One day he said to his brother, "I'll fix that slave driver good and proper. You watch me."

He went to the farmer man and said, "Boss man, I wanna work for you."

"Good," said the farmer man. "You know my workin' men must work good and proper. No idlin', no talkin'. Only workin'."

"Suits me," said the smart fellow.

It was early in the morning, and the farmer man thought he'd get the jump on that working man, so he said, "Had your breakfast?"

"No," the fellow said. In those days working men got their food from their masters.

"I'll give you breakfast. Eat it here. Just eat. There's nobody to talk to." Folks in the Bahama Islands liked to talk while they ate.

He brought coffee and bread and butter, and the working man ate heartily.

Farmer man watched and said to himself, "Hah! now you won't chatter in the field with the other fellows."

Working man was finished and said, "I'm ready for work."

"Had your dinner?" the farmer man asked.

"No, I ain't," the working man said.

"Well, I'm going to give you your dinner. That'll save time o' stopping to eat."

The fellow was pretty full, but he thought he could put in another meal.

Farmer man gave him a piece o' meat and bread and coffee.

Working man ate every bit of it. "All done," he said. "I'm ready for work."

The farmer man closed his eyes for a minute, and then he said with a kinda sly smile, "Had your supper?"

"No, I ain't had supper."

"Have it now, and you can work all day without stopping."

He put before him bread and coffee and greens.

The working man was not a bit hungry, but he remembered that eating gives appetite. He took the first bite and the first sip of coffee. Eating the rest and drinking the coffee was easy till he was all done. He was smiling to himself.

Then the farmer man said, "Now git out and work. You can't waste no time in talkin' an' restin'."

The working man laughed and showed his teeth and said, "No man works after supper. He goes to sleep. I don't work after supper. I go to sleep."

He walked out, and that farmer man, he was so flabbergasted he stood with his mouth open so wide the flies flew in.

E bo ban, my story's en'.
If you don't believe my story's true,
Hax my cap'n an' my crew.

BARBADOS

 The House That Strong Boy Built

Pretty Girl was very pretty. She had black eyes and black, black curly hair and teeth white as pearls.

Pretty Girl lived all alone. She had no father, no mother, no brother, and no sister, and she lived in a hut made of palm leaves deep in the woods of Barbados.

One day she went to the village and saw that her friends had nice wooden houses, so she wanted a wooden house, too.

She wanted and wanted, and worked and worked, and earned money and saved it. Pretty soon she had enough money for a nice wooden house. But she couldn't build a house by herself, and all her friends were too busy to help her.

One sunny morning when the wet on the leaves shone like diamonds, she went through the woods singing loudly.

"Who'll build me a nice house? Who'll build me a nice wooden house?"

Birds listened to Pretty Girl crying for someone to build her a nice wooden house. Ants heard her, and so did butterflies. So did bees and crawling things, but they were all too busy with their own business and had no mind to build a house for Pretty Girl.

A monkey sat high up in a tree scratching his head and looking with beady eyes all around, just doing nothing.

"Who'll build me my nice wooden house? Who'll build me my nice wooden house?"

Pretty Girl kept singing and the monkey listened.

"Pretty Girl, I'll build you your house. I'm a good builder. I built many houses. I'm a fine house builder." Monkey chattered the same words over and over again.

"How much do you want for building my pretty house?"

"Not much, not much. I'll be satisfied with little. Just enough for a good monkey worker. Enough for . . ."

"How much, Mr. Monkey? How much?"

"Fifty pennies a day and enough to feed me well. I have to eat. I eat cooked beans and brown fry-bergs made of fine white flour, good lard, and sweet sugar mixed together and fried deep in lard. And with it I must have good salt fish."

"That's a lot of eating."

"I'll do a lot of building. I'm a fine builder. I build houses and huts, and nobody can build better than I can. Try me, try me and . . ."

"I'll pay you and feed you, but you must build me the nicest wooden house in all Barbados."

"That I will. That I will. That I . . ."

Pretty Girl walked ahead, while Monkey followed. They walked a ways and came to a green clearing with four thick palm trees climbing straight into the sky.

"It's here I want my nice wooden house built," Pretty Girl said.

"You picked a fine place. Plenty of sky, plenty of sun, plenty of coconuts to eat. It's the finest place for a house, your nice wooden house that I'll build right here."

"Less talk and more work. Much talk never brought much food."

"I'm ready, but I'm hungry and I work well when I eat well. Give me beans, give me fry-bergs, and give me salt fish, and I'll be the best worker you ever saw."

"I'll get your food quickly," Pretty Girl said.

She ran to her hut and Monkey followed. She cooked beans, made fry-bergs of flour, sugar, and lard and threw them into the lard to fry, and soon all was ready. But she had no salt fish in her hut.

"I must run to a store and buy nice dry salt fish," Pretty Girl said. "Then, Mr. Monkey, you'll eat your fill and start your work."

She ran to a store and Monkey was alone with the nice brown fry-bergs.

"These fry-bergs smell good. Guess I'll taste one."

He ate one, and there never was a crisper, finer-tasting fry-berg in all Barbados.

"Pretty Girl is a grand cook," he said with his mouth full.

Crunch! Crunch! One after another the crisp fry-bergs were going into Monkey's mouth.

Pretty Girl was in the store buying two pence worth of salt fish.

"Why are you buying so much salt fish? Are you going to have a party?" the storeman asked.

"I must feed Monkey so he will build me my nice wooden house."

"Don't trust Mr. Monkey with anything. You'd better watch him closely."

"I will," Pretty Girl said, and she ran home quickly on her strong bare feet.

Monkey heard her running from afar and hadn't yet finished all the fry-bergs.

"I can't leave any behind," chattered Mr. Monkey. "These are far too good for anyone but me to eat. I'll hide the rest under my hat. Pretty Girl will never find them there."

He put the rest of the fry-bergs under his hat.

When Pretty Girl came in, she quickly saw that all the crisp fry-bergs were gone.

"Where did those fry-bergs go to, Mr. Monkey?" she said, looking straight into his beady eyes.

"The Cat came and ate them, Miss Pretty Girl."

Pretty Girl looked at Monkey's face, saw drips of lard running down alongside his ears. She had her suspicions and remembered what the storeman had said.

"You sure, Mr. Monkey, that Miss Cat ate the fry-bergs? You sure? I got heaps of salt fish for you, but all the fry-bergs I cooked are gone. Are you sure Miss Cat ate them?"

"I saw Miss Cat licking her chops, and you know what that means, Miss Pretty Girl."

Pretty Girl didn't believe a word Monkey said. There was lard running down both sides of his hairy face from under his hat.

"Take your hat from your head, Mr. Monkey. It's a mighty hot day."

"I can't do that, Pretty Girl. I might catch a death of a cold."

"Folks don't catch colds on hot summer days."

"Monkeys are different from other folks."

"You sure are different from honest folk." She looked sideways at Monkey's head and saw the lard still dripping from both sides along his ears.

"Take your hat off like a gentleman before you sit down to eat."

"You want me to die from the cold?"

Pretty Girl kept herself busy around the table and walked up and down with her elbows out, coming nearer and nearer to Monkey where he was sitting on a stump waiting for his salt fish. Then, when she got close to him, she raised her elbows higher, and bang! Monkey's hat was off his head, and heaps of fry-bergs fell from under it.

"Miss Cat must have hidden those fry-bergs under your hat, Mr. Monkey," Pretty Girl said mockingly.

"I . . . I . . ."

"You lie and you steal, Mr. Monkey, and you aren't a man fit to build *my* house."

"No, I'm not going to build your house for you. You're too smart for me," Monkey cried. "You build your own house."

Monkey leaped away as fast as his skinny legs would carry him. Pretty Girl sat down on the grass full of weepy feelings.

"Now I won't have a nice wooden house like my friends who live in the village. I must live in a twig hut in the woods," she cried.

Pretty Strong Boy passed by. "Pretty Girl, Pretty Girl, why are you crying?"

"I'm crying because I have no nice wooden house like my friends in the village. Mr. Monkey said he'd build it for me, but he only cheated me, and now I have nobody to build my house."

There were big tears in her black eyes.

"Don't you cry, Pretty Girl," the Big Strong Boy said. "Don't you cry. I'll build you your wooden house. It will be a house for two. Yes, there'll be plenty of room for two. For you and for me."

Pretty Girl looked up at Big Strong Boy with a laugh in his eyes. Then she got up and said: "That's fine. You'll build a nice wooden house for two—for you and for me!"

"That I will indeed, Pretty Girl."

Big Strong Boy built a fine wooden house for two in the village. Then he married Pretty Girl, and they lived in that house all their lives.

BOLIVIA

The King of the Mountains

The sun, all gold in the sky, and the condor,* the great and strong bird of the high mountains, are worshiped and loved in many parts of Andean South America. Beautiful temples were built to the sun, and large monuments were erected with the condor as the symbol of the land.

There are many stories about both the bird and the sun everywhere in that vast land, and here is one from Bolivia.

This happened long, long ago, soon after the earth first came into being. The birds in Bolivia wanted to have a king. But who would be king? There was so much chat-

* The condor is one of the largest birds in existence. With its wings open in flight, it measures from nine to ten feet. It is also one of the most graceful birds when flying and can go for nearly half an hour without moving its wings—just sailing beautifully through the air. The bird with jet-black feathers, save for a white frill around the base of the neck, inhabits the high mountains of the Andes.

tering and arguing among them about this that the leaves got tired of listening. There was screaming and whistling and singing without end. Every bird wanted to be king.

Finally one wise old bird said, "Let Pachacámac, the great king of the earth, decide; or, better yet, let the one who comes nearest the sun, where Pachacámac has his golden palace, be king of the birds."

This made sense to all the birds, and they agreed, for no one was wiser than Pachacámac. The birds screamed their desire to Pachacámac, and the king of the earth spoke: "Yes, let the bird who flies highest and who comes nearest the sun and my palace be king. The bird who does this will have to be very brave."

Then, at a given signal, all the birds rose into the sky. They were like a great cloud of many colors, and there were so many of them that the sun could not be seen.

Up and up they went, streaking and circling about. Soon some dropped down. Others rose higher and higher. Then more dropped down.

The higher they went, the fewer there were. These few circled still higher. And still more dropped down until there were only three left in the great blue heaven with the gleaming sun. They were the eagle, the hawk, and the condor. Just these three, circling slowly, rising and rising, getting nearer and nearer to the sun.

Up they went, while all the birds below watched in silence. All the animals were watching, too, for it was a sight worth seeing, those three—the fearless eagle, the keen hawk, and the majestic condor—winging their way silently upward.

Soon those watching below saw one of the three becoming larger and larger, and the other two becoming smaller and smaller. It was the hawk who was coming down, while the eagle and condor kept going up.

"I am beaten by those who are stronger and more fearless than I. The heat was too strong for me," said the hawk.

The birds did not hear. They were watching the two left circling and soaring, soaring and circling, rising higher and higher. The birds and the animals on earth watched silently. Which one would win?

Sometimes the eagle looked at the condor; sometimes the condor looked at the eagle. The eagle looked more often. He was feeling hotter and hotter. His skin was burning dry, his eyes were burning hot. He had to shut them; he could no longer stand the golden fire of the sun, and he began to drop. The condor saw him falling. All the birds and the animals saw him coming down. A great stream of pride surged through the condor's body, and he did not feel the heat at all. He had won!

"I must get nearer the sun!" he cried. So he kept circling, circling, closer and closer to the great, shining sun. The feathers on his head were burned. He kept rising, rising, slowly. The feathers on his neck were burned. It was hard for him to breathe the fiery air, but he kept on rising! His eyes became red as fire! Still, he kept them open and kept on rising.

"I must rise to the sun! It matters not what pain I may feel."

Then, suddenly, there was a cool, sweet wind coming from the yellow, gleaming brightness. There was the Golden City of the Sun. And there, in the center, was Pachacámac, the father of all, sitting on his golden throne.

"Hail, great Mallcu, Condor, bird of the sun! Only you had the courage to come so high."

The condor was speechless before all that glory.

"No bird has ever come so close to my City of the Sun. For this you deserve to be king of the birds. You are the king, strong and fearless. Only the strong and fearless can stand the light of the sun that wounds the sight and burns the eyes. You are like me, so I shall take your form when I visit the earth or fly through the air. I am the great king of all that is on the earth, and you will be the great king of all the flying birds. My home is the City of the Sun. Yours will be the highest mountains that are nearest to the sun. Your palace of snow and ice will gleam like my palace of gold. And when you leave the earth, you will come here to me."

Since that time the people of Bolivia know, just as the birds know, that the condor is not only king of all the birds, but that he is sometimes even Pachacámac, king of the earth, flying in the form of the condor; and when they see Mallcu, the condor, they look upon him with love, respect, and worship.

To this day wonderful monuments are still built in Bolivia with the condor on top, wings spread wide, as if it were flying to the sun.

Greed in Heaven, Growth on Earth

This is a story they tell in Bolivia.

In the olden days animals had small mouths, and they always had to look for food on the earth. And there was not too much of it. But the birds were the lucky ones. They could fly up in the trees, and even higher, high up in the sky. And there they had all the food they wanted.

Now, *Tío* Antonio, as they called Señor Fox then, had a very small mouth, but with it he could say big, bad words. And he was always hungry. One day he was trotting along, when whom should he meet but Mallcu, the condor, king of the birds.

"Good day to you, great lord Mallcu," said *Tío* Antonio, bowing low.

"A good day to you, *Tío* Antonio," said the condor.

"Ah! You are truly the lord of the heavens, for you and your fellow birds can eat the finest food in the world, away up high in the sky. We poor foxes are forever scraping around for bits of meat and bones to eat, no matter how old and bad they are. How I'd like just once to go to one of those feasts of yours, high up in the sky. If only you'd invite me to go with you! Just once!"

"Would you really like to eat with us birds?"

"I'd like to do that more than anything else in this world. It would be the joy of a lifetime."

Mallcu raised his head high and said, "I'll take you to one of our feasts, but you must promise me one thing."

"I'll promise you anything!" cried the fox.

"Promise me you'll behave properly and show that you know how to eat correctly among good people. Don't gnaw at the bones and don't throw bones under the table."

"I promise! I promise!" cried *Tío* Antonio very excitedly. "Just take me once, and you'll see."

Then Mallcu the condor picked up *Tío* Antonio the fox lightly in his claws and flew high up in the heavens. He flew up and up until they came to a large white cloud. There Mallcu set down *Tío* Antonio, who looked around with great curiosity. There was a great big table, and on it was every kind of good food. Not a thing was missing. There was corn; there was *quinoa;* there was even *coca.* Every kind of fruit pleasing to the taste was there.

All kinds of birds were standing around. Then everybody sat down, and each one ate whatever he liked and as much as he liked. When everyone was satisfied, the birds got up, brushed their feathers, said good-by to one another and flew away.

Tío Antonio had eaten so much he was about to burst, but he wanted still more. The more he ate, the more he wanted, so he just kept on eating and eating. Even after everyone else had gone and he was the only one left at the table, he still stayed on, eating more and more.

When he saw that he was all alone and no one was watching, he tore wildly into the food, gnawing and crunching the bones the others had left, as if he hadn't eaten for months. It wasn't a pretty sight to see.

Mallcu wondered where Señor Fox was, and he became suspicious. He flew back to the table and saw the ugly sight. He saw *Tío* Antonio doing just exactly what he'd promised not to do.

Mallcu was very angry and said, "You've broken your promise, as you always do. You're cheating, as you always do. I'll punish you for this. You can just stay here. I won't take you back to earth. See how you like it away up here high in the sky!" Then he shook his wings angrily and flew away.

Tío Antonio never opened his mouth, he was so scared. When the great bird was out of sight, he looked around him. He ran to the edge of the cloud and looked down. The earth was far, far away, and it made him dizzy just to look down. He ran over to the other edge of the cloud and looked down there. It made him even dizzier and more frightened. The good earth was so far away! No, he could never jump that far! If he tried, he'd be smashed to pieces. He was crying and sweating with fear.

"How can I get down to earth?" he howled. "How can I get back down there? I can't jump. If I try, I'll break my neck. I'll break all the bones in my body!"

Some small birds called *papachiuchis* flew past, and they heard Señor Fox crying and shouting. They felt sorry for him.

"*Tío* Antonio," they called, "we'll help you get back to earth without breaking your neck. Stop crying and wait until we come back."

Then they flew away. *Tío* Antonio was silent. After a little while the birds came back with a long rope made of the *cortadera* plant. They tied the rope to the cloud.

"Now you can slide down on that rope," they said, and flew away.

Señor Fox began to slide down. It was not easy, and he had to rest often as his paws became sore and raw.

A large flock of parrots flew past. Now, you know Señor Fox. He is a sly fellow and always likes to make fun of others, so he cried, "Oh, you sillies! You're always dropping things where you shouldn't. You always screech foolishly!"

This made the parrots angry. They screamed at him and turned back. "Red tail! Long snout! We'll teach you a lesson. We'll cut that rope and watch you tumbling, tumbling down. Then, crack! and that will be the end of you!"

Señor Fox was frightened. "Oh, please, good birds, don't do that. I was only joking. Really I was. Please forgive me! I'll never do it again."

"Well," said the parrots, "this time we'll forgive you." And they turned around and began to fly away.

Tío Antonio now felt safe, so he opened his silly mouth again. "Dirty feathers! Screeching sillies!" he cried.

Señor Fox began to fall. "Help! Help!" he screamed.

The parrots turned back. "This time we shall really punish you!" they screamed.

"Oh, no! Please!" cried Señor Fox. "I didn't mean what I said. I meant to call you Beautiful Feathers. No bird has more beautiful feathers than you have. They are like rainbows."

Again the parrots forgave him and flew off. No sooner were they at a distance than that stupid, mean fox began his mischief again. "Silly, chattering, longbeaks! Screeching hoddy-doddies!" he cried.

The parrots were now wild with anger. They flew back, screaming, "So that's what we are! We'll show you a thing or two!" They began hacking away at the rope with their sharp beaks and it tore quickly.

Tío Antonio screamed that he meant no harm, but this time it did him no good. He began to fall. Down, down, down!

"Help! *Socorro!* Help!" he screamed. "Hold a blanket!"

But no one heard him. Even if someone had, it wouldn't have done any good, for Señor Fox was known to be a great liar.

"Help! *Socorro!* Help! he screamed. But he kept on falling. Down, down, down! Then, plop! he was on the earth, splattering into pieces like an overripe orange. Everything he had eaten splattered all over the ground—the corn, the *quinoa*, everything scattered all over the earth.

These things became seeds, and grains and fruits began to grow on the earth—and the Indians have been eating them ever since.

The Hero in the Village

The Spaniards say that the Aymara Indians of Bolivia are a cruel and suspicious people and that they are hard to live with. The truth is that the Indians love their freedom and don't want anyone to take it away from them. So they are unfriendly and always on the watch not to be deceived and not to be downtrodden. That's why the white people say it is more difficult to make friends with them than with any other people in the Andes Mountains.

One of these Indians had a burro, and I can tell you that burro had to work. It had to drag wood and carry people and heavy loads all the time. It worked from the time the sun rose until the time it set behind the mountains.

When its work was done, it was tied up and given a little food to eat. Not much, just enough to keep it alive. Just the same, it looked sleek and full. And do you know why? I'll tell you.

Nearby there lived a band of foxes. Every night they came to the gardens of the Indians and ate the crops they had planted. When they saw the burro tied to a tree, they would untie it and let it eat with them.

In the morning, its master would come out and find his

burro untied and the crops eaten. Then he'd beat the burro mighty hard with a stick.

Of course, the burro did not like this. He ate enough, and that was good; but then he was beaten, and that was bad. Since he was beaten in the morning before going to work, he'd remember the beating all through the long day. This went on for a long time: the burro felt fine at night and miserable during the day.

"I must do something about this," said the burro. "But what can I do?"

One day an idea came to him. "I'll play dead, and my master will have to work instead of me. That will teach him a lesson."

Early the next morning, after eating breakfast, the burro lay down on the ground, stretched out legs stiffly and closed his eyes. The foxes were still roaming around eating. They saw the burro and thought he was dead.

"Here is something good for us," they cried. "This dead burro will make fine *charque*."

They began to pull the burro to their den. But the burro was big and heavy, and the foxes were smaller and weaker. They didn't get far, and the sun was coming up.

"Let's tie him to our tails," said one old fox. "Then all of us together can pull him."

The others agreed, and so the old fox tied the burro to the tails of the young foxes, and they began to pull. They pulled a little and then stopped to rest. Then they pulled a little more and stopped to rest again. Every time they stopped, they smacked their lips, thinking of the fine supply of dried meat they would have.

While they were pulling, the burro was thinking. Suddenly he jumped up and began dragging the foxes back to the village.

"Where are you dragging us?" the foxes howled.

"You'll see. I'll show you." And the burro kept on dragging them while the foxes kept on howling. Finally they got to the village, before the Indian chief.

"So it's you foxes who have been stealing our crops!" the Indians shouted. "You thieves! You robbers!"

The Indians beat the foxes until they lay still and did not move.

From that time on the burro was treated like a warrior and a hero in the village, and everybody showed him the greatest respect and consideration.

BRAZIL

So Say the Little Monkeys

In the great, giant country of Brazil there are many mighty rivers. The largest of all is the Amazon, and the next in size is the Rio Negro—the Black River—so called because its wide, flowing waters look black as coal.

Along the Rio Negro live little monkeys that the Indians call "blackmouths" because their mouths are as black as the waters of the river.

Blackmouths live in the tall, waving palms, full of sharp thorns. But these monkeys are silly creatures and stay in the thorny trees, even though the thorns stick them all over. They even sleep there, huddled together, with the thorns digging into their flesh.

At night, when the rains pour down thick as grass mats

and the wind blows with biting cold, young blackmouths, and father and mother blackmouths, wet and shivering, screech and whine and grimace. They are hungry and frightened, for there are many fears in the thick jungle forests along the Rio Negro.

A father monkey chatters, "T . . . t . . . tomorrow I'll build a house so we'll be protected against the cold and wind and rain. W . . . w . . . we'll p . . . p . . . put food in the house, and we'll have something to eat when we're hungry."

Another father monkey, hearing this, answers, "Y . . . y . . . yes! T . . . t . . . tomorrow I'll build a house, too, to protect me and my family against the rain and the cold. I'll have food *too*, so I'll not be h . . . h . . . hungry, as I am now."

Other father monkeys chatter the same words.

And the mothers and children of the blackmouths hear what the fathers say and are glad to know that there will be no more misery at night.

Then morning comes, and they are all happy. For the rain is no longer falling and the wind is hiding in the leaves. The sun comes out and brightens the sky and brings warmth, and the blackmouths, young and old, screech and chatter with joy. They leap and swing among the trees, looking for fruit to eat. When they find some, they eat and jabber shrilly without end. Other monkeys, wild parrots and parakeets, join in the screaming prattle-babble, and the air along the Rio Negro is a thick jungle of noises.

Then a blackmouth mother remembers the words spoken by a blackmouth father the night before, and she screeches, "Let us build the house! You said we'd build a house!"

Other blackmouth monkey mothers and their children

also cry, "Yes, let's build a house! Let's build a house!"

"First let's eat some more fruit. Then we'll build a house," some blackmouth fathers say.

"Yes, let's eat some more. Then we'll build a house," other blackmouth fathers say.

So they eat and eat all morning, while the sun is shining brightly. In the afternoon it is still nice and warm, so they eat some more. Leaping from tree to tree, screeching, chattering, and eating, eating all the time, they think of nothing else until the sun goes down and the jungle forest is again in pitch-black darkness. Then the cold and rain and fear spread over the black forests, and the blackmouth monkeys huddle close together again on the thorny Janarí trees, shivering and frightened. Now they remember what they said the previous night about building houses.

"We must build a house! We must build a house!" the shivering blackmouth mothers chatter. "We must build a house to protect us from the cold, the wind, and the rain. We must build a house where we can keep our food."

Then shivering blackmouth fathers chatter, "Yes, we must build a house! We must build a house!"

But do you think a blackmouth monkey ever builds a house? Never! The next morning they do the same thing they did the day before. They leap from tree to tree, screaming, chattering, and looking for food.

Sometimes mother blackmouths remind father blackmouths of what they said about houses the night before. Then father blackmouths chatter, "Let's eat some more right now. We'll build houses later, *amanhã*—tomorrow."

So, day after day, they keep putting off the building of houses, always saying, "*Amanhã, amanhã!*" But, of course, *amanhã* never comes.

Some people do the same thing; they act just like blackmouth monkeys. And when someone in the great Brazilian tropical forest lands says, *"Amanhã,"* the Indians say, "So say the little monkeys!"

🦅 *Clever Little Turtle*

Along the great Amazon River in Brazil, the Indians tell this tale, and those who listen to it laugh. Now I'll tell it to you.

In the endless wild jungle forest, where ants, animals, and butterflies make their world, Turtle sat in her little house playing her flute. Her song was as sweet as that of any of the birds. *Fing-filoo-fong, fing-filong-fong, fing-filing-foo!* Everyone heard it, over and over again, with its high notes and low notes and middle notes. It was a fine song. Turtle liked it. So did the white herons and the egrets and the snakes and the monkeys. Everybody liked it.

An Indian going by on his way home heard it. He stopped and listened, but not to Turtle's music. He was listening to the tune of hunger in his stomach.

"That turtle will make a fine meal. I'll catch it, take it home, and cook it. Its good meat will make my stomach keep quiet."

He went to the door of Turtle's house and shouted, "Turtle! Ho, there, Turtle! Come out! I want to see the flute on which you're playing such fine music."

Turtle's music stopped and Turtle just grunted, "Uh-hoo . . . crrr."

The Indian waited a little while, and when Turtle did not come out he said again, "Come out, Turtle! Come out so I can see you and your flute that plays such nice music."

Crunch, crunch, crunch . . . Turtle came walking toward the door of her house, and soon she appeared at the opening with her flute.

"Here I am. Here I am. You didn't have to shout so loudly. I heard you. Here is my flute for you to see."

She put out her flute for the Indian to see, but he grabbed Turtle by the neck and began to run through the woods to his hut. *Pit-i-pat, pit-i-pat, pit-i-pat.*

Turtle tried to cry out, but couldn't make a sound, so she closed her eyes and held her flute close to her side.

When the Indian reached his hut with Turtle, his wife and children came out to meet him.

"Here I have Turtle!" he cried. "We'll cook her tomorrow and have a fine feast."

He put Turtle in a cage made of small branches, closed the lid, and put a heavy piece of wood on top. Then the Indian and his wife and children ate and went to sleep.

Next morning they were up early, and the father said to his children, "I'm going to hoe and plant. When the sun begins to go down, I'll come back and we'll cook Turtle. Whatever you do, don't let Turtle out of that cage." And away he went, with his wooden hoe over his shoulder.

The children played near the hut and shouted to the birds and monkeys. Turtle was inside the cage, thinking deeply about what the Indian had said. Then she took her flute and began to play her sweet song: *Fing-filoo-fong, fing-filong-fong, fing-filing-foo.* The children listened and liked the song. They ran to the cage.

"Turtle! Is that you playing?"

"Yes. I'm playing my flute. Listen! *Fing-filoo-fong, fing-filong-fong, fing-filing-foo.*" She kept playing while the children listened. Then she stopped and said, "I can dance as well as I can play."

"Can you really dance?" the children asked.

"I can play and dance at the same time. Would you like to see that?"

"Yes, we'd love to!"

"It's easy. Just open this cage, and I'll show you how I dance and play at the same time. Just open the lid and watch me."

The children took the log off the lid, and Turtle began to dance and play: *Fing-filoo-fong, fing-filong-fong, fing-filing-foo. Thump-crush, thump-crush, thump-crush.* It was a funny sight to see, and the children laughed and laughed.

"Would you like to see me dance and play again?"

"Yes! Do it again!" the children cried.

"Well, then, you must take me out. It's not easy to dance in this little box. My legs are stiff. Just take me out and let me take a little walk to stretch my legs. Then I'll be right back to dance and play for you again."

"We'll let you out because you played and danced so well," said the children, laughing. "But come back quickly. Don't run away."

"You wait right here for me until I come back."

The children took Turtle out of the cage and set her on the ground. Turtle crawled around and around until she got close to the jungle forest. Then she quickly crawled under ferns, leaves, and monkey ropes into the wild jungle, and disappeared. She crept along until she got back to her house, crawled inside and went to sleep.

The children waited and waited. Then they ran into woods, calling and shouting, "Turtle! Turtle!" But there was no answer. They looked everywhere, but they couldn't find her. Again and again they called, but the only answer was the screeching of birds and the chattering of monkeys. The children were scared.

"What will we tell our father? He told us not to let Turtle out; he'll be angry and punish us."

They sat down on the ground. No one said a word. Finally one said, "Let's take a stone and paint it to look like a turtle and put it in the cage. Our father will think it's Turtle, and maybe he won't be angry with us." And that is what they did.

In the evening their father came home and said, "Now I'll put water on the fire, and when it steams we'll put Turtle in and cook her. And when she's well cooked, we'll take off her shell and eat the tender meat."

The children were silent. Soon the water was boiling, and the father put in the painted stone. Then he said, "Now bring the earthen plate, so we can eat."

The children were frightened, but what could they do? They brought in the plate. The father took out the painted stone and threw it on the plate, which broke into many pieces.

The father turned to the silent children. He looked at them for a few moments. Then he said, "You let Turtle run away!"

"Yes," said the children, "we did. We shouldn't have done it. We did wrong."

The father was not angry. He said, "I'll go and see if I can catch Turtle again. But this time, don't you let her run away."

"We won't!" the children cried.

The father went out in the jungle and cried, "Turtle! Turtle! Where are you?"

Again and again he cried, calling to Turtle, but Turtle

did not answer. She was hidden deep down in her house.

The father got tired and went back to his hut. "I'll catch Turtle tomorrow," he said.

Did tomorrow ever come? What do you think?

🏴 *The Boy Who Was Lost*

One day a boy and his mother went out to their little garden. The mother put her basket on a tree stump and began to dig for roots, which are called by many names, such as mandioca, yucca, or cassava. They are all very good to eat. Meanwhile the boy was shooting at birds that were flying about.

Soon he saw a bird, a *bacurau*, flying from tree to tree. When it sat on a branch some distance from him, the boy put an arrow on his bow and shot. But he did not hit the bird, and it flew off and sat on another branch. The boy ran nearer and shot again. But again he missed.

Once more the bird flew off and came to rest on another branch. Once more the boy shot at it and missed. The bird kept flying deeper and deeper into the forest, and the boy kept running after it and shooting at it, missing every time. They got farther and farther away from the garden, and then . . . the bird was gone!

The boy looked around everywhere and couldn't find it,

nor could he find his way back to his mother. He was now far away from her and the garden, and as he had followed the bird from one tree to another, he hadn't noticed which way he went.

"I must get back," he cried, and began to run. But the more he ran, the more lost he became. Finally he reached a wide stream. "I never saw this stream before. There is no such stream near us. My home must be on the other side. It's all the fault of that bacurau bird."

He walked along the river bank but found no place he could cross—no log, no shallows or rocks. He was getting tired and night had come, so he lay down and went to sleep.

Next morning he walked beside the stream again, trying to find a path or someplace to cross. But there was none. He ate some wild fruit and kept trying to find his way all day long. But he had no luck.

Again night came and he went to sleep. The next day he kept on looking, but it was the same. This continued for a few days, and he became very tired and miserable. One day he heard a woodpecker hammering on a tree and screaming.

Said the boy: "If only I could fly like a woodpecker, I'd soon be over that stream and on my way on the other side."

The woodpecker kept up its noisemaking.

"If only that woodpecker were as big as a man, I'd ask him to take me across the stream," said the boy aloud.

The woodpecker flew up and sat down in front of the boy. "What did you say?" it asked.

"I said, if you were as big as a man, I'd ask you to fly me across that stream. I've lost my way."

"Very well," said the woodpecker, and it began to grow bigger and bigger until it was the size of a giant. "Get on my back and I'll carry you across the stream."

The boy got up on the bird's back, and it began to fly. Now, you know the way these birds fly: they skim along close to the earth, and then suddenly they shoot up into the air. When the bird did that, the boy was frightened.

"Let me down!" he cried. "I don't want to fly across."

So the bird dropped him back where he'd found him and flew away. There the boy was again, right where he had been before.

He sat down, not knowing what to do next. He stared at the running water. A big alligator came up slowly, swishing its tail.

"If only that alligator would carry me across the stream!" sighed the boy aloud.

The alligator came up to him and said, "What do you want?"

"I want to cross the stream. I'm lost, but I think my home is on the other side."

"Come, get on my back, and I'll carry you across."

The boy mounted on the back of the alligator, and it began to swim. But when it reached the middle of the stream it said, "You always call me bad names. Call me bad names now."

The boy was quiet. He knew if he did that, the alligator would eat him. He said nothing, and the alligator kept on swimming until it came close to the other shore. But the boy was still afraid, so he jumped off, leaping to the shore, and began to run.

The alligator, who wanted to eat the boy, ran after him, but the boy was far ahead. Soon he came to a lagoon where a heron was standing, looking for fish.

"Why are you running?" the heron asked.

"I'm running from the alligator. It wants to eat me, and is coming right behind me."

"Jump into my fishnet—I mean, my crop—and I'll hide

you there." The heron spat four fish out of his crop, and the boy jumped into it. Then the heron caught up the four fish into his crop again and they lay over the boy, hiding him.

Just then the alligator came rushing up. "Did you see a boy running this way?" it asked the heron.

"No, I didn't."

"You did. His footprints are right here. You swallowed him. Let me see what's in your crop."

"I have only fish in my crop," said the heron, and opened his beak and spat out the four fish.

The alligator looked at the fish and was satisfied, so he went back to the stream.

When the alligator had gone, the heron let the boy out. The boy thanked the heron for its help and went on his way. After a while he came to a broad road.

"That must be the road to my village," he cried. But it was the road over which the Wild Pig people traveled.

He walked and walked until he came to a house where a family of Wild Pigs lived. It was a strange sight. They had thrown off their skins and looked just like human beings.

"Where do you come from? Where are you going?" asked the Wild Pig people.

"I'm looking for my home. I've lost my way and I can't find the river bank.

"If you can't find your home and your people, why don't you stay with us?"

"I'm tired of wandering around, and I don't think I will ever find my home, so I think I will stay with you."

"Here's a Wild Pig skin," said the head of the Wild Pig people. "Put it on just as we do and you'll be a Wild Pig, too. You can hunt with us and live well."

And that's exactly what the boy did. He put on the

"You can stay with us," said the head of the Pig People.

skin and hunted with the Wild Pig people. He liked the life, and he stayed there a long, long time.

One day the Wild Pig people decided to go to look for a garden where they could find potatoes and manioc roots. Next morning they took their baskets and started out. Soon they came to a good garden.

They started to dig for roots, but the boy went off to look around. Somehow he felt that he knew this place. When he saw a tree stump he was sure he recognized it.

"I think this is the stump on which my mother put her basket the day I ran after that bacurau bird and got lost."

He took off his Wild Pig skin. The others did not see him, they were so busy filling their baskets and getting ready to leave. Then they left and never noticed that the boy was not with them. He stood hiding behind a tree.

Soon he saw his mother coming. When she put her basket on the tree stump, as she always did, he came out from behind the tree and she recognized him at once. She began to cry for joy and started to put her arms around him.

He said, "Mother, don't put your arms around me. Just stand where you are."

"Then come home with me, so I can give you something to eat—you must be hungry," she said.

"You go first and I'll follow," he said.

So she went and he followed. The whole family welcomed him home. They were glad to see him and he was glad to see them. But he always kept at a distance from everybody.

He slept by himself in a corner and sang the song of his adventure and the songs he had learned from the Wild Pig people. He couldn't forget their ways. He couldn't forget them all his life.

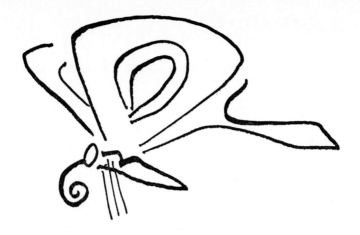

CHILE

Lion and Man

Old Lion and his son, Young Lion, lived high up in the Chilean Andes of Nancagua, where no one could find them. They had been there for a long, long time and had never gone far from their home.

One day Young Lion said, "Sire [such was the title of respect used by all young men when addressing their fathers in Chile], is there anyone or anything braver or stronger than you or I?"

"Yes, son, there is one who is not an animal, who is stronger and more cunning than I am or you are. He is Man. It is because of him that I live in this far-off place. He can't come here, and we are safe. Once I was king of all the land, but I am no longer. He is king now."

65

"I don't believe that," Young Lion growled. "I just can't believe there is anyone stronger than we are, and I won't believe it until I see it for myself. I want to see Man. I'll fight him, and we'll see who is the stronger."

"Son, don't fight Man. He is so cunning that he doesn't need strength."

Young Lion thought about this. Then he went back to his father again and said, "Sire, I want to see Man. I want to see if he is braver than you or I."

"Son, you'll only be sorry, and you may come to harm."

"I want to see the one who is braver than I am."

"What a pity the young will not learn from the experience of the old," moaned Old Lion.

"Father, give me your blessing, for I am determined to find Man."

Old Lion gave his blessing to his son, and then lay down on the ground. He was very tired, and he knew his life was coming to an end. Soon he died.

Young Lion sharpened his claws on the rocks. Then, with his head high in the air and his mane flying in the wind, he set out to find Man. He walked and he walked. He saw Horse eating grass and swishing his tail.

"Are you Man?" Young Lion growled.

"No, I am not Man."

"Where is Man? Who is Man? Is he braver and more fearless than I, Young Lion?"

"Man lives far down in the valley. He is dangerous and strong and, above all, he is cunning. He made a slave of me, and though I am stronger than he is, now I must do everything he says. He makes me work without end. He gets on me whenever he wants to, and if I don't go where he says, he digs iron spurs into me. See, here are my wounds." And he showed the wounds in his sides.

Young Lion looked. Then he said, "You are a fool and

a coward. Man couldn't do that to me. I want to see him and tell him so."

He walked on and on until he met Ox, grazing and swishing his tail.

"Are you Man?" he roared.

"No, I am not Man," said Ox, shivering with fear.

"Where is Man? I want to see him. Do you know him? Is he brave? Is he really strong?"

"That he is, many times over. I am big and he is little, but he can put on my neck a wooden yoke as heavy as a big rock, and I have to pull a cart and Man, too. Sometimes I even pull his whole family."

"You are a fool!" roared Young Lion. "I must see Man. I don't believe it."

"Walk on down into the valley. Man is there."

Young Lion walked on and on, down into the valley. He met Dog, lying in the sun, blinking his eyes.

"Are you Man?" he roared.

"No, I am not Man," barked Dog, jumping up.

"I want to see Man," roared Young Lion.

"You really want to see him?" barked Dog.

"I do, and quickly."

"I can arrange that easily."

"Do you know Man so well?"

"I do, indeed. He is my master. I obey everything he orders me to do, and I love him."

"That sounds strange. You do everything he tells you to do, and you love him?"

"I do."

"I must see Man. Arrange it at once."

"You just wait here," said Dog. "He will come soon."

Dog ran off and found his master working in a field.

"Master!" he barked. "Young Lion wants to see you. Get your gun. I'll bring him here."

Dog ran off and came to Young Lion. "Come," he said, "my master is waiting for you in the field."

Young Lion followed Dog, and they came to the field where Man was working. Young Lion walked right up to him.

"Are you Man?" roared Young Lion. "They say you are braver than I am. I'd like to see that."

Man smiled and said, "I don't know if I am braver than you are. People say what they think."

"Let me see if you are brave. Let me see if you are strong. Battle with me!"

"I have no reason to fight with you. If you call me bad names, then I will become angry and fight with you."

"Good!" roared Young Lion. "You are an unclean thing. You are a bandit, a slave driver, a beater of helpless animals. You are a thief! You are a so-and-so and so-and-so! Show me your courage and your bravery!"

Then Young Lion stopped. He couldn't think of anything else to call Man.

Then Man said, "Now you have insulted me properly, and I am angry. Now I'll insult you, and we'll both be angry and ready to fight. You used many insulting words, but I'll use only one single word. It will be enough for a beginning."

Man raised his gun, aimed it at Young Lion, and bang! it went off, and Man shouted "Bang!" too.

Young Lion felt a terrible burning pain. He became frightened and ran off, shouting "Ow, ow, ow! Ay, ay, ay!"

He ran and ran with the pain in his leg until he was high up in the mountains again, where he had always lived safely with his father. He sat down and licked his wound.

"Ay, ay, ay! Father was right. Man is stronger than I am. He is very strong. I said many bad words to him, and he laughed and said just one word to me out of a stick, and it wounded me, and it hurts. I wonder what would have happened to me if he had used many words. My whole body would have been torn to pieces. I'll never go near Man again."

And he didn't. Lion always stays up in the mountains.

✠ The Fox Who Was Not So Smart

It was a nice warm day in January, which is the middle of summer in Chile. Fox was loping along a path and saw Horsefly sitting on a leaf.

"Horsefly, good friend," said Fox, "let us play together."

"I don't mind playing with you," said Horsefly. "What kind of game do you want to play?"

"Let's play a racing game."

"That's not a bad game," buzzed Horsefly. "I'll play with you."

"Well," said Fox, "let's race from here"—and he pointed to a bush behind them—"to that oak tree over there"—and he pointed to an oak tree a distance away.

"That's a good distance," said Horsefly. "I'll race you there."

"Well, then," said Fox, "let's get ready. Let's both walk back to the bush."

So they walked back together and got ready.

"Now, let's start!" Fox cried, and start they did. Fox ran fast, but Horsefly, instead of running, flew into Fox's bushy tail and quietly sat there.

Fox continued to run quickly, and Horsefly remained on his tail quiet as a mouse. Suddenly Fox saw some ripe red strawberries beside his path.

"I'd like to eat some of those fresh strawberries," Fox said. He looked back. "I don't see Horsefly. She must be slowly crawling along the ground, poor thing. I have plenty of time." So he began to eat the strawberries, one after another. They tasted good.

"They are very sweet," Fox said. "I'm sure I have time to eat some more. I'll get to that oak tree in plenty of time to beat Horsefly."

Horsefly just sat on Fox's tail and smiled to herself. Fox looked around.

"I wonder where Horsefly is. She's so slow, I'm sure I have more time."

Horsefly, still on Fox's tail, could hardly keep from laughing out loud.

"Now I've had enough strawberries, so I'll run on to the oak tree just to be sure to win the race," Fox said.

Lippity-lop, lippity-lop, lippity-lop, along he went. When he got close to the tree, Horsefly quickly flew off Fox's tail, and there she was, at the oak before Fox could get there.

"Ha!" cried Horsefly, "I won the race. I got here first."

Fox looked surprised. "Are you here already?"

"Yes, I got here before you. I won. Now pay me your bet."

"I won't."

"You'd better pay me!"

"I won't pay you. You should be glad I don't eat you."

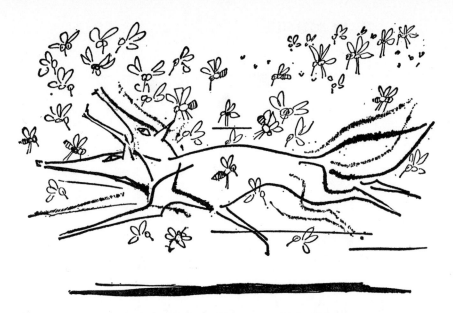

Fox ran and ran, but the horseflies did not stop biting him.

"Pay or you'll be in trouble," said Horsefly darkly.

"I won't pay."

"You'll be sorry."

"I won't pay."

"Oh, you'll pay, you'll pay!"

Then Horsefly called together her brothers and sisters and all her relatives and friends. They came by the hundreds. They crept and flew and buzzed all around and all over Fox. They bit him on the nose. They chewed his ears. They bit him on the belly. They swarmed all over him everywhere.

Fox ran and ran, but the biting did not stop. The horseflies just rode along with him everywhere he went.

Fox jumped into the water, but the horseflies still did not stop biting him. He leaped out of the water and ran off through the woods, but they kept on biting him. He could find no place to go where they did not bite him. And they kept on biting and biting until there was nothing left of Fox.

The Good Man and the Kind Mouse

Once, in Chile, there lived a poor old man called Juan Hollinao. He worked hard in a shabby little shop, but he barely made a living. Just the same, he was a very kind and generous man, ready to share what little he had with anyone who was in need.

In his house there lived Little Mouse, who was forever eating what Juan had. When Juan had bread, Little Mouse ate bread. When Juan had cheese, she ate cheese. And on fiesta days, when Juan had a little meat, Little Mouse ate meat. When there was nothing to eat in the house, the little animal would even gnaw on Juan's old shoes.

Now, Juan knew all about this mouse and what she ate, but he never complained. "Mice have to eat, too," he would say.

Once, when the mouse ate most of the little there was to eat in the house, leaving almost nothing for Juan, he said, "Little Mouse, you shouldn't be so greedy. Remember, I have to eat, too. Eat your fair share and leave me mine."

Little Mouse listened quietly but said nothing. She well knew how kind the poor old man had been to her. She thought about it for a long time, and finally one day she said to him, "Juan, you've been very kind and good to me, and I've taken things from you for a long time. Now I'd like to serve you. I want to reward you for your kindness."

Old Juan listened closely, and the mouse went on:

"Far away from here lives a rich king. He is so rich that he measures his gold in bushel baskets. He also has an elderly daughter who is not married yet. She'd make a good wife for you."

The old man listened and waited for the mouse to continue.

"Now, here's what you must do," said Little Mouse. "You go to that king and ask him to lend you a bushel basket in which to measure your gold, which you will say you have in your cellar."

"How silly!" Juan exclaimed. "Why should I borrow a bushel basket? What gold do I have to measure? I have no gold. That's foolish!"

"Well, if you're afraid to go to that rich king, I'm not. I must reward you for your kindness. Good-by."

Little Mouse ran off. When she came close to the king's palace, she changed herself into a handsome page boy.

The young mouse-page went right up to the gate and said he wished to speak to the king.

He looked so proud and wore such beautiful clothes that the guard told him to go right in.

"Your Majesty," the mouse-page said, "I come from my master, Juan Hollinao. He asks you, please, to lend him a bushel basket so he can measure the gold he has in his cellar."

"Your master must be a very rich man to need a bushel basket to measure his gold."

"Yes, he is a very rich man, Your Majesty," agreed the mouse-page.

"Maybe he is richer than I am," said the king.

"Maybe he is and maybe he isn't, but at this minute he needs a strong bushel basket in which to measure his gold."

"Well, I'll lend it to him, but on one condition: He himself must return the bushel basket to me; if he doesn't, he will pay for it with his life."

"Oh, he won't have to pay with his life. He'll return it, Your Majesty."

The king gave the mouse-page the strongest bushel basket he had, and the mouse carried it off. When he came near Juan's house he changed himself back into his mouse form, and soon Juan saw the little animal dragging the big basket toward the house. It was a strange and funny sight.

"You brought the basket!" Juan cried. "What for? What shall I do with it?"

"Nothing," said Little Mouse. "Just come along and take it back to the king, for if you don't, *zik!*—off goes your head. That's exactly what he said."

What could Juan say or do? A king's command is a king's command.

"How can I go before the king in these rags?" cried Juan, pointing to his old ragged clothes.

"Don't worry, Juan. All will be well."

The two set off through the woods and across the fields. They came to a deep stream. Over it was a bridge of thin ropes. Juan was afraid to cross.

"Don't be afraid. I'll help you," said Little Mouse. She took the old man by the hand and they started to cross the bridge. When they were halfway, Little Mouse ran along Juan's leg, and he tumbled into the water.

Little Mouse jumped into the water and helped Juan out. There he stood, all bedraggled and dripping.

"Now I can never go before the king," he wailed.

"No, you can't, looking like that," Little Mouse agreed.

"We could go back home, but you know what that would mean. *Zik!* Off would go your head. But don't worry, good Juan. Stay here and dry your clothes. Meanwhile I'll attend to an errand. You wait here. I'll be back."

Little Mouse went off, straight to the palace. But before she got to the gate she changed herself again into the handsome page. Then she went right up to the king.

"Your Majesty," the mouse-page said, "a terrible thing has happened. My master was sitting in his carriage, crossing a stream, when suddenly the horses became frightened, threw him into the stream, and ran off. So he cannot come to see you because his clothes are in a terrible condition, and he can't come on foot. You must wait for another time."

"That can be remedied easily. I'll send him some fine, dry clothes and my horses and carriage. I'm eager to see this fine gentleman."

The clothes were brought, the carriage came, and off they went to the bridge where Juan was sitting in the sun, trying to dry himself.

"Here are some clothes, master. Put them on quickly. The king is waiting for you."

You should have seen Juan in those fine, new clothes. He looked twenty years younger. He looked like a rich nobleman. He entered the carriage, and soon they were before the king. All the courtiers thought Juan was some wealthy prince from a far-off land. He was feasted and flattered. And Juan Hollinao was trying the figure out just how Little Mouse had done it.

Now, I told you that the king had a daughter who was not very young. She looked after the palace for her father, because the queen was dead. She thought Juan was a fine and a grand gentleman. She thought more than that. Well, I'll tell you: she really thought he'd make her a fine husband. There's an old saying: Man is fire, woman is straw, and the Devil blows hard.

The king also thought Juan would make a fine son-in-law. After all, there were not many men who had so much gold in their cellar that they had to measure it in bushel baskets.

Juan was a very honest man and he tried to tell the king the truth. He wanted to say that he was not a man to marry a princess. When the king spoke to him about the princess, Juan was ready to tell him the whole truth, but the mouse-page was always by his side, pulling at his coat or hushing him.

One day, when the king thought the time was ripe, he said, "Now, Juan, you can marry my daughter. Then go to your palace and get everything ready, and we'll follow. I'll lend you my carriage and servants to go with you and help you."

What could poor Juan do? He could not tell the truth, as he wanted to, for the mouse-page was always at his side to stop him. So he married the princess, but he was not too happy about it. Then they put him and the mouse-page into the king's fine carriage, and off they went, with everyone's blessing.

"What will the princess say? What will the king say when he sees my little hut?" cried Juan.

"Juan," said the mouse-page, "you worry too much. Have patience. You know that if God wills, it rains when there is need of rain."

Juan did not open his mouth during the rest of the trip. He sat in silence. When they came near his home he had the biggest surprise of all. His old hut was gone, and in its place there stood a palace more beautiful than the king's. Juan looked at the mouse-page beside him, but there was only Little Mouse. She said, "This is your reward for your goodness and patience. This palace has everything in the world you could want, and you and the princess will be very happy in it. Now you must get ready to receive the princess and the king."

There was no time to lose. Trumpets were heard, announcing the king's arrival. He came with the princess and many of his courtiers. Everyone was happy to see the beautiful palace, and the king was happiest of all to see what a rich nobleman his daughter had married.

There were fiestas and celebrations without end, with music and dancing. Juan was so happy he even forgot Little Mouse who had brought him all this happiness.

A long time passed quickly. Little Mouse lived by herself as she had done before, and no one thought about her. One day she died. The princess found her and threw her on the garbage pile behind the palace where they threw things left over from the kitchen.

It just happened that soon after that Juan passed by and saw Little Mouse on the garbage heap. Just imagine how he felt when he saw the one who had brought him all the good luck and happiness, lying there! Tears came to his eyes.

"Dear Little Mouse, to whom I owe so much," he cried, "this is all my fault. I should be punished for this. But now I will give you the finest funeral in all Chile."

He ordered a golden casket and the most beautiful flowers in all the land, then he sat near the casket hour after hour, begging forgiveness. While he was sitting there, Little Mouse suddenly opened her eyes wide.

"Juan," she said, "I am not dead. I just did this to find out if you would remember me and what I did for you. Well, I was very disappointed. You forgot all about me, and when they thought I was dead, they threw me on the garbage pile."

Juan apologized without end. He said he didn't know

what had been done, which was the truth, and he swore that he would think of his benefactor day and night. He picked up Little Mouse and caressed her.

"Now you must come to my room and live with me," he said.

But Little Mouse said, "No, Juan, I am happy to see that you possess the virtue of gratitude, which is a thing most people do not know. Even you forgot it. I will leave now. I don't belong to this world. I've done all the good I can, and now I will leave. I will become an angel."

Then a miracle happened. Little Mouse became an angel with golden hair and white wings and flew right up to heaven. There she became the guardian angel of Juan and the princess and their family, who lived happily for the rest of their lives.

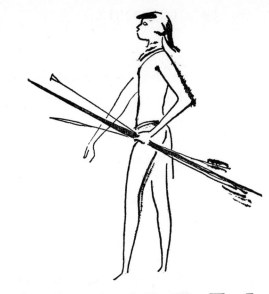

COLOMBIA

The Lord Said, This Is My House

In Santo Domingo, there is a church with a beautiful painting of the Lord. When this church was built, hundreds of years ago, it was the finest church in the city, and the people wanted to have in it the finest picture of the Lord. So they asked many artists to paint such a picture, but none was beautiful enough for the fine church. The people and the priest were not satisfied, and they were unhappy. Nevertheless, they kept on trying to find a true masterpiece.

One day an artist came who asked if he could try. The people said he might, and told him they hoped he could do better than the others had done.

The artist put his canvas on a stand right in the church and got out his paints and his brushes and had everything ready to begin. Then he went off somewhere. Nobody ever saw him again. There stood the canvas with the paints and brushes, but no painter to use them.

But when Sunday came, there was a miracle! On the canvas that had been empty appeared the most beautiful picture of Christ that has ever been seen. People who had traveled all over the world said they had never seen a painting of Christ anywhere as beautiful as this one.

All the people were happy, and there was a great fiesta to celebrate the hanging of the picture in the church.

Soon the day came when the beautiful painting was going to be carried in a procession through the city streets. A special platform was made for it, and the mayor and other important citizens were to carry it.

On that Sunday everybody came from miles around, dressed in their best clothes, to see the procession. The mayor put the painting on the stand, and four men raised it up on their shoulders. Then they started to walk toward the church door.

Now a new miracle happened. The picture began to get bigger. The closer they came to the door, the larger the picture became. When they reached the door, it was so large it could not get through.

When the people and the priest saw that the painting did not want to leave the church, they put it back in its place and did not carry it in the procession.

They tried to take it out many other times, but each time the same miracle occurred. In fact, the painting has never been taken out of the church. So people go into the church to see it where it hangs, because the good Lord has plainly said: "This is my house, and this is where I wish to stay."

The Great Flood

A long time ago, long before Columbus arrived at Colombia, an old, old Indian came to the people of the land. Nobody knew where he came from, or how he came to be there. His name was Bochica.

Bochica wasn't like other people. He had white hair and a long beard. His wife was with him, and her name was Chía. She was very beautiful but she was very bad. Bochica was very good, and he loved the people. He could do many kinds of magic. In fact, he could do anything he wanted to.

Once he said to Chía, "I will help the people of this land."

"Why do you want to help them? They are wild people. They are always fighting," said Chía.

"I will help them just the same. I will teach them good things."

So he taught the people about clothes, how to make and wear them, how to build houses and live in them, and how to grow vegetables in the earth. When the people had learned all this, they built fine houses and big cities, and they lived together peacefully as they should.

But Chía did not like this, for she was an evil woman.

She said, "I will destroy what my husband has done. I will make everything bad again, just as it was."

She waited until Bochica was sleeping, and then she went to the Funza River and began to work bad magic. She worked a long time with that bad magic. The river grew bigger and bigger. She didn't stop; she kept on working, and soon the river was like a big bay. Then it got to be as big as the ocean.

The water rushed in over the villages and the cities. It swept over the gardens and the houses. It tore down the trees and everything that had been planted. It flowed over everything. The people were frightened and ran away with their children, but the water overtook them, and most of them were drowned. Only those who climbed high up on the mountains were saved.

When Bochica awoke from his sleep, he saw what a terrible thing his wife had done.

"Why did you do this?" he asked.

"I told you these people were not good. You never should have helped them as you did," she said.

"They were good, but you see only what is bad. I will punish you for this."

Chía was afraid and did not open her mouth.

"Go from this earth," old Bochica said. "Go far, far away from here and never come back, so you can never harm anyone again. Go now!"

Chía ran away from the land. She ran off the earth until she was so far away that the earth looked like a little island. There she stayed and never came back. She was up in the sky and became the moon. She can come out only at nighttime and shine on the earth. She is still there.

But Bochica stayed with the people who had run up into the mountains and saved themselves. He took pity on them. Though they were all on top of the mountains, there was water all around them. Wherever they looked there was only angry, swirling water.

Bochica was very strong, stronger than anybody, even though he was an old man. With his powerful hands he made big holes in the mountains. He broke huge rocks as if they were sticks of wood. Then the water rushed away wildly, leaping down the steep mountainside. The place where this happened is called Tequendama Falls today. The falling waters make a terrible thunder, and rainbows form in the mist and sunlight.

When the water receded and the land became dry, the green grass began to grow, and Bochica once again showed the people how to build houses and gardens. They lived just as they had lived before—even better, as they do today.

When Bochica saw this, he went far, far away to a holy place, and there he is now.

⚡ The Mysterious Lake

Juan Martin lived in the high Andes of Colombia. Everywhere around his home stood big mountains, like giant houses full of things about which he knew nothing.

Juan Martin lived with his mother and father, who was

a woodcutter. No one lived near them, and Juan had never been to the village. But don't think he was lonesome. He learned to be friends with the birds, the trees, the rocks, and the waters. He lived so close to them for so long that he learned their language and talked to them as he would to friends of his own kind. And the fish, animals, and birds knew him and were not afraid of him. His father told him stories about many things that had happened in the olden days, about the life of the animals and the mountains, and about the old gods of the Indians.

So when Juan was in a cave, or looked at a lake or at the mountains or animals or flowers, they all had friendly and personal meanings for him.

Each day when the sun stood in the middle of the sky, Juan brought his father his noon meal and would sit with him. And when his father finished eating, Juan went home. He walked slowly, stopping to visit with his friends of the outdoor world. Sometimes he would sit down and listen to the birds or to the running water.

One day, when he was sitting at the edge of a beautiful emerald-green lake he knew well, he remembered a wonderful story his father had often told him about this lake. Long before, the Indians had worshiped their god there. Into that lake they had thrown offerings of golden images of birds and beasts, and emeralds and other precious stones. It was said that one day each year a princess in the form of a golden duck came up to the surface of the lake, together with her brothers and sisters, also in the form of golden ducks. People said you could catch these ducks with a blessed rosary, but you would have to catch *all* of them together. If one was missing, they would all disappear. But the person who could catch them would be richer than anyone in the world.

Juan was sitting at the edge of the green lake, recalling

the story for the hundredth time, when suddenly a large duck waddled out of the ferns, followed by a *zancudo*, a little bird with long legs.

They stopped at the edge of the water and looked at Juan, but they did not run away. They were talking. The duck was saying to the zancudo, "Good friend Zancudo, I am leaving. The cold winter is coming, and I am going where it is warmer."

"Good friend Duck," said the zancudo, "must you go today? Stay just one more day and you will see a wonderful sight. Tomorrow is the day when the Golden Duck and Ducklings will come out of the lake. It is the only day in the year when they come out, and that is a sight worth seeing."

"Then I think I'll stay," said Duck, and the two birds walked away.

Juan jumped up excitedly. So tomorrow was the day! He'd be there, too. He went home, but he did not say anything to his family. He never talked much. However, he was so excited that he couldn't sleep that night. Very early the next morning he rose before the sun, took his mother's rosary, and went quickly to the lake.

The water was greener than green, and very still. There was not even the smallest wind blowing. The forest stood in silence. The birds were not noisy, as they usually were in the early morning. All the animals were quiet, too. It seemed that everyone was waiting for something important to happen.

Then, from the middle of the lake, rose a beautiful golden duck with seven golden ducklings. Their golden glow was like that of the sun in the sky. Juan stood hidden and did not move. Golden Duck was speaking to the Golden Ducklings.

"That blue up there high above us is the sky. Around

us here are the mountains, covered with trees. The clothes on the trees are leaves."

So she went on explaining to the Golden Ducklings all the things around them. At first the Ducklings listened, but after a time they became restless and swam away. Juan was watching for his chance to catch them, holding his rosary ready in his hand.

Now they came close to the shore. He threw the rosary! It fell around . . . six of the Golden Ducklings. The seventh had swum off in a different direction.

Big Golden Duck saw Juan and let out a cry. Then she and all seven Ducklings disappeared under the water.

Juan walked home slowly.

"I'll wait for them next year," he said sadly to himself. "They come every year."

He waited patiently, and he prepared. He got a big long rosary and practiced throwing it.

Finally the year passed and the day came. As the sun appeared, Juan was at the lake, waiting. Just as it had been the year before, the lake was still, no wind blew, and all the animals were silent. Juan stood in the bushes, his rosary ready in his hand.

Soon there was a rippling on the surface of the water, and Golden Duck appeared with the seven Ducklings.

Again she began to tell them all about the things around them, and again they listened for a little while, and again they became restless and swam away. When they came near the shore, Juan saw his chance. He threw out his large rosary, and there they were—all seven of them within it.

Now a wild wind rose and bent the trees to the ground. Angry waves jumped toward the sky. The wind pushed the waves, and the waves beat against the shore. The water nearly blinded Juan.

Suddenly everything became quiet again, and Juan saw before him a beautiful girl of bronze-gold color, and seven children just as beautiful and of the same color.

"You shouldn't have done that," said the girl.

"Who are you?" asked Juan.

"I am Quira, the Chibcha princess. I have lived in this lake for many, many years, but now we can't go back because of what you did."

"Are these your children?"

"No. They are my brothers and sisters. None of us can go back to our palace of emerald and gold under the lake."

"How can you live in the lake, under water? Only fish live there."

"We live in the lake, too, in a beautiful palace of gold, with sparkling green emeralds. The floor and the roof of our palace are covered with emeralds; that is why the water of this lake is so green. We have lived there for hundreds of years.

"Once there was a great temple here where the Indians worshiped their god. But when the white men came and wanted our gold and emeralds, and even our lives, my father put a powerful magic on us, and we went under the water. We come up only once a year, for one day, as golden ducks. Then we go back down to our palace at the bottom of this lake. But now that you have broken our magic with your rosary, we cannot go back. We will all be unhappy."

It seemed to Juan that the princess was about to cry. He was a kind boy and felt very sorry for her and her little brothers and sisters.

"I'd like to help you," said Juan. "I'm sorry for what I've done."

"You *can* help us," the princess said.

"How?"

"You are the only one who has seen us. No one knows yet what has happened here, so we can all go back down in the lake . . . if you will come with us."

"I, go down into the lake!"

"Yes, that is the only way. Come and live with us. Our home is very beautiful, and you will have everything you want."

"Can I never come back to my home and see my parents and brothers?"

"Yes, you can come up once a year for a day, just as we do. . . . This is the only way. . . ."

Juan was silent for a long time. Then he said, "Suppose you're not telling the truth? The water is cold and deep. I might drown."

"A lazy ox never gets fresh water. Courage makes a real man."

Juan stood thinking. He looked into the shining, wet, sad eyes of the princess. Then he cried, "I'll go with you!"

So Juan and Princess Quira and her seven brothers and sisters went down into the lake, and . . .

Once each year they come back up for a day to look at the world above the waters. But now there are eight little Golden Ducklings. One always stays a long time near the shore, looking at the woods and the trees and the mountains.

Where is that lake? I mustn't tell you. It's not good for you to know. If I told you, then too many boys and girls, and even grownups, might leave their homes.

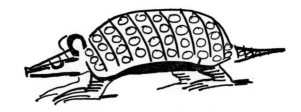

COSTA RICA

Juan in Heaven

Juan of Costa Rica was a silly fellow, and his head was as empty as a bell without a clapper. He was forever doing things the wrong way, and everybody was always laughing at him and teasing him. But he simply couldn't help being silly—that was the way he was.

Sometimes he felt sad that he was so foolish, but more often he just laughed at his silly ways, along with the rest of the people. They couldn't understand that. They didn't know he was having a good time.

Juan loved the darkness of the night, for then no one teased him, no one laughed at him, and he dreamed nice dreams. Really, there is nothing nicer than to dream nice dreams.

One night he lay on his mat looking for a long time at

the stars. Suddenly there he was, standing on a big stump of a mahogany tree. It was a big, round stump, and he was standing in the middle of it. It wasn't night; it was day. The sky was blue and the sun was shining.

Pop! That stump began to go up away from the ground, higher and higher in the sky. Juan looked down. Sure enough, there was that big tree stump rising higher and higher into the air! It was going fast.

Now it was higher than the trees! Now it was near the clouds! Now it was in the clouds! Now it was above the clouds! Now it was in heaven! He was right before the big golden gate, and there was St. Peter standing before him, with a golden miter on his head and a golden staff in his right hand.

"Is that you, St. Peter? And is this heaven?" asked Juan.

"Yes, good Juan, this is the gate to heaven," answered St. Peter in a kindly voice.

"I'd like to go into heaven," said Juan. "Nobody will tease me or laugh at me there. On earth everybody teases me and laughs at me."

"You can't come in. You're not ready for it."

"But I want to go into heaven!"

"That isn't a good enough reason."

"I'll be happy in heaven."

"Even that isn't reason enough."

"I never did harm to anyone."

"That is in your favor, but it isn't enough reason to go into heaven. But, Juan, since you've been so good, I'll let you into the big waiting room, where people wait before they go into heaven. There no one will bother you, and you'll live in peace."

Juan was satisfied and went in. It was nice there. All kinds of people sat around, but nobody teased him or even looked at him.

"This is a fine place. It's just the place for me."

He walked around, looked at everything and everybody, and he was happy. He was very good, and after a time St. Peter let him wander around in other rooms. He came to one that was filled with burning oil lamps. Some burned brightly and some burned weakly.

"Why are all these lamps burning in this room, St. Peter?"

"Every lamp represents the life of a living person."

"Why are some strong and some weak?"

"Those that shine brightly show that the people they represent will have long lives. Those that shine weakly represent short lives."

"Which one is mine, St. Peter?"

"That one," he said, pointing to one with a dent in its right side.

"The light in it is not very bright."

"That is your life, Juan. Now you must go out of this room. You can't stay here."

Juan went out, but as soon as he saw St. Peter at the gate, he went back quickly into the room with the lamps. He cleaned the wick in his own lamp and put fresh oil in it. As he started to go out, there was St. Peter, standing right behind him.

"So that is what you do behind my back! I let you walk around here freely, and at once you do things you shouldn't."

Juan tried to say something, but there was nothing he could say. He knew he had done wrong.

"From now on you'll stay in the waiting room. You must not go out of there any more. The next time you do something you shouldn't, you'll have to go back to earth."

So Juan was back in the waiting room, watching the endless number of souls waiting to get into heaven.

One day he saw a soul coming in, followed by a large number of angels who showed great respect toward that soul.

"Whose soul is that?" asked Juan of one of the angels.

"It is the soul of the blessed Pope going to the Lord."

The diamond gate opened wide, and the soul flew in, followed by the angels. Juan went along behind them, and soon they were before the jeweled golden throne of the Holy Lord, who greeted the Pope's soul. Then He noticed Juan.

"Juan," said the Lord, "you should have wings like the angels when you come before me. Let someone get wings for Juan."

An angel ran up with a pair of wings and put them on Juan's shoulders. They were too large and too heavy, but Juan didn't mind that. He was happy to have wings like the angels and to be in heaven.

"So that is what you do behind my back!" said St. Peter.

Music was played on golden harps, and food was served on golden plates. Juan thought the food tasted very good.

The music kept on playing, but it changed to the singing of birds and grew louder and louder, and suddenly Juan sat up, wide awake. The window in his room had no glass. The sun was shining in through the open window brightly, and a great company of birds was twittering and whistling in the trees.

Juan knew now that it all had been a dream. But what a fine dream!

"What happens in my dreams is much better than what happens when I'm awake," said Juan.

CUBA

 The Silly Owls and the Silly Hens

There is a narrow, deep, dark valley in Cuba where the sun never shines. Only a little patch of blue sky, high, high above, can be seen from this valley. Long ago, away down in its gloomy shadows there lived thousands of owls. They sat there all day long, on ledges and branches, thinking of nothing but looking very wise. Now and then one owl or another would look up into the blue sky, but the strong light would blind him and he would close his eyes.

One day a young gentleman owl looked up and saw a few flowers blooming on a rock ledge.

"Where do they come from? Where do they go?" he asked. No one answered him. The owls didn't want to be disturbed.

But this young owl was different from the others. He was adventurous and curious, and he wanted to know more about the world. So one moonlit night he flew up to see what was there. He flew higher and higher, until he reached the tops of the mountains that closed in the valley. He flew still higher, until he was up in the fast-moving clouds.

"How nice it is to be in clouds and to be carried along by them!" he cried.

The clouds carried the young gentleman owl across the sky until he saw below him a city with lights and people.

"Those down there might be owls. They stand around just as we do, but their feathers are different. I think I'll go down there and look around."

So down he went, and landed in a chicken yard. The yard was full of hens. When the hens saw the handsome young owl there was great excitement.

"A fine young gentleman has just come down from the moon!" said some. "How handsome he is!"

"How different from the roosters!" said others.

"Let us have a fiesta in his honor," cried one young hen. "He looks lovely in his gray-green clothes."

All the hens, young and old, agreed this was a splendid idea, and in no time at all they arranged a fiesta.

A great banquet was served. There was singing and dancing, and much flapping of wings and fluttering of hens' hearts.

The young owl had never enjoyed himself in all his solemn life as much as he did that night. It was so nice to be flattered. It was so nice, in fact, that he forgot the time. Suddenly he noticed the first rays of the sun. "What time is it?" he hooted anxiously. Just then a rooster crowed. "I must be off! I must hurry home!" the owl cried uneasily, and off he flew, without even so much as saying "*Adiós.*"

Back in his dark valley, he told all the owls who would listen about his exciting adventure with the hens. How kind they were! What fine food they served! How they sang and danced! All the young gentlemen owls listened and wished they had gone with him.

The story of his adventure spread rapidly through the owl colony. "We should all enjoy such adventures," said some. "We should all eat such fine food," said others. "Let us all visit these marvelous hen people!" Some of the young gentlemen owls said to him, "Let us all go back there together tomorrow night. You show us the way."

The next night the adventurous owl flew up into the clouds, followed by nearly half of the younger members of the owl colony.

"We'll all go and make friends with those wonderful people," they cried. And, with a whirring of wings and a pushing of the clouds, they soon came to the city of the hens.

When the hens saw the large flock of gentlemen owls coming in, there was terrible excitement among them. They all talked at once. You never heard so much talking. There was no end to the clack! clack! clack! of hen chatter.

"Look how many young men are coming! We can all have dancing partners tonight!" they screamed. "Saints of the land! So many of them!" And they fell over one another in their excitement. "Now we can really have a grand time. We'll have the biggest fiesta this chicken yard has ever seen."

The few roosters who lived there refused to have anything to do with the owls and looked on angrily. What could they do? What could they say? There were so few of them and so many hens and owls.

The fiesta began. First they ate meat and cakes, and then the dancing started. It began slowly, then went faster and faster, until the whole yard was a whirling mass of

When the hens saw the gentlemen owls, they all talked at once.

feathers. The dance grew wilder and wilder. Eggs were broken, forming pools of yolks and whites on the ground. The yard became slippery, and dancers began sliding all over the place.

Everybody in the neighborhood joined in. Frogs in a nearby pond started to croak. Birds in the trees awoke and began chirping. Only the few roosters did not join in the fun. They stood in a dark corner, silent and angry. But the big, bright moon looked on and smiled.

"I didn't know there were so many men," said one rooster.

"A curse on them!" said another.

"How can we put an end to this?" asked another.

"There are many more owls here than there are roosters," gloomily said one old rooster.

So, while the hens and owls danced and danced, roosters argued and argued. But they could never agree on what to do. Finally some of the older roosters fell asleep, but the younger ones went on talking about the terrible invasion of the owl men. In the end they decided to go and ask Pedro Animal what to do.

First I must tell you something about the great Pedro Animal of Cuba. His fur is thick and twisted like rope. His fists and muscles are stronger than iron. His teeth are as long as a crocodile's. He is quicker than a monkey. He has more courage than a lion, and he is the wisest of the animals.

But he is lazy. My, how lazy he is! His favorite word is *mañana*—tomorrow. He puts off everything till *mañana*.

"*Hoy* [today] is too soon," he says. "We mustn't be too hasty. Let's think about this and do it *mañana*."

But when he shoots his long, straight arrow, it moves swiftly and surely, *zoom!* And it lands exactly where it is aimed. When he bathes in the river, his strong arms and legs shoot out, *güéchene, güéchene*, and his body moves through the water like a streak of lightning. When he is thirsty and opens a coconut to drink, *gloco, gloco*, he empties it before you can bat an eyelid.

All animals have great respect for Pedro Animal, for he knows not only as much as all the animals know but also what all men know as well. Therefore, he is wiser than either animals or men.

So the young roosters went to his house.

"Don Pedro Animal!" they called. "We are in great trouble!"

"Go away! Don't bother me!" he mumbled, half asleep.

"We need your help!" crowed the roosters.

"Oh, let me alone!" yawned Pedro Animal from within his house. "I want to sleep. Come back *mañana*."

"Tomorrow will be too late. We need help today."

"Go away! We'll talk *mañana, mañana*."

"Please! Please help us!"

They crowed and cried and groaned so loud and so

long that finally Pedro Animal was completely awake.

"What's the trouble?" he asked.

"The owls! The moon!" they shrieked.

"What about the owls and the moon?"

"They are terrible. The owls have invaded our chicken yard, and the hens are dancing with them. There's a wild fiesta going on there right now. And the moon is smiling on them and encouraging them."

"How's that?" asked Pedro Animal.

"The moon keeps the sun from coming up, so they can have a long, long night, and they just keep dancing on and on."

"That's bad! That's very bad!" said Pedro Animal.

"It's worse than bad! What do those silly hens see in those ugly owls when they can look at handsome roosters like us? Help us, Pedro Animal! Help us!"

Pedro Animal sat down, his head bent over. He was staring at the ground. He was thinking hard. Finally he spoke.

"Listen carefully, and do as I say. You arrange a big fiesta. Invite all the animals, from the elephant to the flea. Tell everyone it is in honor of the owls. Eat and dance and enjoy yourselves. But let no rooster crow to warn the owls that the dawn is coming. Wait until the sun has come up and it's broad daylight. Then the hens will see what fools they are, making such a fuss over those ugly owls. The whole animal world will laugh at the silly hens, and that will put a stop to their foolishness."

The roosters did exactly what Pedro Animal told them to do. They arranged a big fiesta and invited all the animals. Not one was left out, and everybody came. Even the Queen of the Owls was there. There was tasty food to please everyone, and everybody danced and was happy. You never saw so many different kinds of dancing. The roosters stood around the walls, watching, and kept their beaks closed. The singing and dancing went on and on, hour after hour. No one cared about the time. Only the Queen of the Owls asked now and then what time it was, and the roosters answered, "It's the middle of the night. Go ahead and dance a while longer."

And that is what they did.

Then the first golden streaks of dawn appeared in the sky. For the moment the roosters forgot what they were supposed to do, and simply did what roosters always do at dawn. They crowed. *"Kick-key-ree-key! Kick-key-ree-keeeey! Cock-a-doodle-doo! Cock-a-doodle-dooooo!"*

The owls looked up, saw the light of dawn, and quickly flew away.

The roosters had forgotten to keep their beaks shut. They were angry with themselves. "We acted like fools!" they all cried.

Once again they went back to Pedro Animal.

"We are ashamed of ourselves," they confessed to him. "We forgot to keep quiet when the dawn came."

"I'll help you just once more," said Pedro Animal. "This time we'll hold the fiesta at *my* house. We'll invite everybody just as before, and we'll even invite some people, too. But remember! No crowing! *Don't crow!*"

So the invitation went out. The biggest and the best fiesta ever held would take place at the home of the highly respected Pedro Animal. Everybody was invited, both animals and people. And everybody came, including the owls, of course. Pedro Animal's house was so packed that there wasn't even room for a falling feather. But not one rooster was in the room; they were all outside.

Pedro Animal was outside, too, closing all the doors and windows and sealing up the cracks with mud, so not a single ray of light could get into the house. Then he took some string and tied the beak of every rooster. He wanted to be sure there would be no crowing at dawn.

Inside, the music played wildly and the dancing was wilder. This way, that way, around, around, boo-see-*kee*, boo-see-*kee*, boo-see-*kee*, the feet shuffled and twisted.

"Is the sun coming up? Is the sun coming up?" asked the owls anxiously every little while.

"Not yet. No, not yet," the hens would answer softly.

The singing and dancing and eating and drinking and merrymaking went on and on and on. After hours and hours some of the animals got so tired they could not dance any more and just fell asleep standing up. There was no danger of falling down, for there were so many people that there was no place to fall. Finally, even Master Thousand-Legs got so tired he couldn't dance any more, and *he* fell asleep, too. Nobody saw the first rays of the sun shining on the palm leaves. And, of course, the cocks did not crow. How could they, with their beaks tied up?

When the sun was well up in the sky, Pedro Animal opened all the doors and windows and untied the cocks' beaks, and the bright sunlight streamed into the room. All the fur and feathers gleamed in the golden sunlight—all except the dull gray owl feathers. They looked as if moths were nesting in them.

The owls, frightened and ashamed to be seen in all their ugliness in broad daylight, quickly flew away. They were night animals and should not be seen in daylight. Whirring and bumping into one another—for they were blinded by the bright sunlight—they fled back to their dark valley, ashamed and disgraced.

So were the hens. How could they have preferred moth-eaten owls to their proud, handsome roosters? From that day on, roosters are kings in the henyard and owls stay in the dark. That is as it should be.

DOMINICAN REPUBLIC

Who Rules the Roost?

In a small town of the Dominican Republic there once lived two men who were good friends. Both were merchants. One, José, sold yucca and corn. The other, Francisco, sold yams. These two often talked together, about this, that, and the other.

One day José, the older of the two, said to his friend Francisco, "From the oldest days, from the days when the world began, from the first days Christopher Columbus saw our blessed Island of Hispaniola, and right on down to our day, woman has been the ruler of the house. She is not only queen of the house, but also king."

"Now, José," said Francisco, "I say you are wrong. True, I am not married, as you are, but I say man rules the house, and woman follows. The man heads his home, and his wife obeys him."

"My good friend Francisco! You are a thousand times wrong. Am I not married? I should know! Look around you, right here in our town, and on all the farms around the town. Look as far as you like, for that matter. You will always find that I am right, no matter where you look in this world. Woman rules the roost!"

"You are wrong, José, dead wrong. I tell you man is the rooster of the house, and woman just cackles."

And so they argued, but neither convinced the other he was right. It got so that every evening after their work was done they would look for each other and begin to argue the same question over and over.

One evening the argument became livelier than usual, and José said he would *prove* he was right.

"I'll tell you what we'll do, Francisco. You say that man rules the house, I say that woman rules the roost. We can argue this question until Judgment Day, and we'll get nowhere. Let us put the matter to a test. Whichever of us wins, the other must admit that he was wrong. Agreed?"

"I agree," said Francisco.

"Here's what we'll do. I'll take a dozen horses, and you take a dozen cows. We'll go from house to house and talk to people and find out whether the man of each house or his wife is master. If it's the woman, we'll give her a cow. If it's the man, we'll give him a horse. What do you say to that?"

"That's a good plan. I agree!" said Francisco.

Bright and early the next morning, José was at the meeting place with his dozen horses, and Francisco with his cows. They set out with the animals behind them. "Remember," said Francisco, "the first one who gives away all his animals loses."

When they came near the first house, they could hear before they ever reached the door who was master there. The woman was screaming at her husband for not having locked up the pigs the night before. The husband stood with head bowed and did not open his mouth.

"Give her a cow!" said José victoriously. And Francisco sadly did so without saying a word.

They went to the next house. While they were still out in the road they heard a woman shout, "Go and get the bread! Be quick about it, and don't argue with me!"

Francisco looked at José in despair and meekly gave that woman a cow.

And so they went from house to house, and quickly found out who was the head—the woman, of course! Poor Francisco had to give away cow after cow. Finally he had just one cow left, but José still had his twelve horses. Francisco's face had grown longer and longer, and José's smile had grown broader and broader.

At last they came to the house where the judge of the town lived. The judge was home, but his wife was out.

"Good morning, *buenos días, Señor Juez,*" they both said respectfully. "We are trying to find out who is the master of the house in the different homes of our community, the man or his wife."

"I say the woman always rules the house," said José with great certainty.

"And I said the man is master in his home," said Francisco sadly.

To his surprise, the judge said, "You are right, Francisco. Here in my house *I* am the head and master. Whatever I say goes. *My* wife does as I say."

"I'm glad to hear that, Señor Judge," said José.

"Yes, it's been that way from the day we were married," the judge said proudly.

Poor Francisco had just one cow left.

"You're a lucky man, Señor Judge," said José. "The Lord has blessed you."

"It's really quite simple," continued the judge, encouraged by this respect and admiration. "All you have to do is to begin the very first hour you are married to show your wife that you are the head of the house."

"You are the first man we have found to say that," said Francisco, his spirits rising.

"In this house, my word is law," continued the judge.

"I'm delighted to hear that, indeed," said José, "even though I lose a horse by it. You see, Señor Judge, we decided to give a horse to each man who is master of his house. You are the first to get one. I have a dozen horses here. Please come out and choose the one you like best."

"Do you really mean this?" asked the judge.

"Yes, I do," said José. "Come and take the one that pleases you most."

"This is my lucky day," said the judge joyfully. "You say there are twelve to choose from?"

"That's right!" said José. "See, here they are."

The judge came out and looked them over carefully. "Just look at that black one," he said. "He looks as if he could run a good race. But that brown one! He looks strong and healthy. And that spotted one! He is certainly a handsome horse. Well, well, well! It's really hard to choose. I tell you, José, just wait until my wife comes back. She's a fine judge of horses. Besides, I'd like to please her. It's funny, but she's right most of the time."

"Father in heaven!" cried José. "He's no better than the rest. Give him your last cow, Francisco. Unfortunately for us men, I win. You can easily see who rules the house here."

Francisco did not say one word. Sadly he handed over his last cow to the judge. Then he turned to José and said just two words: "You win!"

Now everyone knows who rules the roost in the Dominican Republic, just as in all the rest of the world: the woman!

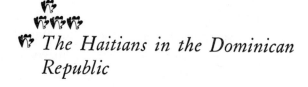

The Haitians in the Dominican Republic

Between Cuba and Puerto Rico lies one of the islands Columbus first saw when he came to the New World. It used to be called Hispaniola, but now it is divided into two republics. On the west lies the Republic of Haiti, on the east lies the Dominican Republic. Since Haiti is the smaller of the two, and has more people, Haitians are forever wanting to go to the Dominican Republic, for the Dominicans have plenty of food, and good eating makes for good dancing, and the Haitians love to dance.

One day three Haitians went over the mountains into the green land of the Dominicans to look for work. But the Dominicans speak Spanish and the Haitians speak a French dialect, so the Dominicans could not understand them.

"When you come to a land where the people dance on one foot, you must learn to dance on one foot, too," said one of the Haitians.

"We must learn the language of this country if we want to eat," said another.

"Let's listen to them talk. Then we'll repeat what they say, and so we'll learn Spanish," said the third.

Some girls came along the road, talking in Spanish.

The Haitians heard one of the girls saying over and over, "*Nosotras mismas* [we ourselves]."

"What this girl says must be important," said one Haitian, "so I'll learn to say it, too." And he repeated the words over and over until he could say them in his sleep. "Now I can speak their language," he said proudly. "We'll get along fine."

They kept on walking. Two boys came along talking very loudly. One was asking the other why he and his brother had done such and such a thing.

"*Porque quisimos* [because we wanted to]," the boy said over and over again.

"These words must be very important words in the Dominican language," said the second Haitian. "I will learn them. That will help us get work and we can then live like the Dominicans."

He repeated the words over and over again until he knew them perfectly.

"Now I, too, can speak the language of this land," he said proudly. "We'll succeed here."

They walked on and came to a village where the police were talking, in great excitement, about escaped prisoners who had committed a great crime.

"They'll be punished for this, so they'll remember it all their lives," shouted one of the officers.

"*Y bien hecho* [and rightly so]," roared another one of the policemen over and over again.

The Haitians listened. Said the third one of them:

"These three words must be terribly important if a man in uniform shouts them so loudly so many times. I'll learn them. I am sure it will help us get along in this land." He repeated the sentence again and again until he knew it perfectly, and he was very proud of it.

"Now all three of us can speak Dominican and so we are Dominicans."

They walked on and came to the next village. The police there had already heard about the crime and were looking for the criminals. They saw the three Haitians and were at once suspicious.

"Who are these three?" they asked. "They don't look like Dominicans. What are they doing here? Maybe they are the criminals! We'll question them." And so they began questioning them.

"Who are you?" they asked. "What are you doing here?"

The Haitians of course did not understand a word, but they wanted to show that they could speak Spanish, so each one began to shout over and over again the one sentence he knew, and all at the same time:

"We ourselves," said the first.

"Because we wanted to," said the second.

"And rightly so," said the third.

The suspicious policemen did not understand the gibberish, so they took the men before the judge, who was sitting in his big leather chair.

"*Señor Juez*," said the police, "we think we've caught the fellows who committed the crime."

Again each of the three Haitians began to say his only Spanish sentence over and over. But they all talked at once and so fast that the judge could not understand them, either.

"Silence!" shouted the judge.

The Haitians did not understand the word, but they understood the tone, and were quiet.

The judge glared at the first one and said, "Who committed that crime? If you know who it was, tell us. Did you?"

"*Nosotras mismas*," answered the first Haitian, saying the only Spanish words he knew.

"Ah! So you are confessing your terrible crime! Why did you do it?" thundered the judge, looking at the second Haitian.

"*Porque quisimos*," answered the poor fellow, using the only Spanish he knew.

"You will all be properly punished for this horrible crime. You'll be hanged for it. We will make an example of you," cried the judge, glaring at the third one.

"*Y bien hecho*," said the third Haitian, proudly showing that he could speak Spanish, too.

"Of course, rightly so. I'm glad you realize that," cried the judge. "Take them away, to be hanged at dawn tomorrow."

They were put in jail. But they were lucky. That same day the real criminals were caught, and the Haitians were set free the next morning.

So you see, the Lord takes care of cows without tails.

ECUADOR

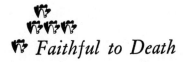

Faithful to Death

This happened in the olden days of long ago in Ecuador, when the *chiltota* bird sang beautiful songs that delighted the ear.

In those days there was a great Indian *cacique,* or chief, who was ambitious and hard not only with his own people but with the neighboring lesser chiefs. He was so hard that in the end the people and the other caciques revolted against him.

It was a fierce rebellion, in which many persons fought and died, and many towns were destroyed. But the Indians wanted to be free men and not slaves, so the fighting went on for a long time.

Among the rebels, there was one who had a beautiful

111

daughter named Apanatl, who was not only beautiful but also courageous.

When her father fell on the field of battle, Apanatl joined the warriors and became their leader. She led them, fought with them, and encouraged them by her fearless example.

Apanatl loved the creatures of the mountains and the woods, but most of all she loved the birds. When she led the men, she always had a *nahual*—a bird—with her. Even in the midst of the fiercest fighting, a chiltota bird always sat on her shoulder, and the songs it sang inspired her and the warriors to great deeds.

One night, after a long, hard march, the men lay down to sleep, but Apanatl could not go to sleep. She arose and, with the bird on her shoulder, quietly left the camp and went into the woods.

She did not come back.

The next morning her followers searched for her and found her . . . dead!

No one was there to tell how she had died, and the faithful chiltota bird who was with her could not speak. The bird was sitting on a tree, under which Apanatl was lying, breaking twigs for a nest and throwing down beautiful flowers on the dead princess.

Apanatl was buried with great honors and great sorrow. The war was won, and the men went to their homes. But the faithful chiltota bird stayed in the tree over Apanatl's grave, always singing its song to her, as it had sung to her when she was alive.

One night, when the moon from the deep sky shone over the silver Andes, the faithful bird sang its last song and fell dead on the grave of the princess it had loved so much.

That was the last time a chiltota bird was ever heard to sing. When these birds open their mouths now, only a croaking sound comes out.

🦋 The Head of the Inca

There is a great legend in the land of Ecuador, and this is what it tells.

The soothsayers of the rulers, called the Incas, had foretold for many years that strange white men would come and bring black disaster to the land. There would be bloody wars, and poisonous plagues, and fierce earthquakes that would shake the mountains and the earth.

Then what the soothsayers had said happened. The white warriors came and, with them, terrible tragedy. Many Indians died, and the Inca chief, Atahualpa, Son of the Sun, became the prisoner of bestial men.

For the white Spaniards wanted gold and more gold and more gold.

"Set me free and I will give you as much gold as this chamber will hold and as high as I can raise my hand above my head," the Inca said.

Francisco Pizarro, the Spanish commander, agreed. Gold drinking-vessels, gold images, gold ornaments were brought from every part of the land until the chamber was full.

"I want another chamber full of silver," the greedy Pizarro then demanded.

This, too, was done.

Then these men, who knew neither pity nor manhood, made up false charges, and Atahualpa, whom the Indians loved and worshiped, was condemned to be burned.

The Indians cried in despair, and all nature was in deep sorrow. Most of all, the volcano Cotopaxi was angry. This proud peak raises its head nearly ten thousand feet above Ecuador's nearby capital, Quito, which itself is nearly ten thousand feet above sea level. Shaped like a cone and covered with snow, it seems almost to touch the sun. It is a beautiful sight to see. Night and day Cotopaxi roared in wild fury, belching forth flames high into the clouds, hurling smoke and ashes in all directions, burning and destroying everything for miles around. Cotopaxi was angrier than he had been for centuries because Atahualpa was to be burned alive by the white men! Atahualpa, Son of the Sun!

The Inca ruler was kept in chains until the unhappy deed was to be performed. Then a good Spanish priest offered Atahualpa the chance to be strangled instead if he would become a Christian. Atahualpa was silent.

The Indians cried to the sun. They could not fight against these men on their strange horse beasts, who held in their hands sticks that spat fire and lead.

There was death everywhere, and Cotopaxi bellowed his volcanic roars more fiercely than ever.

The black, flaming day of the execution came. The people, the priests, the soldiers—everyone stood around the wood-stacked pile, ready to watch its horrors. Every heart was bitter with helpless fury.

The Spaniards wanted more gold and more gold.

In the distance Cotopaxi roared again, spitting out fierce flames and hot liquid rock.

Then the awful moment came. The Inca said he was **a** Christian, and the horrible, un-Christian deed was done.

It was a frightful, tragic day for the people of the Inca. Then, the legend tells, a strange thing happened. Out of the top of the volcano Cotopaxi was hurled a gigantic carved rock. It fell against the side of the cone-shaped mountain, and there it lay! And there it is still lying. It has the shape of a noble Indian face, turned upward, toward the sun. The face of Atahualpa, the last Son of the Sun, looking at the sun!

It is a noble head, lying there dark against the snow on the mountain: *La cabeza del Inca*—the head of the Inca, the head of Atahualpa, murdered by Pizarro.

Cotopaxi's great volcano mouth is silent now. He no longer roars with fire and sand and smoke and ashes and rocks. His silent cone stands clothed in snow, gleaming in the light of the sun, god of the Indians. And on his side lies the giant *cabeza del Inca*, the head of the Son of the Sun, for all to remember.

The Indians do remember, and they still tell the tragic legend to their children. But Cotopaxi, with his head raised twice as high above the sea as lofty Quito down below, tells it to the sun and to all the world.

EL SALVADOR

How Much You Remind Me of My Husband!

Once, there lived an old Indian and his wife in Huizúcar, in El Salvador. The old Indian worked and hunted as best he could, and his old wife worked as best she could. And so they lived through the years until one day the old Indian died.

His wife was quite sad. She was lonely now, like a person lost in a great forest. She worked a little, but most of the time she just sat on a wooden bench in front of her hut, in the shade of a large tree that grew there. She sat thinking of the days when her husband was living and they were happy together.

One day, as she was sitting on the bench shaded by the tree, she was saying, "How much I miss you, husband!

How much I miss you! How I wish you were sitting by my side!" She wished very, very hard, but it was no use. She still was sitting there all alone on the bench.

She looked up into the sky and saw a big buzzard flying around, moving in great circles. The buzzard looked down on the hut, the bench, and the woman. Then he looked at the tree beside her and decided this tree would be a fine place for him to rest. Slowly he flew lower and lower, and when he had selected the branch of the tree he liked best, he settled on it and made himself comfortable. The old Indian woman watched him flying around and around and finally alighting on the branch. She sat there looking at the buzzard, and the buzzard looked at her. They looked at each other for a long time.

Then the old woman said, "Oh, Tío Buzzard! How much you remind me of my dear dead husband! May his soul rest in peace! How much he looked like you! You are dressed just the same as he used to dress—his clothes were always black, just like your black feathers. He really looked like a buzzard. Oh, Tío Buzzard! How much you remind me of my dear husband!"

She paused, and then continued talking to the buzzard. "He wore a little white cap on his head just like yours. How you remind me of him! He always sat just as you sit, with his legs under him, hunched up. His head was always sunk deep between his shoulders, just like yours. How much you remind me of my dear, dead husband! May he rest in peace."

She kept on talking and talking. The buzzard gazed at her solemnly. Suddenly he moved around in the branches, ruffling his feathers. As he did so, he broke off a thick branch. Buzzards are heavy birds, and his weight was too much for the branch to hold. It fell down on the old Indian woman, hitting her hard on the nose and cheek.

"Oh!" she cried. "That's just the way my husband used to hit me with a stick in the face! How much you remind me of him!"

Then the buzzard rose from the tree and slowly flew high up into the sky.

As he flew away, the old Indian woman gazed after him and said, "And there you are, flying away to Heaven, just as my husband did. How much alike you and my husband are!"

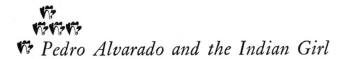

✦ *Pedro Alvarado and the Indian Girl*

Pedro Alvarado, fiery, terrible Spanish conquistador, or conqueror, was sent to capture Cuscatlán, now called El Salvador. But the people of Cuscatlán did not want to be conquered. They did not have weapons like those of the invaders from across the ocean, they fought in their Indian way.

When the Spaniards came near their villages, they left the villages and attacked their cruel enemy from the mountains. For that reason Alvarado destroyed their towns and burned their nobles when he caught them. But the Indians continued to resist. They did not want to be slaves.

The Spanish warriors in their shining armor came near the village of Izalco, which is close to the Izalco volcano.

It was a large village, divided by a river that becomes a raging torrent of water in the rainy season.

Not a soul was in the village when Alvarado arrived, and he set fire to the Indian huts and went on his way. For Alvarado was in a black fury because he had not found the Indians waiting for him—waiting to be enslaved. As he rode along on his great horse he came to a small hill that had a deep ravine running beside it in which there swirled a raging mass of wild water. He did not notice the stream, for his mind was full of plans about how to conquer these Indians who were forever running from him and fighting him at the same time.

Suddenly he saw between two green scraggly bushes a beautiful dark-brown Indian girl. She was standing still, looking at him, half frightened, half curious. She had heard everyone speak of the terrible white men. Some called them gods and others called them beasts with hairy faces, sitting on giant, strange animals—men who only wanted gold and who burned towns and killed Indians! Here was one of them, looking like some fierce god! She did not move; she just looked.

Alvarado called to her in his own language to come to him. The sound of his voice frightened her, and she ran back a little. He got down from his horse and followed her.

The frightened girl turned and ran into the bushes. Alvarado ran after her. Now she ran away swiftly, but the Spaniard still pursued her. But the Indian girl wore no heavy armor and she knew the ground well, so she could go faster than he. Soon she came to the ravine with the rushing, swirling water, which cut off her escape.

Now Alvarado felt sure he would catch up with her. But he did not know the Indian girl's mind. She was more afraid of the unknown man or god or beast than of the

Suddenly he saw a beautiful Indian girl.

wild water. She leaped into the rushing stream, which carried her away swiftly, hurling her body and tossing it this way and that, along with branches and everything else in its path. Alvarado leaped in after her to save her, but the angry, rushing stream was stronger than the conquistador, and carried the girl away before Alvarado could help her.

When he came out of the stream, he walked with heavy, angry steps to his horse. Everything in Cuscatlán defied him, even the water. His face was set. "I'll conquer them just the same," were the words that kept passing through his mind as he and his horse continued on their way.

The people of Izalco say that the footsteps of Alvarado and his horse were so heavy with anger and disappointment at losing the Indian girl that they sank down deep into the stone, where they can be seen to this day. There they still stand: the imprint of a horse's hoofs and of the big boots of the conquistador.

GUATEMALA

 The Great Blessing of the Land

Bitol and Tzakol are the father god and the mother god of all the gods of Guatemala. They created everything, and are wise and old and gray.

One day they were talking about the land and the people in it. While they were talking, four animal-people came running up to them. They were Parrot, Coyote, Jaguar, and Eagle. They had bodies of people and heads of animals. They were very excited, and all of them spoke at once.

"Bitol and Tzakol," they cried, "come, let us show you a boy who is more beautiful than Butterfly."

Bitol and Tzakol arose and followed the four animal-people who led them through the woods, to the River, where a lovely boy was playing.

Now, I must tell you that in those days the sun and moon, stars and flowers, water and animals—all were people and had children. They were very happy.

A sunbeam from the sky had fallen in love with River, who sang and danced over the stones day and night. Sunbeam and River were married and had a beautiful son. That day the boy was lying on the riverbank, playing with his water mother, and he shone bright as the sun on the water.

"Where did this beautiful child come from?" asked Tzakol.

"Golden Sunbeam shot down from the sky and fell in love with River. They married, and this is their child."

Bitol and Tzakol looked at the shining boy and their hearts opened to him at once.

"Let us take him home with us to live with our children," Tzakol said.

And that is what they did. They called him Teosinte, and Teosinte grew up quickly into a fine young man, strong and graceful.

The old gods Bitol and Tzakol had many children of their own, and the most beautiful of them all was their youngest daughter, Ma-ix. She was lovelier than a *quetzal* bird gleaming in the sunshine. Teosinte loved her, and she loved Teosinte. They loved each other so much that they were married.

"Now that we are married," said Teosinte, "let us leave your home and go to live near River, where I was born. There we shall listen to my mother's song all day long. It is a song without end."

"Wherever you go, I shall go," said Ma-ix.

Bitol and Tzakol, the old gods, were sad, and even angry, when they heard this news; they did not want their daughter to live so far from them because they loved her dearly.

But Teosinte and Ma-ix went away to live beside River, where Teosinte had been found.

And though Bitol and Tzakol were angry, they did not say anything.

Teosinte and Ma-ix found a cave beside River, and there they made their home. But they were not very happy because they knew that Bitol and Tzakol were still sad and angry.

Many months passed, and Bitol and Tzakol were worried and grieved because their children did not come to visit them as children should. What had happened to them?

One day they decided to go and see Teosinte and Ma-ix. They walked a long time, until they arrived beside River. They looked in the cave, they looked everywhere, but there was no sign of the young people. Where had they gone? Although Bitol and Tzakol looked in every place, the young couple was nowhere to be found. All they could find were two tall, very graceful plants in front of the cave, waving and dancing in the wind to the singing of River. They were beautiful plants. Both had long ear-leaves wrapped around a fruit, from which silken red hair hung—exactly the kind of hair that Teosinte had. And the fruit inside had little white pearly teeth, just like those of Ma-ix.

"The two have turned themselves into plants. These plants are the spirits of our children," said Tzakol.

"Yes," said Bitol, "the tall, straggly one is Teosinte, who took our daughter from us. Let it stay here alone in the wind and the rain. The other lovely plant is Ma-ix, our daughter. Let us take her with us. We shall cultivate

"The two have turned themselves into plants."

her so that she will grow stronger and more beautiful. The plant that is the spirit of our daughter will be a great blessing to the land, just as Ma-ix was a joy and a blessing to us."

So they took the plant, and watched it and tended it and helped it to grow strong and beautiful and to multiply. Now they called it Maíz. It spread all over Guatemala, and the Indians ate it and grew strong. Today people everywhere eat it, for the Spaniards found it when they came to the New World, and they took it back to Europe.

But Teosinte was not cultivated, and grew wild all over Guatemala, and is just a weed.

The Little, Little Fellow With the Big, Big Hat

You can hear the story of *El Sombrerón* in many different places in Guatemala, but most of all in Antigua, the ancient capital of that land. Ask any Maya Indian, or even a *ladino* —a person born of European or of mixed European-Indian ancestry—for a funny story, and he will tell you one about El Sombrerón.

Who is El Sombrerón?

Once there lived an Indian woman in Santiago de los Caballeros de Guatemala, as the old capital was called, who gave birth to twin sons. This made the father, who was a hatmaker, very proud.

One of the boys grew up to be a fine fellow, but the other one had the Devil in him. He always did what he should not do.

He was in the habit of taking things that were not his: he broke into other people's gardens and took fruit and flowers. He made trouble in the marketplace, turning over jars and stacked piles of food. And he was always playing tricks on boys and girls that made them cry.

Finally his father called the *brujo*. *Brujos* are wise men of the Maya people who give them advice, cure them when they are sick, and get them out of trouble. The brujo came and listened to the long tale of trouble the boy was always getting into.

"I must think about this overnight and pray," the brujo said. "Come to see me tomorrow, and I'll try to help you."

The next day the boy's father went to the house of the brujo, who said:

"God told me to tell you what to do. Make a very, very big sombrero, the biggest one you have ever made. When you have it made, bring it to me. I'll put magic in it, and it will teach that boy a lesson he'll never forget."

The hatmaker went home. He worked for a long, long time, and when he was done he had made the biggest sombrero that had ever been made in Guatemala. It was so big and heavy that it was hard to carry, but carry it he did, straight to the house of the brujo.

"Leave the sombrero here until tomorrow. Come back near evening, when I will have it ready for you."

The hatmaker went home.

The brujo lit candles and put rose petals on his altar before the images of saints and idols, asking them to bring his prayers to the attention of God. The next morning he prayed a long time. Then he wove a strong magic into that big hat. It took a long time because the magic had to be very strong.

When the volcanoes near the city pointed their long shadows eastward, the hatmaker came back.

"Take the sombrero now," the brujo said. "There is magic in it. Put it in the middle of the floor of your house, and your son will do the rest."

The man went home and put the sombrero right in the middle of the room on the earth floor, exactly as the brujo had told him to do. Then he went to sleep in a little room nearby.

After a while there was a great noise of something falling. It woke up the hatmaker.

"What's that noise? It sounds as if a pot fell and broke. Maybe it's that son of mine taking the money I keep in it. I'm sure it's that boy making trouble."

He got up and went into the big room to see what had happened. The moon was shining right on the sombrero, still lying in the middle of the floor . . . but the hat was moving. He went up to it and pushed it and pulled it and pushed it and pulled it until he turned it over. And there was a sight to see!

His troublemaking son was under the hat, kicking his legs, and the hat was tight on his head.

"Father, please! Take this sombrero off my head."

"How did you get under it?"

"I was 'borrowing' some money from your jar. I wanted to buy candy tomorrow. It's market day. The pot fell down. I heard you coming so I ran and hid under the hat. Now it's on my head and I can't get it off."

"Serves you right!" the father said. "That will teach you not to 'borrow' what does not belong to you."

Then the father tried to take the sombrero off the boy's head, but he could not do it, either. It seemed to be glued

"Take the sombrero off my head," cried the son, kicking.

on, and nobody could take it off. From that day on the boy had to wear it all the time, and people began to call him *El Sombrerón*—The Big Hat.

El Sombrerón did not grow any taller. That hat was so heavy, it kept him down. So he stayed short in size though he was getting longer in years.

And all the time he went right on making mischief. With each passing year he brought more trouble to people, and they did not know what to do about it.

El Sombrerón had learned magic, and that made him worse. With his magic he was able to make himself invisible so no one could see him. He could climb up straight walls, and even go right through them. He would ride other people's horses at night, so they were lame the next morning. He would frighten people. Everybody was afraid of him and wished he would go away. Then one day he did go away, and it happened in a funny way.

El Sombrerón was full grown in years, though not in size, and he wanted to marry. He saw a girl he liked and began to visit her house and bring her presents, as is the custom among the Maya Indians.

The mother of the girl did not like El Sombrerón courting her daughter and tried to drive him away, but he would not go. She locked the door against him, but he got in just the same. She saw that the only way to get rid of him was to go far, far away without telling him where she was going.

She told no one about this because she was afraid the fellow would hear of it, but she had to tell her daughter. And what do you think the daughter did? She told El Sombrerón.

"I'll take care of that," he said, laughing. "Just you wait and see."

The woman got her things together, hired a cart, and

she and her daughter left very early one morning when only the birds were awake.

They rode and they rode for many days, for the mother wanted to make sure El Sombrerón would never know where her daughter had gone.

Finally they came to the place in which they planned to live, and the woman and her daughter began to unpack their belongings. When they were almost finished, the woman saw that her big cooking pot, her *olla*, was not there.

"A curse on that Sombrerón who made us come here and who made me forget my olla. I wish I had never laid eyes on that worm with two legs."

As the last word was out of her mouth, she heard someone laughing just outside the door.

"That's not a nice way to talk about me. I knew you had forgotten your olla, so I brought it to you."

She ran out, and there was El Sombrerón, laughing and holding her olla in his two hands.

What could she say? She saw there was no escape from that devilish creature, so she shut her eyes and let him marry her daughter.

After he was married, do you think El Sombrerón changed his ways? No, indeed! He just kept on plaguing folks and playing tricks and doing things he shouldn't do all over Guatemala for as long as he lived. And people still talk about him and his tricks to this very day.

❦ The Sweetest Song in the Woods

This is an old-time story of something that happened many thousands of years ago. There lived then a Maya Indian king who had a beautiful daughter. Her name was Nima-cux. The king loved her more than his kingdom, and he was always with her. They were like two friends, for Nima-cux loved her father as much as he loved her.

These two were very happy together, but one day there came an end to this happiness. Nima-cux was then fifteen years old. She became sad and would not speak to anyone—she wanted to be alone. Her father tried in many ways to bring back her happiness. He had the most beautiful birds and the finest beads in the land brought to her. He had the young people sing and play games before her. But nothing the king did would make her speak, or laugh, or even smile. When the king saw this, he was very sad.

"I must have my daughter as she was," he said to his counselors.

He called together the wise priests of his land and asked them what to do.

Many of them came to his palace and listened to what he had to say. Then, after much thinking and talking, they said to the king, "We know the cause of your daughter's trouble, and we know what you should do. Your daughter has reached the age when she should be married. When she is married, her sadness will leave her, and she once again will be as she was."

"She shall be married," said the king.

He ordered all the young noblemen of his land to come to his palace on a certain day, to show that they were as noble in deed as they were in birth. Then Nima-cux could choose from among them the one she would take as her husband.

The young noblemen of the kingdom came on the day set. There were a great many—the most handsome, strong, and skilled in the land. They were all beautifully dressed in gold and feathers. Each one showed what he could do before the king and his daughter: some in strength, some in skill, and some by their gold and beautiful clothing. But the princess did not smile. She sat in silence and took little notice of what was going on.

As the sun was sinking and the games were coming to an end, one more young man came up the path. He was from a noble family, but he was poorly dressed. He carried no weapons, and he had no gold or jade around his neck. He walked up singing a beautiful song in a beautiful voice. It was the loveliest singing the princess had ever heard, and her eyes opened wide and became bright. There was a smile of pleasure on her face, and she looked the way she used to look.

"Let that young man come to my palace," the king ordered.

When he came in, the king told him that he could marry his daughter.

Nima-cux smiled sweetly and said, "You sing more beautifully than anyone I have ever heard, but you do not sing as sweetly as the birds. I will marry you when you sing for me as sweetly as a bird."

"I can do anything for you," the young nobleman said, "and I can learn to sing for you as sweetly as a bird. But you must give me time to learn."

"How much time do you want?"

"Four moons will be enough."

So the young nobleman went out into the woods to listen to the singing of the birds. Day after day he listened to their singing and tried to sing as they did. He practiced all the time. But, although he tried endlessly, his singing could not match that of the birds and he grew very sad. The days were passing swiftly, and there was little time left. And, try as he would, he could not sing as sweetly as the birds.

Only a few days were left, and he sat silently in the woods. He had given up hope and had decided not to go back to the palace. Suddenly the Spirit of the Woods stood before him.

"Why do you look so sad?" the Spirit asked.

The young man explained the cause of his grief.

"Do what I tell you, and you will sing as sweetly as the birds," said the Spirit, smiling. "First, cut a small branch from that tree."

The young nobleman took his black stone knife, and cut off the branch, and handed it to the Spirit, who shaped it and hollowed it like a tube, and then made holes in the side of it.

"Now blow through it and learn to move your fingers along the holes," the Spirit said.

The young man did as he was told, and from the hollow stick came music as beautiful as a bird's song.

"This is a *chirimía*," the Spirit said, and continued, "play on it, and its music will be as sweet as the song of a bird. Learn to play it well, then play it before the princess, and she will marry you." Then the Spirit was gone.

The young nobleman practiced the whole day long on his chirimía, and soon the music he played was even more beautiful than the song of the birds. It was the sweetest song in the woods.

He went back to the palace, and when the princess heard this new song, she said it was the most beautiful she had ever heard.

So Nima-cux and the music player were married and lived happily ever after, and the Maya peoples have played the chirimía ever since.

Golden Goodness

There are a thousand golden tales of goodness told in Guatemala about Brother Santiago de los Caballeros de Pedro. He was always doing good for all those in need, and most of all for the Indians and black slaves, who were so harshly treated by the Spaniards. He did this because he loved everyone and followed the word of God.

His own home, a broken-down thatched hut, he made into a hospital for the poor. The people lovingly called his hut *"la casita del Hermano Pedro"* (the little house of Brother Peter).

At night Hermano Pedro walked through the streets of the city ringing a little bell, to remind people to praise the Lord and thank Him for their many blessings.

People, poor people, came day and night to the little house of Hermano Pedro, and he cured them of their ills and taught them to read and write.

One day there came to his hut an Indian dressed in rags. He was crying.

"Good Hermano Pedro, my wife is ill and in great pain, and I need medicine for her. My children are starving, and I need money to buy food for them. Hermano Pedro, you help everybody. Help me!"

"Good Brother Indian," said Pedro, "I have herbs that will cure your wife, with the help of God, but I have no money to give you to buy food for your children."

Pedro stood with bared head in the warm light of the sun shining high in the blue sky. "Sweet Lord in Heaven," he said softly, looking lovingly upward, "help me to give this poor man money to feed his children."

Then he looked down on the earth. Not far from where he stood was a grayish-white rock, and on it lay a tiny green lizard with shining emerald eyes, sunning himself. Hermano Pedro looked at the lovely little lizard for a while, then took it up gently in his hand.

"The Lord in Heaven feeds this tiny lizard," he said, "and He will feed those little children who need food."

Suddenly the small lizard was no longer warm and soft, but hard and heavy. Pedro looked at it closely, and lo! a miracle had happened. The live lizard had turned into a solid gold lizard.

The poor Indian looked on this miracle with great surprise. But Hermano Pedro was not surprised at all.

"Our sweet Lord has turned this little animal into pure gold so you can feed your hungry children," said Pedro. "Here, take it, sell it, and with the money it brings you, you can feed your children for a long time."

"I thank you from the bottom of my heart," said the

grateful Indian. "May the Holy Mother of God bless you for your goodness!" And with a smile of bliss on his face, the medicine in his pocket, and the gold lizard in his hand, the Indian went off to a jewel merchant.

"Lend me money," he said to the merchant, "and I will leave with you this gold lizard Hermano Pedro gave me. When I have earned enough, I will come back and return your money to you and take the gold lizard back to Hermano Pedro."

The medicine cured the Indian's wife, and the money he got for the gold lizard multiplied many times. He became a rich man. True to his word, when he had enough money, he went back to the merchant.

"Good merchant," he said, "you will well remember the money you loaned me when I left that gold lizard with you. It was blessed by the Lord, for it helped me to earn much more. Here is the amount you loaned me. Now, give me back the little gold lizard, for I must return it to Hermano Pedro."

The merchant gave him back the precious animal, and with shining eyes and a light heart the Indian went to the house of Hermano Pedro.

"Here, Hermano Pedro, I have brought back your miraculous lizard," he cried. "It has given me both wealth and health. Now I give it back to you. God bless you for your kindness!"

"Thank you, good brother," said Pedro. "God was good to you, and I hope you will be good to others, as He has been to you."

Hermano Pedro took the little gold lizard in his hand and looked at it for a while. "Little creature," he said, stroking its gleaming body, "you have brought joy into the world, as God wants all creatures to do, and I thank you for it, in God's name."

He put the little gold lizard back on the rock from which he had first taken it. The sun shone on it just as it had that first day he saw it. And then another miracle happened—the gold lizard turned into a live lizard again and ran into a crack where it lived.

Then Hermano Pedro spoke. "You see, good Brother Indian, the Lord on high takes care of all His creatures, and He wants us on this earth to do the same—to help Him by helping others."

Those were the words of Hermano Pedro.

THE GUIANAS

 Bahmoo Rides the Wrong Frog

Bahmoo was a boasting fellow. He boasted about doing things that he could not do or that he had never done. And he was not very smart, either.

One day he went to a village to visit some friends and to find a wife. In the village everybody knew Bahmoo, and they thought they'd have a little fun with him.

"Bahmoo," one said, "come and hunt frogs with us. We have the finest frogs in the land. They are as big as bush hogs, and they are fine to eat. We'll go tomorrow morning."

Bahmoo was glad to be asked. He liked cooked frogs, and he had never seen frogs as big as bush hogs.

139

In the morning everybody was ready to start. Every man had his weapons.

"Bahmoo," a friend said to him, "take a club of hard mahogany wood. Those frogs need the hardest blows."

Then Bahmoo began his old boasting game.

"I don't need any weapons to hunt frogs. If they are that big, I'll jump on their backs and twist their necks," and he did not take any weapon. Then Bahmoo and his friends went into the woods and the swamps. On the way, Bahmoo kept saying, "I don't need any weapons. If I meet a big frog, I'll jump on its back and twist its neck."

It so happened that the chief of the frogs was hiding in the big leaves and heard Bahmoo's foolish boasting.

"I'll teach that boasting fellow a good lesson," croaked the chief to the other frogs.

The hunters went in different directions. Bahmoo was alone, and the chief of the frogs followed him. After a time the chief jumped ahead and lay down in the swamp water nearby and half closed his eyes.

Bahmoo was walking in that direction. Around him there was a whole army of frogs making a terrible noise with their croaking: *boro-ohk, boro-ohk, boro-ohk*. It was almost like thunder, only it didn't stop. The people who lived there were used to it, but Bahmoo didn't like it because it hurt his ears. He was worried. Some of the Indian hunters passing by saw the fear in his face and laughed at him.

"They think I'm afraid," Bahmoo said in a low voice. "I'll show them!" But the sweat was running down his forehead.

He saw the chief of the frogs lying there, asleep, he thought, and he leaped on the chief's back. The chief was a giant frog. He turned his legs and twisted them around Bahmoo's neck.

"Ho there!" the chief of the frogs croaked. "Come with me to my house, young fellow. I don't live far from here. Come along, young fellow!" He leaped into the water, holding Bahmoo tightly around the neck. Bahmoo howled and tried to get away, but the chief of the frogs was very strong and held him tight.

"Come, don't be afraid," he said. "We'll get through this water. Let's sing as we swim." *Boro-ohk, boro-ohk, boro-ohk,* the frog kept singing. And all the other frogs around them croaked: *boro-ohk, boro-ohk, boro-ohk.* It was enough to split one's ears. Such a thunderous noise had not been heard in Guiana for a long time.

Bahmoo was terribly frightened, but he could not escape the strong hold of the chief of the frogs. He howled and the frogs croaked. His friends heard the noise and rushed to see what was happening.

When they saw Bahmoo flopping around in the water, they laughed and laughed and laughed.

"Twist the frog's neck! Twist the frog's neck!" they screamed. "You don't need any weapons. Show us what you can do."

The chief of the frogs pulled Bahmoo across the water to the opposite side. "Young fellow," said the chief, "I brought you safely to shore. I hope you liked being with me and had a good time." Then he threw Bahmoo over his head and onto the ground. "Now I must go and help my people. Your people are killing them. I showed mercy to you, but your friends show my people none." Then the chief of the frogs hopped away.

Bahmoo felt ashamed. He went back to his friends in the village and told them that he had acted foolishly. He did not like people to laugh at him—and that's why he had acted as he had.

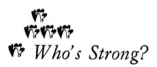

Who's Strong?

Jaguar was walking in the jungle, growling and stalking. He growled at everything, at all the animals and even at the trees. He was hungry.

Lightning was working, making himself a big club. He didn't see Jaguar, but Jaguar saw him and thought he was an animal and would be good to eat.

"I'll get him!" cried Jaguar, and leaped on Lightning. But of course he just leaped through fire. That made Jaguar very angry.

"Are you strong?" he growled.

"I am not strong," said Lightning.

Jaguar began to boast. "I'm not like you. I'm as strong as a giant. I'll show you how strong I am, brother-in-law. I'll show you I can break branches from all these trees."

He climbed up one tree, tore off all its branches, and threw them down on the ground. Then he came down, leaped up into another tree, stripped it of all its branches, and hurled them to the ground. He did the same thing to a third tree. Then he sprang to the ground and tore up the grass and the earth all around him with his sharp claws, just to show Lightning how strong he was.

But by this time he was very tired, and all wet with

sweat. His mouth was open, his tongue dripped, and he was breathing hard: *aif . . . aif . . . aif . . .*

"Do you see, brother-in-law, how strong I am? I am very strong; I'm not like you."

Again he jumped on Lightning and tried to eat him, but of course he couldn't. How could he chew fire? So he said:

"Now, show me how strong you are."

"I told you I'm not strong. I'm not strong like you, brother-in-law," said Lightning.

"Well, if *you* are not, *I* am. Look!" And Jaguar again began to rip branches from the trees and tear up the grass and earth. Lightning just watched him and didn't say anything.

Soon Jaguar was huffing and puffing and sweating again. He was tired, so he sat down, his back to Lightning.

Lightning picked up his club, swung it around, and quick as a flash there was roaring thunder and pouring rain.

"What's this? What's this?" screamed Jaguar, frightened. Quickly he climbed up a tree, shivering all over.

Lightning smashed the trees all around and Jaguar fell to the ground with a thud.

Then Lightning picked up Jaguar by his legs and flung him far, far away. Jaguar jumped up, ran away in fear, and hid in a rocky cave. Lightning struck the rocks and broke them apart.

Jaguar ran out of the cave and climbed up into a big tree. Lightning cracked that tree in two with one stroke.

Jaguar ran into a deep hole in the earth. A giant snake lived down there. Lightning cracked the earth apart all around the hole.

Jaguar ran this way and that way, up trees, down in the earth, behind rocks, but, wherever he went, Lightning was after him, smashing everything to splinters.

It was getting colder; a heavy rain was falling. Jaguar was freezing, wet, and sick with fear. He lay down on the ground, rolled up, and let the cold rain beat down on him.

Then Lightning stopped and said, "See, brother-in-law, the way I am. I am strong, too. You shouldn't boast so much. You are not the only one who has strength. I am stronger than you are; you have just seen that. Now, brother-in-law, I am going away." And off he went, leaving Jaguar lying on the ground, shivering and ashamed of himself.

He lay there for a long time. When he was sure that Lightning had gone, he got up and limped home.

That day he learned a lesson he never forgot. When thunder, wind, and rain come, he knows Lightning is there, and he is scared. Now you know why.

Smart Dai-adalla

"Dai-adalla, will you come with us to a great feast our friends are giving?" That's what Dai-adalla's father asked his little daughter.

"No, Father, I'll stay in the hut, do the things that have to be done, and look at the butterflies and monkeys."

"Dai-adalla, come to the feast," said her mother. "There will be young boys and girls playing, singing, and dancing. There will be fine fruits and good armadillo meat."

"No, Mother, I'll stay here and do the work for you. You and Father can go to the feast."

So Dai-adalla's father and mother went to the feast, and Dai-adalla stayed home in her hut. She swept it, and then she lay down to look at the macaws and parrots with green feathers and the funny toucan birds.

In the afternoon she heard a noise. She went out and there stood her dearest friend, whom she had not seen in a long time. They were such good friends that they had exchanged names, as the Indians often do. But it was really *not* her friend. It was an evil wood spirit who wanted to harm her and who had taken on the form of her best friend.

"You are all alone, Dai-adalla," said the disguised evil spirit.

"Yes, I'm alone. My father and mother went to a feast."

"I am glad we two can be alone," the evil spirit said. "I'll stay the night with you."

"That's good. I know my parents will not be home until the moon has gone."

Night came, and it was filled with the great night noises of the jungle forest. Loudest of all was the noise of the frogs.

"I know you like frogs," said Dai-adalla to her friend. "Why don't we go and catch some? We'll have a fine meal."

"Good!" said the disguised evil spirit. "Let us go into the woods." There the evil spirit could do even more harm than in the light. "You go one way and I'll go another. We will call to each other and tell each other how many frogs we've caught."

Each went in a different direction, calling out every now and then how many frogs she had caught.

But in the black, noisy jungle night, the evil spirit became excited and forgot himself, and when Dai-adalla asked once how many frogs her friend had caught, the evil spirit cried, "I'm catching many, many, and I eat them as fast as I catch them!"

Dai-adalla was frightened. People did not eat frogs alive; only evil spirits did that. This was an evil spirit, not her friend. It was an evil spirit disguised as her friend. Her father and mother had told her to beware of evil spirits, for they could harm her, even eat her! What could she do to escape?

The evil spirit was calling to her, "How many frogs have you caught, Dai-adalla?"

Dai-adalla thought quickly. "Sh! Hush!" she cried. "You are frightening the frogs, and I can't catch any to put in my calabash."

The evil spirit was silent. Dai-adalla ran home as fast as she could. Inside the hut she turned all the earthen pots upside down, for Indians always did this when evil spirits were near. Then she climbed up on the roof and waited to see what would happen. She did not have long to wait.

The evil spirit was calling Dai-adalla and there was no answer. He called again—again no answer.

"That girl has tricked me," he said and ran to the hut. It was dark and there was no fire. He touched everything with his hand.

"Ah, here are pots upside down. Maybe she is hiding under one of them," he exclaimed, turning over each pot. No Dai-adalla.

"Where are you? Where are you?" he screeched. "If I had known you were a trickster, I would have eaten you with the frogs."

He kept running around and around, looking everywhere for Dai-adalla. She was afraid, but she stayed quietly on the roof and did not move. The stars were be-

"I'm eating the frogs as fast as I catch them," said the evil spirit.

coming pale in the sky, and she knew the evil spirit would go away when day came.

When the first sign of the sun came, the evil spirit ran away. Dai-adalla came down from the roof and waited for her mother and father.

When they returned, she told them how the evil spirit had come, disguised as her best friend, and all that had happened. Her parents listened carefully and then her father said, "Now, when we ask you to come with us, you will do it."

Dai-adalla said she would, and she did.

A Promise Made Should Be Kept

This happened in the time when bees and honey were everywhere in South America, and particularly in the Guianas. Indians ate honey all the time.

Now, at that time there was one young Indian who was famous because he was a very great bee hunter. He could find honey where no other Indian could find it. Every time he went into the woods, he came back to his hut with plenty of honey.

One day he was walking in the green jungle, looking for honey. He came to a very large, hollow tree, standing all alone. It looked like the right kind of tree to have honey.

"I know there is honey in that tree," he said, and he felt glad. "But I must chop it down to get it."

He raised his ax and began to chop—chip, chop, hack, hock. He chopped away, and the splinters flew on all sides.

All of a sudden he heard a voice in the tree saying, "Stop! Don't chop! You'll cut me in two!"

He stopped chopping, mouth open, and looked all around to see who was talking. No one was there.

"That voice came from the tree. Someone is in it. I must be careful."

He began to cut again, but now he worked slowly. Soon he made an opening in the tree, and in it he saw a beautiful Indian girl.

"Who are you? And how did you come to be in that tree?"

"My name is Maba. I live in this tree."

"You are Maba?"

"I am Maba."

The Indian honey hunter knew that Maba means the Mother Spirit of honey, the queen of honey, and he realized he was very lucky to find her.

"You are Maba, the beautiful Mother Spirit of honey," he said. "I am very lucky to find you. Let me get moss from the trees to make you an apron."

He wanted to please her. He ran around here and there and everywhere, gathering soft gray and green moss. From it he made a fine apron.

"Here it is, beautiful Maba," he said when he had finished it. He told her how happy he was to find her, and of how he had hunted for honey for years and years, always hoping to see her someday.

They spoke of other things, and then he asked her to marry him. She said no. Then he begged, and in the end she said she would, but only if he would promise that he would never call her by her name before friends or strangers, for she did not want anyone to know who she was. He promised, and they were married.

For many years the two lived together happily, he hunting and she tending to the housework.

From that time on he had more luck with honey hunting than he had ever had before. Everybody knew about his luck. And he had luck at home, too. Maba was a fine wife, and she made *kashiri* better than any woman. This is a sweet drink the Indians love. Not only that. When she made a *trog* (a barrel) of it, it was enough to make everybody happy. No one else could do that.

One day Maba's husband invited a large gathering to a great feast. They sat in a circle eating juicy armadillo meat and drinking the fine kashiri Maba had made. They drank until there was not a drop left in the trog.

Everyone was feeling wonderful, and the host got up and said, "Friends, you have eaten good armadillo meat, and you have drunk the best kashiri there is. That is the way it should be. It is late and you can go, but you can come again another time. I promise you that Maba will—" and suddenly he stopped, remembering that he must not speak his wife's name before others. But her name had escaped from his mouth before he had thought about it.

The minute that word came out of his mouth, Maba got up from the earth and flew away like a bee. She flew far, far away to her bees.

The Indian stretched out his arms to hold her back—but she was gone! He sighed and sorrowed, but it did no good. She was gone!

Maba was gone and so was his luck. From that time on he no longer could find honey as he had before. Now he had to hunt for it long and hard. And none of the other Indians could find honey as easily as they had before, either. That's the way it has been ever since then—all because an Indian didn't keep his promise.

When a Man Is Foolish

There are noodleheads all around the world, and South America is a big part of the world, so there are many noodleheads there, too.

One day a party of Indians in Guiana set out in their *corial* to visit friends in another village. They glided along the river bordered by jungle forests on each side. In the front of the boat sat the leader, an old, wrinkled Indian who was a wise medicine man. In the back of the boat sat a man who was very foolish. The other Indians were in the middle.

They paddled along the river for a long time, watching carefully for giant bushmasters, the fiercest of all snakes, and for boa constrictors, another snake greatly feared, too, and for jaguars.

One morning there was nothing to eat, and all the men were hungry.

"Go hunting, men," said their leader, the medicine man. "Shoot your arrows at any animal you see. Take your clubs along, too, for you may need them. Bring the game back here, and we'll have plenty to eat."

The men took their bows and arrows and their clubs of hard mahogany wood, and they went into the jungle to hunt. The only one left in the boat was the old medicine man.

All the others went off in different directions, each one watching for game. Every man found some game, shot it, and dragged it back to the corial. But the foolish fellow could not find any game, so he made a hammock of twigs, curled up in it, and went to sleep.

He slept all day long, and when the sun was low he awoke and thought it would be a good time to hunt.

Soon he came upon a long, gray anteater, sound asleep. The anteater's little eyes were closed; his long, thin mouth was curled up; and his large, bushy tail was spread over him like a fan. When the foolish Indian saw him, he stopped.

"Ho!" he cried. "Here is some good meat to eat. That anteater lies very still. He must be dead. I don't even have to waste an arrow on him to shoot him."

He came close to the sleeping animal.

"Are you dead or are you not dead?" he cried.

The animal was fast asleep and made no sound.

"He is dead. I know he is."

He touched the animal with his bare toe, but it was fast asleep and did not feel it.

"Who killed you and when?" the foolish Indian asked. "You are very fresh and still breathing, and you feel warm. Your meat will be very good to eat."

The anteater was breathing quietly and did not wake up.

"You are a big fellow and I'll need strong cords of bark to carry you to the boat. I'll go and get them."

He went off into the jungle forest to find strong strips of bark on which to carry the anteater.

It was hard walking in the jungle, and it was hard to find the right bark. But he found it, cut it into strips, and went back. It took him a long time to come to the place where the anteater was. When he got there . . . it wasn't there!

He looked everywhere. He crept through the brush, he climbed up the trees. No anteater.

"I left that anteater under this tree—I can still see where he was lying dead. I touched him with my toe. He couldn't walk away because he was dead. Someone stole him. When I catch that thief, I'll let my club dance on his head."

He looked around a little while longer, then went back to the camping place. All the other Indians were sitting there, eating.

"Where is your game?" the medicine man asked the foolish fellow. "Didn't you see any animal to shoot?"

"I saw a fat anteater. He was dead but still fresh. Some other Indian stole him."

"How was he stolen if you were there?"

"He was stolen when I went to get some strong bark to tie him on my back to carry him."

"Did you shoot him or club him?"

"I didn't shoot him and I didn't club him. I found him dead and he was still fresh."

"How did you know he was fresh?" one asked.

"He was blowing up and down, and his tail was moving up and down. His whole body was moving."

"You mean he was breathing?" asked the medicine man.

"He was, but he was very still. I even touched him and he didn't move. He was dead."

The medicine man laughed. All the Indians laughed.

"You fool!" said the medicine man. "Don't you know that an animal that blows up and down is not dead? It is just sleeping. When you went for the bark, it ran away."

"I didn't know that," said the fool.

"You should have shot him," another cried.

"I'll remember that next time."

But you know what the promises of fools are worth. The next time he did something else just as foolish as this. He acted that way all his life. Once a fool, always a fool.

HAITI

 Uncle Bouqui and Little Malice

Cric!

  Crac!

There was a king in Haiti, and he had a fat sheep he loved more than silver and gold. This sheep was his pet, and he had it near him all the time. He played with it as if it were his child. He combed its fleece and put red ribbons on it, and called it My Joy.

Day and night he watched his sheep because he was afraid someone would steal it. More than anyone else he was afraid of the trickster Malice, the smartest and most cunning fellow in all Haiti.

Now, little Malice had seen that fine fat sheep, and he had a fine fat appetite. Besides, he loved sheep meat more than any other kind of meat. He had made up his mind he

155

was going to eat the king's sheep, and he could think of nothing else except how he could get it.

Well, believe it or not, it didn't take too long. Soon the king's sheep was in Malice's yard, in Malice's pot, and, before you could count five, in Malice's mouth. He enjoyed a great feast of sheep stew.

When the king missed his sheep, he ran around the palace wildly roaring, "Where is My Joy?" But nobody knew where My Joy was. So the king sent for the very best *houngan* (witch doctor) in all Haiti.

When the witch doctor arrived, the king shouted, "Find me My Joy! Find me the thief!"

"I'll find the thief," said the houngan. "Give me a candle, a pot of water, and money."

When these things were brought to him, he lit the candle, made a cross with the money, and put the water in front of it. Then he prayed and sang and danced.

Finally he said, "King, My Joy is dead. A thief stole it and ate it."

"Who was the thief? Tell me his name quickly!" roared the king. "Where is he? Who is he? He'll never steal again!" he screamed, stamping and shouting at the top of his voice.

"I can't tell you his name," the witch doctor said, "but I can tell you that he is the smartest man in all Haiti, and you know who that is. Now, pay me. I must go to a fisherman who can't catch fish."

The king paid him. He knew who the smartest man in Haiti was, and he was determined to catch him.

"Chief of the guards, come here!" he shouted.

The chief of the guards came running. "Go and find Malice," said the king. "Put him in chains and bring him here."

"You know, King, it's hard to catch that scoundrel. He

is a crafty fellow," mourned the chief of the guards.

"You bring him here in three days or I'll do to you what I want to do to him," warned the king darkly.

Sadly the chief of the guards went out to look for Malice.

The king was still unhappy, so he decided to hold a prayer meeting and give a feast in honor of the dead My Joy. He invited every important person to come to the feast.

You can be sure that Malice knew all about what had happened: that the king had sent the chief of the guards to look for him and bring him back in chains. He was very worried and kept thinking hard how to get his neck out of that noose.

"I'm an honest man until I'm caught," he said, and went where the guard could not see him. He went to the house of Bouqui, that stupid Bouqui of Haiti, who loved to eat more than anyone in the world. Bouqui came to the door.

"Honor!" cried Malice.

"Respect!" answered Bouqui.

That was the proper manner of greeting in Haiti.

"Uncle Bouqui," said Malice with an innocent expression on his face, "Uncle Bouqui, have you heard of the great prayer and feast the king is offering for his lost sheep?"

"No, I have not, Malice."

"Everybody must come in carnival clothes. There will be a song contest, too. He who sings the best song and wears the finest costume will receive as a prize three big fat oxen, five sheep, and other good things. That is a prize for you!"

"Really?" cried Bouqui, his eyes as big as saucers.

"Yes, it is exactly as I tell you," Malice assured him.

"Ah, my dear Nephew Malice! You know how much I

love you. Three fat oxen! Five sheep! You know how I love ox and sheep meat. You said three oxen and five sheep, didn't you?"

"That's exactly what I said."

"Here is money, Nephew Malice. Go and buy me the finest costume and teach me the finest song, so that I can win that prize. I promise you half of all the king gives me."

Malice took the money. Then he took the skin of the sheep he had stolen from the king, and from it he made a fancy coat for Bouqui. He brought it to him and put it on his back, and looked at Bouqui with the greatest admiration.

"That coat looks fine on you, *Nonc* Bouqui. Now I'll teach you a song nobody can beat, and you are sure to win the prize."

"Teach me, teach me quickly, Malice. I want to win those oxen and sheep."

"Now, listen carefully while I sing, *Nonc* Bouqui," and Malice began to sing:

> *"I am Bouqui the Great,*
> *who took My Joy*
> *in the king's palace.*
> *In the king's palace*
> *I took My Joy.*
> *You can see the proof right on my back.*
> *I ate My Joy*
> *in the king's palace.*
> *In the king's palace*
> *I ate My Joy."*

"That is a wonderful song," cried stupid Bouqui. "I'll learn it and I'll win the prize."

"Don't forget that half is for me," said Malice slyly.

"How can I forget, my dear Nephew Malice, after all you have done for me?"

Bouqui learned the song, and when he knew it well, he and Malice went to the king's palace. The building was all lighted up and there was a grand company of important people. Bouqui went in, but Malice stayed out in the bushes, saying he did not feel well.

Bouqui walked around with his head high in the air. Everybody was talking about the terrible loss of the king's sheep and how the thief would be punished, and everybody ate stew and yams and plantains, deliciously cooked by the king's own cook. And they also drank the king's fine rum.

Bouqui ate more and drank more than anyone there. He felt very happy and sang the song Malice had taught him, hoping the king would hear it and that he would win the prize. It did not take long for his song to reach the king's ears.

"What's that song I hear?" shouted the king. "What's that song? Who is singing it?"

"It's me, King!" cried Bouqui. "I'm the one who's singing that song. Listen!" And again he sang:

> *"I am Bouqui the Great,*
> *who took My Joy*
> *in the king's palace.*
> *In the king's palace*
> *I took My Joy.*
> *You can see the proof right on my back.*
> *I ate My Joy*
> *in the king's palace.*
> *In the king's palace*
> *I ate My Joy."*

"Turn around!" roared the king at Bouqui.

Bouqui turned around, and the king saw My Joy's skin on his back.

"Oh, my poor sheep!" cried the king. "So you are the

"Oh, my poor sheep!" cried the King. "So you are the thief."

thief and the robber! Ah! You won't ever steal sheep again. Guards, take him, beat him, and broil him! Be quick!"

The guards took poor Bouqui away. Then Malice came out of the bushes and said in an innocent voice, "King, you must pay me the prize because I helped you to find the thief who stole your sheep."

"Hm!" said the king. "A snake is not far from its hole, and Malice is not far from my chief of guards. Maybe the saying is true: Set a thief to catch a thief. You are too smart, Malice. Maybe you had a hand in all this. The witch doctor said the smartest man in my land did this, and Bouqui is *not* the smartest man in my land. Guards, take Malice, also. It will do no harm to punish him a little, too."

So the guards took Malice and bound him in chains, and there were Malice and Bouqui in the same prison, waiting to be punished.

"It's you who got me into this mess, Malice, you scoundrel!" cried Bouqui.

"I know I did, Bouqui, and I'm very sorry for it. I love

you even when I do such things. But now I'll get you out of here. Let us both leave and live happily together."

Malice knew how Haitian guards were, so he gave a little money to some, and presents to others, and before long they were both free.

Bouqui swore he would never listen to Malice again.

Do you think he kept that promise?

Of course not!

HONDURAS

 How the Caribs First Came to Honduras

This happened a long, long time ago, before the Caribs, the Carib black folks, the Spanish, or the English were here. It happened before any kind of people were in Honduras.

The Creator looked around and saw that there were trees and flowers and butterflies and animals and fish and fruit to eat, but there were no people to eat them. There was no woman, or even any man.

"There should be people to find pleasure in these things, and to fish and hunt. I'll make people," He said.

He took some clay and wet it in a stream. Then He kneaded and kneaded it like dough, and twisted it and shaped it. When he was finished, there were a man and a woman—a nice black man and a nice black woman.

"That's fine," He said. "Now all is done."

Then the heavy rains came and fell on the clay man and clay woman, and they lost their shape and just melted away. It was a sad sight to see.

"I must do better," said the Creator.

He thought about the matter for a time. Then He took cork and cut it and shaped it, as He had done before with the clay. Soon He had a man and a woman made of cork.

"That's better," He said.

The cork man and woman stayed on the earth, but they couldn't work well. They were so light that they flew around in the wind and floated away on the water. One day a volcano spat fire and stone and water, and the man and woman were burned up.

"I must make a better man and woman," the Creator said. "The cork man and woman were no better than the clay ones. I must make a man and woman the fire can't burn or the water melt."

He thought about it for a long time. Then He took corn and made a man and woman out of this. They were as beautiful as the ripe corn and their teeth were as white. Their hair was as fine and silky as its tassels. They were the Caribs, the first people in Honduras. Fire from the volcano did not destroy them. Water from the heavy rains did not wash them away. They have been here ever since.

🖼 The Virgin of Honduras

All through the lands of Latin America, the people love their patron saints, and, most of all, the Holy Virgin. Often they have legends that tell how they chose their patron, or why their patron's holy shrine is located where it is, or how their patron's image first appeared. The people of Honduras, the Silver Mountain people, tell how the image of their patron, the Holy Virgin of Suyapa, first appeared.

It happened many years ago, when the land was still peopled with Indians and there were only a few Spaniards, when the roads were still trails, and the beautiful temples of Copán were already very old.

One day two Indian boys were going home after working all day in the fields. They had worked hard and were tired, so they walked slowly, and night overtook them while they were still far from home.

"Let us sleep right here on the mountain," said one. "I am tired, and it will be late in the night before we get home."

"I am tired, too, and the way is long," said the other. "Here is a good place, on the soft grass beside this tree."

They had come to a great mahogany tree with yellow-red leaves that stood proudly and alone. That is the way mahogany trees grow. Beside it the grass was soft and there was no brush.

They spread their blankets on the ground and lay down to sleep. It was nice to lie there and listen to the singing of the night birds and the buzzing of the insects.

They had not been there long when they began to smell the sweetest perfume they had ever smelled. It was sweeter than the fragrance of any flower.

"I have never smelled such a sweet odor," said one. "It can't be from the flowers."

"I, too, have never smelled anything so sweet," said the other. "Where do you think it is coming from?"

"It must be from some flower, blown to us by the wind."

"It is so sweet I can't sleep. I would like to know what it is."

"I can't sleep, either. Besides, there is something under my blanket that is digging into my side."

"Let's get up and clean away whatever is under your blanket."

The two Indian boys got up, lifted their blankets, and cleaned the ground beneath them with their hands. While they were doing this, the hand of one of them struck something. They couldn't see what it was in the dark, but it felt like a small stump or piece of wood, so they threw it away.

They put their blankets back down on the ground and lay down again. But still they couldn't sleep. The perfume smelled stronger than before. Its fragrance was so heavy that it seemed they could almost touch it. And again one of the boys felt something hard under his blanket.

"That stump is back again under my blanket," he said somewhat impatiently. "It is hard and hurts my side. I wonder how it got back here again."

He reached under his blanket, felt the piece of wood, threw it away, and lay down again. But no sooner was he on his back than he felt that stump again, and again he reached under the blanket, took it out, and threw it away as far as he could. Once more he lay down, only to feel the stump again. The same thing happened twice more. Now he was wide awake. "I wonder what this queer coming-back thing is," he said. "Let's light a fire and see."

The two boys got up, hung their blankets on a branch of a tree, and made a fire. When the fire was bright enough so they could see clearly, they began to look around on the ground for the stump.

"Here it is," said the one who had thrown it away so many times.

He picked up a small bundle covered with cloth. They took off the covering cloth and saw by the light of the fire a small statue of the Holy Virgin Mary, more beautiful than any they had ever seen.

"How did this Virgin come to be here?"

"I don't know."

"Neither do I. It must be a miracle. It must have come from heaven!" Both boys were very excited.

"We must take it to the village at once, and show it to the padre and to the people."

The boys ran, excited and stumbling, through the dark woods, holding the precious statue carefully. When they came to the village they woke the priest and all the people. They showed them the statue and told how they had found it, and about the perfume.

Soon everybody in Honduras heard about the miracle, and people came from everywhere to see the precious image and to worship it.

A fine church was built on the spot where it had been

found, to house the marvelous image of the patron of Honduras, the Holy Virgin of Suyapa.

🖋 *When Boquerón Spoke*

The great, cruel Spanish nobleman, Diego de Alvarado, took from the Indians their gold and their lands. Among these lands was Honduras, and there he helped to start the town of San Jorge de Olancho. It was close by the Volcano Boquerón, which stood clear and high in the sky, full of a burning strength inside.

The volcano watched in silence the building of the town beside it. It watched the Spaniards drive the Indians to work, without peace or rest. It watched the white men rob the Indians of their gold. The Spaniards were savage taskmasters, and the Indians worked day and night while the town grew bigger and bigger. For no reason except greed, the Spaniards kept looking for Indian gold and grew richer and richer. They tried to learn where the Indians got their riches, but the Indians would not speak. The Spaniards tortured them, but still the Indians remained silent.

The Spaniards got so much gold they didn't know what to do with it. They put it on their horses and saddles, they put it in their homes, and they sent it back in ships to Spain for the king and queen. So the town and its Spaniards all became richer, while the Indians were treated worse than beasts. And the volcano Boquerón watched silently.

One day the rulers of San Jorge de Olancho decided it was time to thank the Virgin for their riches and their town.

"Let us make an image of the Virgin out of pure gold, the like of which is not to be found in all Honduras. That will please the Holy Mother who has been so good to us."

Everyone agreed, and they ordered a great artist to do the work. They told him to make the image of solid gold, which they gave to him. After this they felt that they had done enough for heaven, so they turned their attention again to trading and to robbing the Indians.

The artist and craftsmen worked hard, and they cast a beautiful statue of the Virgin. It was so clear and sharp, it seemed almost to be alive. But they did not have enough gold to make the crown to place on the head of the lovely image, so they went to the priest and told him about their difficulty.

"Go to the nobles," he said, "and tell them you need gold for the crown."

The artist went to the nobles but found them too absorbed in their business to listen to him. They told him to come back some other day.

The artist returned to the priest and said, "The nobles are too busy with their own affairs. They wouldn't even listen to me."

The priest was very angry when he heard this.

"They are too busy with their own affairs to attend to the affairs of God? For shame! Go and speak to them again. Tell them to give you the gold to make the crown for our Heavenly Mother who has blessed them with their possessions."

Once more the artist went to the nobles, but he had no better luck than before. The nobles and the merchants were too deep in their money-making affairs to listen to the needs of the Holy Virgin. The artist returned and told the priest what had happened.

"Blasphemous sinners!" cried the priest. "They have sinned in the eyes of heaven and of earth and nature. They will be punished for this! I will put them to shame for their ungodliness."

He did not know that the volcano was watching and listening as he spoke.

The priest took coarse, raw cowhide, cut it into pieces, and from them he shaped a crown that he set upon the head of the image of the Blessed Mother of God's Son.

When the people came into the church and saw the cowhide crown, they laughed and made sport of the priest for placing it there.

"You will regret this day," the priest said to the people. "You will pay dearly for it. You will fall from your heights like the idols, and be shattered to pieces."

But the rich nobles and their followers mocked him and laughed at him and called him a fool. They went about their business of getting more gold and of driving the Indians to work harder. They thought no more about the Virgin's cowhide crown.

The richer they became, the less they thought about God. Finally, they did not go to church at all. They said they were so rich they did not need the Lord's help any longer. But heaven heard what they said, and so did the volcano Boquerón.

The priest kept begging them to mend their ways, but

nobody listened to him. At last God himself spoke to them through Boquerón.

It was a black night when Boquerón spoke to the people of Olancho. His voice roared like thunder and shook the earth with its angry and furious tones. He spat down fire, rock, and hot ashes, which poured over the town and covered the people and their houses. Buildings crashed to earth and men were buried under the ruins. Soon there was no San Jorge de Olancho—there was only rubble, wreck, and ruin. And a ruin it has been ever since.

This terrible tragedy happened in the year of our Lord 1611.

JAMAICA

✾ Anansi Play With Fire, Anansi Get Burned

*"I go away, I go away,
  Perhaps I come another day."*

There was great running around all over in the woods, for Tiger was getting married. Everyone, leaping, walking, crawling, and flying, was invited. Only one was not asked, and that was Anansi. Anansi—sometimes a spider, sometimes a man, sometimes half a man and half a spider —Anansi with a spider face who was always playing tricks and making trouble and cheating everyone in the forest and village. No, Anansi was not invited by Tiger to the wedding feast, because Tiger was angry at Anansi for playing so many mean tricks and cheating him so often.

Anansi was very angry, for he liked eating and dancing most of all. "I must do something about this," he said.

He walked up to Tiger's house, where Tiger was busy cooking and cleaning and getting everything ready.

"Good day, Bredda Tiger, it's a fine day and I see you are cooking fine-smelling food."

"Grrrrrrrrr," Tiger growled, not even looking at Anansi.

"Heard you were getting married tomorrow to a fine girl."

"Grrrrrrrrr," Tiger growled again.

"Heard you invited everybody, but you didn't invite me, your friend," and Anansi smiled sweetly.

"*Grrrrrrr*," Tiger growled louder at Anansi, the troublemaker.

Anansi made believe he did not hear.

"Never thought you would treat me that bad, and I am such a good friend to you."

"Get out of my eyes, you cheat, you thief, you liar," roared Tiger. "Get away from here before I tear you to pieces for the many times you cheated me. I don't want to spoil my wedding day."

That was too much for Anansi—he was boiling with anger. "I'll spoil your wedding day good and strong. If you want fire, you'll get it. I'll give you plenty trouble. I'll put a spell on you. You'll remember me all your life for this insult."

Then he ran away, for Tiger was getting ready to go for him.

Tiger growled and kept on working. Pretty soon he began worrying and thinking. "Folks say Anansi is a magician man. He can put curses on folks. He might put a curse on me. Maybe I should have invited him, even though he has lied to me and cheated me so many times. I better go to see my bride and talk things over with her."

Tiger went to his bride and talked to her of such nice things that he forgot all about Anansi.

But Anansi did not forget. Every one of his thin legs were shaking with anger. "I must fix that mean Tiger so that he remembers me all his life. I'll show him how to insult me! Not to invite me to the feast! When everybody'll be eating good food, I won't. I'll teach him something. But how? . . . How? . . . I know! I know!"

Anansi went back to Tiger's house. But he did not go straight—he was the kind that couldn't go straight. He went round about till he came to Tiger's house. He stopped and looked all around on all sides. Not a sound from the house.

"Just fine. Just what I wanted," Anansi said.

He ran in back of the house where there were trees and bushes, looking for the cowitch creeper. That's a creeper growing on trees. It has nice, soft, fluffy-velvety pods. But look out! If you touch those pods, your skin will burn and itch so you'll want to jump in the river. And you'll scratch and scratch until the blood runs, and then you'll scratch more and more.

"Those cowitch creepers will fix Mr. Tiger so he won't forget me," said Anansi as he climbed up a tree that had plenty of cowitch creepers hanging from it. He cut some of the streamers, holding them in his hands, in which he had put some leaves.

When he came down he went into Tiger's house holding the poison plant far away from him. On the table lay Tiger's wedding clothes nice and ready. Then mean Anansi rubbed the fluffy pods all over Tiger's clothes so that when he put them on, the fluffy things would rub his skin and make him itch to beat Carnival. When he had finished that mean work, he ran off.

After Tiger had talked with his bride and come back to

his house, he was still worried. Even when he went to sleep, he kept thinking and worrying about Anansi and what he would do.

Early next morning Tiger put on his wedding clothes, and soon all his animal friends started to come: Dog, Horse, Cat, Monkey, birds, frogs, land turtles—everybody came except Anansi. Tiger was beginning to itch. Guests were greeting him and talking, but poor Tiger was itching terribly. Soon he couldn't stand it. He tore his clothes off and looked at them. So did all the animals, and they saw the cowitch plant all over those clothes.

"That was that devil Anansi. That's the revenge he said he'd take," roared Tiger, and then he told the animals what had happened.

Now, all the animals had a great grudge against Anansi for he had done some wrong to each of them, and they decided they would take revenge on him.

"Let's pay him back for what he has done to us. Let's finish him so he can't do any more harm," shouted each one, from the ant to the horse.

"We'll invite him to the wedding, and when he's here we'll . . ."

"I'll bring him," zoomed Bee, "I'll bring him quick." She flew off, but she did not have to fly far. There was Mr. Anansi hopping around not far from Tiger's house, hoping to be asked to the feast.

Bee told him quickly that he could come: Everyone was waiting for him, and there was plenty left to eat. Anansi was such a glutton he did not smell anything wrong, so he went to Tiger's house. Yes, everybody was waiting for him. Anansi looked at Mr. Tiger, now dressed in different clothes, and thought everything was fine.

All the animals gathered around Anansi, and when there wasn't a hole the size of sand for him to get through, Tiger roared: "Now we have you and we'll show you how to put cowitch on my wedding clothes. You just wait!"

Anansi turned as white as chalk. He looked around and saw there was no place to run, for all the animals were gathered close. Tiger and Horse and Cat ran out to the trees and came back with heaps and heaps of cowitch creeper and laid them on the ground. They brought more and more and made a thick bed of it. Anansi looked on, shaking like a leaf in the wind.

"Now you'll get some of your own medicine," Snake hissed. "We'll put you on the bed of cowitch and roll you around and around in it. That'll pay you for trying to put it on Tiger's wedding clothes."

"You can't do that," Anansi howled. "It'll kill me. I'm your old friend, Mr. Tiger. I just played a little joke."

"Now I'll play a little joke," Tiger roared. "You put the cowitch on my clothes, and now I'll put it on you."

"Bredda Tiger, please don't do that. It'll hurt terribly. I was just playing a little joke."

"You didn't mind hurting me, did you? Now I'll play the same little joke on you."

Then the animals threw Anansi down on the cowitch and rolled him over and over and over. Anansi began to burn and itch like dry grass on fire, and when he saw they were not going to stop, he began thinking fast how he could escape. Even with the terrible burning and itching he had an idea.

"Bredda Tiger," he cried, "the Queen is coming down the road. Do you hear that noise far off? That's her coming this way."

"You are lying. You are up to some old trick," the animals cried.

"I'm not lying. It was in all the papers. You were too busy with the wedding to listen to it."

And though the animals doubted Anansi's word, some of them began to think he might be telling the truth and looked toward the road.

The wind was blowing high in the trees, making a lot of noise in the leaves.

"Don't you hear the noise of the people?" Anansi cried, for he couldn't stand the itching any longer. "That's the folks coming with the Queen," he screamed so you could hear him from one end of the island to the other. (But he really screamed because of the pain from the cowitch.) "There she is coming on the road! Run quick if you want to see her."

All the animals ran to see the Queen who was not there, and Anansi, he ran the other way to scratch himself. So you see, Anansi got paid what he deserved, but he got away just the same. That was just like Anansi.

Jack Mondory, me no choose none.

The Gold Table

Fate won't let a man go if it has its teeth in him. You want a story? I'll tell you one to show what Fate does. It's about a gold table on the Río Cobre at Three Meetings, where the rivers meet at Enson. There's a deep black pool over there, an' that's where that big gold table comes out.

If you stand in the sticky thorn bushes when the sun is shinin' hot at twelve o'clock an' look at that pool, you'll see the table. But you trouble it never. If you do, you're a dead one—fire out, ashes dead.

That table's been there a long time, from pirate times. And it's a pirate's table. It's from the gold the pirates robbed from ships.

But only one man got it. His name was Jackson. Master Jackson was a ship's carpenter. He was a smart one, an' ambition bit him hard. But you know, licky-licky (gluttonous) fly goes with coffin in a hole. He was licky-licky, an' he trusted no man.

The pirates robbed ships an' ships till their pirate ship was full o' gold. Then they said it was time to divide the gold between 'em an' quit an' live in peace.

All pirates said that. Jackson 'd just shake his head. He didn't talk much. An' nobody smelled a rat.

The pirates divided all the gold, an' each fellow put his share in a strongbox. One stormy night, when nobody could see 'em, they landed it just off Great Pedro Bluff, on the south coast of Jamaica. But before they left the ship they put all the kegs o' shootin' powder in the ship's bottom to blow it up, so nobody would know they were there.

Said Jackson, "Before we do that, let's have one great big party; then we'll blow up the ship. Let's go an' bury our strongboxes. Then we'll come back for the big feast."

They went, all of 'em, to Jack's Hole, near Pedro's Plains, and buried their strongboxes deep in the earth. Then they went back. Jackson don't say anythin'. Cross cow keeps its tail close. But he was gettin' ready to thief away with all that gold.

When they got back to the ship, an' nobody was watchin', Jackson put strong sleepin' powder in the keg o' rum. The pirates drank, but not Jackson. They sang an' danced. Then they all fell asleep so no storm could wake 'em.

That mean Jackson put light to the powder in the bottom o' the ship an' rowed off in a boat quickly. Soon the ship blew up with all the sailors in it, an' nobody ever heard a word from 'em after that.

Jackson went to town workin' at a trade and playin' his fiddle at weddin's. He was a fine fiddler an' a fine carpenter, so he made good money. He fiddled an' he worked until one day he found a place not far from here, that's Old Spanish Town, an' built a fine house with a strong cellar. He was a mighty good carpenter and made a good strong house, but the strongest was the cellar.

Then, a little at a time, he brought those strongboxes full o' gold an' jewels from Jack's Hole to the cellar. He did it in the nighttime when nobody saw him, an' after a while he had all the strongboxes full o' gold in his cellar.

Now he was the happiest man in all Jamaica, for he loved that gold more than anything in the world. He loved that gold so much that he always stayed with it. He never went out, he never spent a penny. So time passed: Jackson always with his hands in the gold in the strongboxes.

All the time he loved that gold more an' more, so much that he was no longer satisfied to hold it in his hands. He wanted to hold it in his arms and close to his heart. He wanted to hug that gold just as you hug your mother or your sweetheart.

One day he had a grand idea that made his eyes shine. He began to work hard with wood, and soon he had a fine big fancy table. When that table was finished, the next thing he began to do was take the gold pieces and nail them to the table, one piece after another, close, close to each other, so close you could see no wood. In the end it was a

The ship blew up and Jackson took the strongboxes of gold.

table o' gold, a big round table o' gold a man could take in his arms an' hug close an' tight.

Then Jackson was really the happiest man in the world. Now he could hug that gold table just as you do your love, an' he hugged an' loved that table deep down in his cellar. He was a happy man, never saw anybody, and just lived with his gold table, lovin' and huggin' it all the time.

But I told you Fate won't let a man go if it's got its teeth in him. An' Fate had its teeth deep in Jackson, watchin' to make him pay for the wrong he did piratin' and the wrong he did the pirate sailors the night he put sleepin' powder in the rum.

Jackson spent all his time in his cellar huggin' an' lovin' that table, while the world was goin' along. It was goin' along much. It was rainin' hard. It was rainin' in Jamaica as it never rained before. Lawd! The sky was pourin' out rivers an' oceans o' water. But Jackson never saw it. He was busy lovin' his gold table.

One morning he looked out o' the window an' saw the rain, rain pourin' and pourin'. The Río Cobre was big as a lake now, runnin' all over the land, maybe three or four feet deep. He looked and looked, an' fear bit him. It bit him hard, an' he don't know why.

Then, sudden-like, that rain stopped, an' Jackson saw the sun coming up. But the water kept roarin' around the house as if devils was pushin' it. The water broke the windows and rushed into the house. Jackson rushed down to the cellar and took his gold table in his arms, huggin' it to his heart, shoutin' and cryin'—just sounds, no words. But that did no good. The mighty water rushed in an' begun to tear that house to pieces. The house was nothin'. Then the wild water pulled Jackson and his gold table deep in the black pool of water that was there.

People came from nearby and stood on a hill to see if Jackson's house was still there. It was then just noontime. They didn't see anythin' of Jackson's house 'cept some swirlin' wood. But right then, for just a few seconds, they saw a gold table come out of the black pool, high up and shinin', bright like the sun, over the crazy runnin' water. It was there for just a few seconds. The gold shone so strong that people had to close their eyes. When they opened their eyes again, the gold table was gone. It had sunk down into the black pool of the Río Cobre.

An' every day when the sun shines hot and you stand near that black pool of water you can see the gold table come up out o' the water. But you must never trouble it. If you do, you'll die."

MEXICO

❦ The Love of a Mexican Prince and Princess

Among the ancient Toltecs of Mexico there was once a king who had a daughter as beautiful as a flower. So many fine noblemen courted her that she could not decide which one to marry. So the years passed, and she was still unmarried.

One day there came to the capital city of Teotihuacán a Chichimec prince, to buy and to trade. He came on a golden litter, dressed in colored robes and adorned with brilliant feathers. Many warriors accompanied him, as was befitting a prince. But the Toltecs looked down on the Chichimec people—whom they called the dog people— who lived in the great Ajusto mountains, hunting and fishing, and they had little to do with them.

The prince and his followers went around the market, examining the blankets, animals, carvings, and golden ornaments. On that very day the beautiful Toltec princess was also in the market, buying embroideries and woven baskets and colored blankets for her palace. The prince and the princess looked at each other, and suddenly it seemed to both of them that the sun was shining more brightly and the birds in their cages were singing more sweetly. Each felt a deep love for the other, though each knew this was a forbidden and hopeless love. A Toltec princess could marry only a man of her class among the Toltecs. Similarly, a Chichimec prince could select his bride only from among his equals in the Chichimec nation. Such were the laws of their lands.

But love does not think of silly laws. The two felt that life would not be worth living without each other.

The maidens who accompanied the princess saw this in her eyes and understood it well. But they, too, knew the laws of their people and of the Chichimecs, so they hurried the princess back to her palace.

The prince also returned to his home with his men, burning with anger at the thought that he could not be with the princess he loved. He tried to put her out of his mind, to forget her, but he could not.

One morning he put a shining ocelot skin about his shoulders, and around his loins a cloth woven of the finest maguey fibers. On his arms and about his neck he put jewels of jade and precious stones, and on his head he set a gleaming headdress of green quetzal feathers. Thus arrayed, he set out with his followers and again came to the great Toltec capital of Teotihuacán, where he wandered about, close to the palace of the king.

It was not long before the princess knew he was there, and soon she came out, adorned in rich white lace. Her

The prince and princess were in the market on the very same day.

beautiful black hair hung down from her proud head in graceful braids bound in colored bands and jewels.

The prince and princess met and spoke to each other, and the prince said he would come for her shortly and take her to be his wife.

Soon messengers of the Chichimec prince came to the Toltec court and, on behalf of the prince, asked the king for the hand of his daughter in marriage. The brow of the Toltec king grew dark with fury.

"My daughter will marry only a Toltec noble, never a stranger, beneath her station!"

The messengers bore this sad reply to their master, while the angry Toltec king hid his daughter where she could not see anyone. But true love always finds a way. The princess was attended by a maid who did not believe the king's course of action was just, and the princess sent her with a message to the prince, telling him where to meet her as soon as she was free again.

When the king thought his daughter had forgotten the prince, he set her free. Soon she went to the meeting place in the woods, and the two lovers went up into the mountains together, planning their future.

The next day the princess returned and revealed to her father that she and the Chichimec prince were married.

"Please forgive me, my father, I know that our custom forbids me to marry a Chichimec, but I love him, and love is greater than custom."

When the king heard this, he was angry beyond words.

"Get out of my sight!" he cried. "You have brought shame upon me. I banish you, and I forbid any Toltec to give food or shelter to either of you. May wild animals devour both of you!"

Heartbroken, the princess left the palace.

The same thing happened to the prince. His father, too,

felt that his son had greatly shamed him by marrying outside his own people. The king banished his son and forbade
any Chichimec to give food or shelter to him or his wife.

The prince and princess met and set out on their sad
wanderings. Through mountains and valleys, over rivers
and streams they went, and no Toltec or Chichimec would
give them food or shelter. They lived on fruits and herbs
and berries, for the prince had no weapons with which to
hunt. The cold winds came, and the two began to lose
their strength. But as their bodies grew weaker, their love
grew stronger.

The prince knew that when the icy winds became more
biting they would die.

One night they were in a little valley from which they
could see the proud capital of Teotihuacán. A mountain
rose on either side of the valley. The icy cold penetrated
to their bones. The princess was thinking of her home, and
the prince was able to understand her thoughts, for he
loved her dearly.

"My princess," said he, "we chose love above life, so life
is not important to us. The cold winds are coming. No one
speaks to us; no one wants us. We cannot rest anywhere.
Soon we shall be so cold that we shall die. Let this be our
last night together in the lands where we are not wanted.
Tomorrow we shall part and enter the world of spirits,
where all people are the same and there is no difference
between Toltec and Chichimec. Here we committed a
crime against our peoples. In the other world there is only
one people, and all live together in peace.

"Tomorrow you go to the lower mountain that watches
over your city, and I shall go to the higher mountain that
also watches over your city. On top of these mountains
your body and mine will find resting places. I shall watch
over you and your body, and our spirits will become one."

The princess knew that her husband's words were true.

They spent their last night in each other's arms. When the red sun rose above the mountains, they bade each other a last farewell. Then each one turned to the appointed mountain and began to climb. The princess went up Ixtaccíhuatl mountain. She climbed slowly, while the icy wind blew, penetrating her body, and the thick snow fell over her. The wind helped her upward. Soon she reached the top and lay down, her eyes staring fixedly up at the sky.

The snow kept falling, slowly, softly, and soon covered her to protect her from the icy winds. White snow is always on top of Ixtaccíhuatl, protecting the princess from the biting cold winds.

The prince also climbed his mountain, and when he reached the top he, too, lay down and was covered by the thick snow.

After a time, smoke came out of the mountain, and the bowels of the earth grumbled and growled. The people called it "Smoky Mountain," or Popocatépetl. It is said that the smoke and the grumbling are caused by the Chichimec prince crying for his Toltec princess.

Coyote Rings the Wrong Bell

In Mexico there are many tales about animals, but most of them are about Hare and Coyote. These two always argue and try to outwit each other; they are rivals in hunting and in everything else. Since Coyote is much the stronger, Hare has to match his wits against Coyote's strength.

Now, one day Hare finished a fine meal and lay down under a tree for his siesta. Sometimes he gazed up at the blue sky, and sometimes he just closed his eyes. Finally he was fast asleep. Coyote came along, very quietly, looking for Hare. He was hungry. When he saw Hare sleeping, he approached very slowly and silently, and when he was near, he took a great jump and *plppp!* he landed squarely on top of Hare with all four paws.

Hare awoke with a frightened start and saw at once that he was in deep trouble. But he was not afraid.

"Now I have you, Hare!" said Coyote. "You must have had a fine dinner, for you feel nice and fat. Mmm, what a meal you will make!"

Hare was thinking fast.

"Yes, I did have a fine meal, and I don't mind if you eat me, for my flesh is old and dry and I don't have much longer to live anyway. But just be patient and wait a bit.

Perhaps I can give you something to eat that is much more tender and softer than I am."

"I wouldn't mind having something more tender, but I don't see anything better to eat around here. So it will have to be you, Brother Hare. Ho, ho, ho!"

Hare did not laugh.

"I know," he said, breathing hard, for Coyote was sitting right on top of him and he was heavy. "I know you see only me right now, because all the tender little hares are in school, but that is just a little way from here. They are all there, soft and juicy, and just the right age."

Coyote licked his lips.

"I know," he said, "that these little hares are very soft and juicy. Where is that school, Brother Hare?"

"Just a little way down the hill. They are waiting for me to ring the bell for them to come out and play. But I can't ring it for a long time, not until the sun reaches the tops of the trees up on the hill. Then I can ring the bell. It's right up here in this tree." And he pointed to the tree under which they were lying and in which there was a big brown hornets' nest.

"Will the little hares come out if you ring the bell?" asked Coyote.

"They will, indeed, but I have to wait a long time. It's too early now. They must stay there a long time yet."

"Would they come out if you rang the bell now?"

"They would, but I won't ring it now. I must wait for the right time."

"Brother Hare, I'm not hungry, and I won't eat you. See, I am letting you get up. Why don't you go for a little walk, to stretch and get the stiffness out of your joints? I'll stay and ring the bell for you at the right time."

Coyote got off Hare, and Hare stretched himself slowly.

"I don't mind running off if you will promise that you will stay and ring the bell. But don't forget; you must not ring it until the sun reaches the tops of the trees on the hill."

"I won't forget. But you must tell me how to ring the bell."

"It's very easy, Brother Coyote. All you do is shake the tree very hard. Then they will hear it at the schoolhouse. But shake it violently, so they will be sure to hear it."

"You can be sure I'll shake the tree hard enough, Brother Hare. Now, run along!"

Hare was off like a flash. When he was at a safe distance, he shouted, "Be sure to wait for the sun to reach the trees, Brother Coyote."

"I won't forget, Hare. Now, be on your way!"

Hare ran off, while Coyote watched. No sooner was Hare out of sight than Coyote rushed up to the tree and began shaking it with all his might. He shook it and shook it; but no bell rang. Finally, he threw all his weight violently against the tree, and *klppp!* down fell the hornets' nest and landed squarely on his back. Suddenly the air was filled with hornets as they flew out in fury from their nest, stinging Coyote all over his body, from the point of his nose to the tip of his tail. You couldn't see his fur anywhere for hornets.

He ran as fast as he could, howling, but the hornets were after him all the way, stinging him at every step, to teach him a lesson for knocking down their nest.

And so Coyote had sharp stings instead of juicy little hares.

✾ The Sacred Drum of Tepozteco

Long ago, in the valley of Tepoztlan, a valley in Mexico where there is much copper, Tepozteco was born. He was born to be different from other children, for he was destined to be a god.

In a short time he was a fully grown man, rich in wisdom and great in strength and speed. He could hunt better than other men, and he gave counsel that brought success.

So the people made him king. And as he grew in wisdom and understanding and strength, they worshiped him and made him a god.

He was known for his virtues even to the farthest corners of his kingdom, and he was loved and respected by all. The other kings feared him, although they never dared to say so.

One day the king of Ilayacapan asked Tepozteco to come to a great feast to be given in his honor. Other kings and nobles and men of strength were also invited.

The king told his cooks to prepare food such as had never been eaten before. He had new dishes painted in bright colors, and he ordered new blankets of lovely designs.

And the most beautiful blanket of all was to be for Tepozteco to sit upon. This was to be a feast of feasts.

On the appointed day, the kings and nobles arrived wearing their richest robes and jewels of jade and gold. It was a wonderful sight to see the great company seated on the many-colored mats, with the richly painted dishes before them. All around were beautiful servants ready to bring the fine food.

They sat and they sat. They were waiting for the great guest, Tepozteco.

They waited and they waited. After a long time they heard the *teponaztli,* the drum that always announced the coming of Tepozteco.

Soon he was seen, approaching with his followers. But he was not dressed for the feast. He was dressed in hunting clothes, with an ocelot skin thrown over his shoulders and weapons in his hands. His followers also were dressed in hunting clothes.

The king and his guests looked at them in silent surprise. Then the king spoke.

"Noble Tepozteco," he said, "you have put shame on me and my land and my guests. This feast was in your honor, and we came properly dressed to honor you, but you have come in your hunting clothes and not in your royal garments."

Tepozteco looked at the king and his company and did not say a word. For a long time he was silent. Then he spoke.

"Wait for me. I shall soon return in my royal clothes."

Then he and his followers vanished into the air like a cloud.

Again the company waited a long time, and finally the drum of Tepozteco was heard once again. Suddenly the whole company saw him.

He was alone, dressed more beautifully than anyone there. He was all covered with gold. From his shoulders hung a mantle in colors that gleamed more richly than birds in the sunlight. His headdress was of the most brilliant quetzal feathers ever seen. Gold bands bound his arms and jade beads encircled his neck. In his hand he held a shield studded with jewels and richly colored stones.

The king and his company were greatly pleased at the sight.

"Now you are dressed in a manner befitting this noble gathering in your honor. Let the food be served."

Tepozteco did not answer. He seated himself on a mat, and the food was served by beautiful maidens. Everyone ate except Tepozteco, who took the dishes and poured his food on his mantle.

Everyone stopped eating and looked at the guest of honor in surprise.

"Why do you do this?" asked the king.

"I am giving the food to my clothes, because it was they, not I, that you wanted at your feast. I was not welcome here in whatever clothes I chose to wear. Only when I came in these, my feast-day clothes, were you pleased. Therefore this feast is for them, not for me."

"Leave my palace," said the king sharply.

Tepozteco rose and left.

When he had gone, a great cry of anger rose from all the guests.

"He is not fit to live among us," they cried. "We must destroy him!"

Everyone agreed to this, and the kings and nobles gathered a great army of warriors and marched on Tepoztlán.

Tepozteco knew he could not do battle against this great army, for his soldiers were too few. So he went up on the Montaña del Aire—the Mountain in the Air—where a vast temple had been built for him by his people.

There he stood, drawn up to his full height, almost

reaching the sky. He raised his hands and waved them in all directions. The earth quaked and trembled and roared. Trees fell and rocks flew in every direction. Masses of earth rose into the air. Everything fell on the army that had come to destroy Tepozteco and his people, and the enemy was wiped out.

The temple of Tepozteco still stands on that mountain, and at night, when the wind screams through the canyons that the earthquake created along the Montaña del Aire, one can hear the sacred drum of Tepozteco, telling his people he is still there to guard and protect his city.

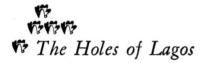

The Holes of Lagos

"Lagos! Where is Lagos?"

"Far, far away."

"How far?"

"As far as far can be in Mexico."

"How far is that?"

"Well . . . I can't tell exactly."

"What part of Mexico?"

"I can't tell. Maybe any part of Mexico. Some people say one place; some say another; but, wherever that town is, it is full of foolish people."

"Aren't there foolish people everywhere?"

"Yes, but in Lagos *every* man is a *bobo*. The people of Lagos are different from those of any other town in Mexico. Everywhere there are *some* fools; but in Lagos they are *all* fools."

"That can't be."

"Oh, yes it can! In Lagos they do things people would do nowhere else. Take, for example, the time they found a deep hole in the center of the plaza, not far from the church."

"What happened?"

"Well, this is what happened."

One morning the mayor of the town was walking in his bare feet across the plaza, on his way to the city hall. When he got near the church, he discovered a deep hole, big enough for three men to fall into. He stopped and looked at the hole for a long time.

"How did this hole come to be in the plaza of Lagos?" he cried. "Who put it there?"

When no one answered, he called to the town policeman, who had a big torn sombrero on his head and a thin stick in his hand.

"How did that hole get there?" cried the mayor.

"I don't know, Señor Alcalde."

"If you, the guardian of peace in Lagos, do not know, then nobody knows."

"That is true, Señor Alcalde."

"It's dangerous to have a hole like that in our town plaza. If people walk to church or to the city hall, they might fall into it and get hurt."

"Quite true, Señor Alcalde."

"Well, then, it must be closed at once."

"That's right, Señor Alcalde."

"Get the men of Lagos immediately and have them fill up that hole."

"Si, Señor Alcalde."

The mayor went into the city hall to attend to business, and the policeman went to assemble all the men of Lagos who were sitting on their heels. And there were plenty of these. They took shovels and began digging up the earth from a place nearby and threw it into the hole. When the sun sank behind the hill, the hole was filled and the earth over it was smooth as a leaf. Everyone was satisfied with the day's work and went home to eat tortillas.

Later, when the mayor came out of the city hall, the policeman said politely:

"Señor Alcalde, you see that the hole is filled. The men did a fine job."

"I'm glad to hear it. We have good men in our town, better than any in Mexico."

"Thank you, Señor Alcalde. *Buenas tardes.*"

"*Buenas tardes.*"

The mayor walked away. He hadn't walked far until he came to a second hole, the one from which the earth had been taken to fill the first hole. He stopped and looked at it in surprise.

"Another hole!" he exclaimed. "How did *this* hole get here? I didn't see it this morning. . . . Carlos! Carlos!" he shouted.

The policeman came running.

"Yes, Señor Alcalde."

"There is a hole here. Look!"

"Yes, Señor Alcalde, there is," said Carlos, looking at it.

"People going to church or to the city hall could fall into it and break a leg, or even a neck."

"Well they might, Señor Alcalde; they certainly might."

"It must be closed at once, Carlos."

"Yes, it must be closed at once, Señor Alcalde," agreed

Carlos, taking off his sombrero and scratching his head, "but the men have all gone home to eat their tortillas and go to bed. Everybody will be sleeping now."

"That's true," said the mayor. "Then *mañana*."

"Tomorrow it will be done, Señor Alcalde."

Early next morning Carlos had the men of Lagos digging up the earth not far from the new hole.

The mayor passed by on the way to his office, watched the men at work, and smiled in satisfaction.

"There are no workmen in all Mexico better than the workmen of Lagos," he said aloud, and went to the city hall.

The men all heard what he said and were pleased, and they continued their work with greater zeal. Soon the second hole was filled and the earth smoothed down.

At the setting of the sun, the mayor came by and saw the hole filled and the ground over it as smooth as a church floor.

"Carlos, that is good work."

"The men of Lagos are good workers, Señor Alcalde," agreed Carlos.

The mayor walked on; but he hadn't walked far when he came to a new hole.

"*Madre de Dios!* Holes grow in Lagos like weeds in a corn patch. How did this hole come to be here? Carlos! Carlos!"

Carlos came running.

"What's happened, Señor Alcalde?"

"There's another hole here in the ground. Look!"

Carlos looked. "Yes, Señor Alcalde, there is another hole in the ground."

"It must be filled."

"Yes, it must be filled, Señor Alcalde."

"People crossing the plaza might fall into it and break a leg."

"They might indeed break a leg, Señor Alcalde."

"Fill it at once."

Carlos removed his sombrero and scratched his head.

"The men have gone home to eat their tortillas, and soon they'll be asleep."

"True," said the mayor, ". . . quite true. Well then, *mañana*."

"Yes, Señor Alcalde."

Next morning, bright and early, the good men of Lagos were out digging again. From a spot nearby they dug up earth and filled the hole. When the sun set, it was done.

The mayor passed by on his way home.

"This is good work, indeed," he said when he saw the hole filled, smooth as glass. "What excellent workers these men of Lagos are! There are none finer in all Mexico."

"That's true, Señor Alcalde," Carlos agreed.

The mayor continued on his way, and soon came to a new hole.

"*Madre de Dios!*" he cried, "a new hole! There is a curse of holes on our town. Some evil spirit has wished them on us. Carlos! Carlos!"

Carlos came running.

"There is a new hole. See!"

"So there is, Señor Alcalde."

"It must be filled. At once. But the men will be asleep. Then *mañana*, Carlos."

This went on and on. Everyone in Lagos tried to figure out how it happened and why there were so many holes in their town, but they couldn't. They were just that kind of people. So they kept on filling holes by digging new holes until they came to the edge of town.

Now, the people of the next town had been watching the work of Lagos day by day, laughing and saying nothing. But when the hole was next to their own town, they filled it with things lying around that they had been wanting to bury for a long time.

When the mayor of Lagos saw the last hole filled, and could not find another, he was very happy and said, "The men of Lagos never give up a job until it is finished."

The men of Lagos were happy, too, for they said they were getting a little tired of so much digging every day.

So everyone was happy, and there were no more holes in Lagos.

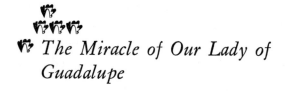

The Miracle of Our Lady of Guadalupe

On Tepeyac Hill, overlooking the beautiful Valley of Mexico, stood the temple of the goddess Tonantzin, goddess of earth and corn. At the bottom of the hill there were two smaller temples, one to the Mother of Gods and the other, over a spring, to the Goddess of the Waters.

Through the centuries, Indians came to these temples from far and wide to worship and pray. For the Earth goddess gave them corn, which was their daily bread, and the Mother of Gods cured them of all their ills.

When the Spaniards, with their strange horses and steel

weapons, overran these fair lands, they tried to eradicate the Indians' religion as well. They tore down the temples and baptized the Indians. But though the temples were shattered and the people were christened, they kept coming to worship their gods on Tepeyac Hill.

On a Saturday morning, the ninth of December, in the year 1531, a poor Indian who had been baptized as Juan Diego was on his way to the church of Santiago. As he passed Tepeyac Hill he suddenly heard angels singing. Then the singing stopped and there was a great light. In it stood a beautiful lady dressed in garments of blue and gold.

"Juan, my son," she said softly, "I am the mother of you, and of all mankind. Go and tell the bishop to erect a temple for me here where the ancient temple stood."

Obediently Juan went straight to the bishop's palace, and finally the servants let him enter.

"Holy Bishop," he said, "I saw a shining lady dressed in blue and gold. She said you should build her a church where the old temple stood on Tepeyac Hill."

"My good man," said the unbelieving bishop, "you must have been dreaming. Go home and tend your corn. Consider this matter well and, if you still insist, come again. Then I shall hear you in more detail and consider the purpose that has brought you here."

The Indian started home, and when he came to Tepeyac Hill, he found the shining lady in blue and gold waiting for him.

"Beautiful lady, I gave the bishop your message. But he did not believe me and said I was dreaming."

"Son, go again tomorrow to the bishop. Tell him again to build me a church where the old temple stood."

The following morning, which was Sunday, Juan left his home and went straight to the church. After the service he came before the bishop and, with tears in his eyes, knelt before him.

"Holy Bishop, believe me, I am telling the truth. I saw the shining lady again and she said she wants you to build her a church where the old temple of our goddess Tonant- zin stood."

"Good man, go back to your shining lady and bring me some token of her so I may know this is not a dream. Then I will do as she says."

Juan walked back slowly. The way was long and the road was full of stones. There, on the rocks, the lady in blue and gold was waiting for him again.

"The bishop told me to bring him a token from you. Then he will believe me and build the church."

"Come tomorrow and I will give you a token," she said.

The next day, Monday, Juan could not go because his Uncle Bernardino was very sick. The doctor came, but he said he could not help the old man.

"Tomorrow bring a priest to give your uncle the last sacrament," he advised Juan.

In the morning Juan set out on his sad errand. He did not think of the shining lady and he took a different road. Or perhaps he was more anxious to bring the priest to his uncle than to carry the message to the bishop. But soon, there the shining lady was standing before him. . . .

"Juan, don't worry about your uncle—he is all well by this time. Now, go up to the hill where you saw me first and pick the roses you will find there."

"Roses between the rocks, where there is only spiny cactus? Are you sure?"

"I am sure, Juan. Pick the roses and put them in your *tilma* and bring them to the bishop as a token from me."

Juan ran up the hill, and there, instead of green and gray sticky cactus, were beautiful, sweet-smelling roses. He picked them and put them in his cape. Then he went to the bishop, but the servant would not let him in.

"I am bringing the bishop roses I picked among the rocks on the top of Tepeyac Hill."

"I don't believe you," said the servant. "There are no roses up there. Show them to me and I will let you see the bishop."

Juan opened his *tilma* and the servant saw the roses.

"I want one," he cried. He put his hand into the cape and—there were no roses. There were only painted roses on the cloth!

The servant was frightened. "Go to the bishop," he cried. "Show him your . . . roses."

Juan came before the bishop. "I have brought you a token from the shining lady. Here are roses from a place where roses never grew." He opened his cape, the roses fell out, and there on the cloth was . . . a painting of the Virgin.

"A miracle!" the bishop cried, falling on his knees and begging to be forgiven for his doubts. He put the miraculous cape on the altar of his chapel and said:

"Juan, you must show me the place where the church must be built."

The very next day Juan took the bishop to Tepeyac Hill, and very soon a chapel was built there. They put the *tilma* with the miraculous painting of the Virgin over the altar, and they called the church Our Lady of Guadalupe.

Later, a more beautiful basilica was built there—perhaps the most beautiful basilica in all Mexico—to house the miraculous painting of the Holy Virgin.

To this basilica thousands of people from all parts of Mexico come every year to pray and to worship, even as the Indians had worshiped their ancient gods. And often they pray to these old gods, too. They come throughout the year, but especially on the twelfth of December, the day on which the Virgin appeared to Juan Diego for the last time, ordering him to give her message to the bishop.

Pancho Villa and the Devil

Do you want to hear a story about the Mexican people? Then I shall tell you one about a man who is *all* the Mexican people. He is a great hero whom every Mexican loves: Pancho Villa.

He was stronger than any Mexican who ever lived— that is what people say. He knew everything—just ask any Mexican. He understood all things about men and animals, and he was not afraid of anything in the world. He was not even afraid of the Devil himself. Yes, that's right; not even of the Devil himself.

People say he sold himself to the Devil, and the Devil, in return, made him strong and brave. Maybe he did, but that was just to fool the Devil in the end, for that is exactly what Pancho Villa finally did. All his life he waited for the chance, and in the end he got it.

Pancho Villa had a horse with feet like dancing flames. Not only was this horse as swift as a tornado, but it was also as smart as a hare. It was a horse for a hero of Mexico— for Pancho Villa.

Villa's horse was always helping him. When he was hungry, the horse would lead him to a place where he could find something to eat. When he was thirsty, it would lead him to water. When he would lose contact with his soldiers, it would show him where they were.

To tell the truth, that horse actually *was* the Devil, waiting to carry off Pancho Villa to . . . you know where I mean.

Do you think Pancho Villa did not know who that horse really was? Of course he knew! And he was just waiting for the right time to show him which one of them was the smarter. He let the horse do everything for him. He gave it plenty of food. But he kept his eyes wide open, just the same.

Things went on that way for a long, long time, the horse doing everything for Pancho Villa, and the great hero accepting it but always watching, watching.

Now, you know they finally killed Pancho Villa. The fools! They did not know he was the greatest Mexican who ever lived. Ask any true Mexican, and he will tell you.

The only one who knew he was going to be killed was that horse, the Devil. It could talk, but it never said a word. It just kept waiting to carry him off to the Hill of Box, where the Devil lived, just north of San Juan del Río. It was there that Pancho Villa sold his soul, so he would become a great hero.

As soon as Pancho Villa was shot, the horse spoke.

He said, "Now, you come with me. I have kings and princes in my hill, but I don't have anyone there as fearless as you."

But that Devil-horse had forgotten one thing.

Said Pancho Villa, "You are right. I am fearless, and I am not afraid of anything, not even of *you*, Devil! I have gone to church ever since I gave up soldiering, and now you can't take me. I have a cross around my neck, so you can't touch me. You go back to your hill and I'll go the other way, where all good Mexicans go."

The Devil-horse couldn't answer that, so he galloped off, screaming and neighing, in the opposite direction. Fire and brimstone shot from his hoofs.

And Pancho Villa went off in the other direction, to heaven, where he really belongs.

NICARAGUA

 *Uncle Rabbit Flies to Heaven*

Tío Conejo—Uncle Rabbit—was walking down a road one day in Nicaragua. He walked and he walked and he walked.

"I walk so much you would think there was only walking in this world," he grumbled.

He came to a place where there were many trees and bushes full of fruits and berries.

"This is the right place for me," he said, and he ate and ate as if there were nothing in the world except eating.

A big buzzard came up to him.

"Good day, Tío Buzzard."

"I'm glad to see you, Tío Rabbit," replied Buzzard.

But of course Buzzard was not really glad to see Rabbit, for Rabbit had played many tricks on him, and he was waiting for a chance to get even. Tío Rabbit did not know this.

"I haven't tasted such good fruit in a long time, Tío Buzzard."

"Yes, that is very good fruit," agreed Tío Buzzard, "but it is not nearly so good as the fruit you'd eat if you came to a feast held high up in the clouds. They have the best food in the world at those feasts up in the clouds."

"I have never been to any of those feasts, Tío Buzzard."

"Why don't you come to one?"

"How can I? I can't fly."

"Well, I'll tell you what to do. There is a great feast going on up there right now, and if you'll bring along your guitar, I'll take you up there. It would be nice to have some guitar music at the feast."

"I'll get my guitar right now. Just wait for me and I'll go with you."

He hopped off as fast as he could go. Tío Buzzard waited for him.

"This time I'll get even with Rabbit for the many mean tricks he's played on me," Tío Buzzard said to himself.

Tío Rabbit came back quickly with his little guitar.

Tío Buzzard saw him coming and cried, "Come quickly and get on my back. Hold onto me under my wings and I'll fly up with you."

Tío Rabbit climbed up on Tío Buzzard's back and held tight, with his paws under Buzzard's wings.

Tío Buzzard flew up. He flew higher and higher, and all the time he was flying he was planning how to get revenge on Rabbit. He went higher and higher. Now they could see the world spread out below them.

"Now I'll pay you back for all the mean tricks you have played on me," cried Tío Buzzard.

"What did you say, Tío Buzzard?" cried Tío Rabbit.

But Tío Buzzard did not answer. He bent his head and began to fly around and around, up and down, zigzag, and upside down. He did everything to try to make Tío Rabbit fall off. But Tío Rabbit held on tightly. His stomach seemed to jump up into his mouth, and his head to swim around and around in circles.

"Stop! Stop! Stop this crazy flying. I'm dizzy. I'll fall."

"I always fly like this when I get up close to heaven."

"I'm dizzy!" cried Tío Rabbit. "I'm almost dead! You'll kill me!"

"We are getting nearer to heaven," said Tío Buzzard, and he flew worse than before: backward, sideways, around and around, upside down.

"We're nearer to heaven! We're nearer to heaven!" screamed Tío Buzzard.

"Get nearer to earth! Stop flying in such a crazy way," shrieked Tío Rabbit.

But Tío Buzzard flew more crazily than ever.

Then Tío Rabbit took his guitar and gave Tío Buzzard a whack on the head with it. He hit him so hard that Buzzard's head went into the guitar and he fainted and began falling to earth. But Tío Rabbit held Buzzard's wings outspread, and they floated slowly down to earth together.

When they landed, Tío Rabbit jumped off Tío Buzzard's back, and Tío Buzzard slowly came to his senses and opened his eyes. His head was still stuck in the guitar.

"Take that guitar off my head!" cried Tío Buzzard.

"Ha! Ask your friends in heaven to take it off. This will teach you to try to play tricks on me." Then Tío Rabbit ran off laughing.

Tío Buzzard tried to get his head out of the guitar. He tried and he tried. He pulled and he pulled. In the end his head came out of the guitar but left lots of feathers behind, for he skinned his neck clean.

Those feathers never grew back, and his children never had any feathers on their necks, either, and that's the way it's been with buzzards ever since.

A Sacred Pledge Should Not Be Broken

One of the most beloved saints in Nicaragua is Santo Domingo de Guzmán. His feast days are celebrated with singing and dancing, fairs and fireworks, games, rodeos, and horse races.

The statue of this good saint rests in a little church in a town named after him, not far from Managua, the capital city of Nicaragua. From the day the statue was placed in the little church high up in the mountains, the good saint showed his love for the people by helping those in need and those who were sick. The glad news of this spread swiftly and soon came to the ears of people who lived in the capital. There, too, many were in need of help, and they asked the villagers of Santo Domingo de Guzmán to lend them the wonder-working statue of the holy saint.

The good people of the village said they would lend their beloved statue to the people of Managua for two weeks to help them in their need.

Now, I must tell you that Santo Domingo de Guzmán

Horsemen galloped around the procession and rockets were fired.

was a sailor before he became a saint, and for that reason his image is not on a stand but in a boat set in a glass case. So the holy image was carried over the mountains to Managua in that glass case.

The people of the capital came out on the road with a decorated cart, and the glass case with the statue was placed on it. Then the procession went into the city.

The people of Managua were happy to see the good saint come to their city, and the villagers were happy to help their countrymen. Everybody was happy. As the procession marched into the city, horsemen galloped around it and rockets were fired up into the heavens. People threw their hats into the air and cried with joy. "Viva Santo Domingo de Guzmán!" they shouted. "Long may he live with us."

The image was taken off the cart and carried on the shoulders of the men into the church. Then the people of the city celebrated the presence of the holy saint with a great fiesta, horse races, and other sports. After the celebration, everyone went into the church to pray and then lay down on the stones to sleep.

But they didn't celebrate just with games and prayers; they also carried out all the promises they had made during the year, so that they would have good luck during the year to come. That was what the good saint would want them to do. And he helped the sick to get well and the needy to better their lives, and they all rejoiced.

The festivities and good deeds continued day after day. Everyone was so happy that the people of Managua said they would like to keep the saint longer. "Our city is bigger than Santo Domingo de Guzmán, and we have many more people here. The saint can do much more good here," they said. And when the two weeks were over, the people of Managua showed no sign of returning the image. They did not know that the saint loved his little church in the village in the mountains more than any other place and had decided to return to it after the two weeks had passed.

On the morning of the fifteenth day, the people who slept in the church got up and looked at the place where the image had stood. The image was not there! Its place was empty! A great cry arose and soon the whole city was in turmoil.

"Someone has stolen the saint! The holy statue is gone! Some other city has taken him!" they cried in despair.

Fear seized the people, and the priests prayed in the church. Then some villagers arrived from Santo Domingo de Guzmán.

"A great miracle has happened!" they cried. "This morning we went into our church, and there was the statue of our beloved saint, standing in its usual place. He returned to his old place all by himself when the time was up on which we had agreed."

The men of Managua were silent. But soon they began to rejoice, for they were blessed to have had the holy image even for two weeks, and they thanked God for this blessing.

Ever since that time, the people of Managua have borrowed the statue every year for two weeks, and then faithfully returned it. They know that if they try to keep it longer, the saint himself will return to his church in his mountain village. But during the time he is in Managua, there is no end to merrymaking, fiestas, games, and fairs.

Ha! Tío Rabbit Is Bigger

Tío Rabbit saw all the animals around him, and he was angry because he was not bigger.

"I'd like to be as big as a horse, or a bull, or even a full-grown tiger. I don't like being so small," he said again and again. "Here I am, smarter than anyone, but I'm so small! I must do something about it."

So he decided to go to see Papa Dios (Father God), who lives up in heaven.

He walked and he walked, and finally he met Tío Dog.

"Where are you going, Tío Dog?" asked Tío Rabbit.

"I'm going to see Papa Dios, to beg him to give me the power of man. I want to be as smart as my master."

"I'm going to see Papa Dios, too. I will ask him to make me as big as a horse. Why don't we go together?"

So they walked together until they came to the gate of heaven. St. Peter was standing at the gate and watching all the time.

"Good day," said St. Peter. "What do you two animals want?"

"We want to see Papa Dios," they both said.

"I'm sorry, but I can't let you in. There is no room for animals in heaven now. Come back later."

"Please let me in, St. Peter," said Tío Dog. "I must ask Papa Dios for something very important."

"I'm sorry, Tío Dog. I told you there's no room for animals in here now."

"But this is very important, St. Peter. It's something really important."

"I wish you wouldn't bother me, Tío Dog." St. Peter was getting impatient.

"I want to see Papa Dios. I want to see Papa Dios," Tío Dog barked and growled over and over again.

St. Peter was getting angry. "Stop!" he cried. "Stop! I said 'No.' "

But Tío Dog was angry too, and wouldn't stop. St. Peter looked around for a big stick to chase Tío Dog away. He found one, and Tío Dog ran off yelping, with St. Peter after him.

All this time Tío Rabbit had stood to one side, never opening his mouth. But the minute St. Peter left the gate to run after Tío Dog, he took the keys that were hanging on a hook, unlocked the gate to heaven, and walked inside.

He saw Papa Dios sitting on his golden throne.

"Good day, Papa Dios," he said.

"Good day, Tío Rabbit. What do you want?"

"Papa Dios, I've come to ask a favor of you."

"What favor do you want?"

"I want to be bigger. I want to be as big as a horse or a bull."

"Tío Rabbit, be satisfied as you are. Each one of us should be satisfied to be the way he is."

"But I want to be big. I'm smarter than the other animals, but I want to be bigger. Please, Papa Dios, make me as big as a horse."

"You are just the right size."

"Then make me as big as a bull."

"I told you that you are just the right size."

"Please, Papa Dios, it costs you nothing to make me bigger, and it will make me more important."

Papa Dios was getting tired.

"I told you that you are the right size. You make enough trouble, small as you are. If you were bigger, you might cause more trouble."

But Tío Rabbit kept on begging and begging. No matter what Papa Dios said, he kept on begging. Finally Papa Dios said, "I'll tell you what I'll do. I'll make you bigger if you'll bring me the skins of three big animals. Bring me the skin of a tiger, the skin of a big monkey, and the skin of an alligator ten feet long. Then I'll make you bigger."

Tío Rabbit ran off, bippety-bop, bippety-bop, bippety-bop, to get those three skins.

He came to a river, and there was a fierce tiger drinking water.

Tío Rabbit saw Señor Tiger, and then he began to cut some thick vines that were hanging from the trees. He kept cutting and cutting, and never even looked at the tiger.

"Why are you cutting those thick vines, Tío Rabbit?" Tío Tiger asked.

"A terrible storm is coming. It will tear down the trees and fling animals into the air. I'm cutting these vines to tie myself tight to one of the strongest trees I can find, so that the storm will not carry me away."

"Are you sure it will be such a terrible storm?"

"I wouldn't say so if I weren't sure."

"Well, then, it might be a good idea to tie me, too."

"You are big and don't have to be afraid of the wind."

"But you said this would be a terrible wind."

"So it will be—the most terrible wind there ever was."

"Then tie me, too, if the wind will be so strong."

"No, no, Tío Tiger. I don't think I will."

"Come, Tío Rabbit. We're old friends. You must do this for me. Tie me good and strong and find me a big tree to hold me down."

"Well, if you really want me to, I'll do it for you."

Tío Rabbit took some thick, strong vines and wound them around and around Tío Tiger. He wrapped them tightly, pulling as hard as he could and tying them in hard knots.

"You are tying me awfully tight, Tío Rabbit."

"You don't want to be flung against the rocks and trees by that wild wind that's coming, do you?"

When he had Tío Tiger tied so that he couldn't move an inch, he said, "Tío Tiger, I'm going up on that hill to look for a strong tree."

He went up the hill, but he didn't look for any trees. He looked for a big rock. When he found one, he rolled it down on the fierce tiger, and when it hit him, there wasn't any fierce tiger any more.

Soon Tío Rabbit had his tiger skin. He put it in a big bag and off he went, bippety-bop, bippety-bop, bippety-bop, through the woods until he came to a place where he heard a great jabbering. Up in a big tree the monkeys were chattering like the falling rain. The biggest of the monkeys was a mean fellow, always bullying all the other monkeys. Tío Rabbit knew him.

Tío Rabbit made believe he did not see the monkeys. He slowly put his bag down on the ground under the tree, opened it wide, and said aloud, "If anyone goes into that bag to see what I have hidden in it, he will have to pay dearly for his curiosity." Then he walked away, but he did not go far. He hid behind some nearby bushes and then sneaked back close to the tree where he had left the bag.

The monkeys had been watching him all the time, and they heard what he said.

As soon as he went away, they all rushed down to the bag, thinking there was something good to eat in it. But the big, mean monkey pushed all the rest aside and ran up to the bag, roaring, "I'll take what's in there!"

He stuck his head inside the bag to see what was there. It was dark inside, so he went all the way in to look around.

When Tío Rabbit saw the big monkey all in the bag, he dashed out and tied the opening with a string, tight, very tight.

"Thief! Robber!" he screamed. "So you went in there to steal my corn! I'll teach you a lesson." He picked up a stick and beat the bag with all his might, and soon the big, mean monkey jumped around no more inside the bag. Then Tío Rabbit skinned the monkey and put the skin inside his bag.

"This makes two skins. Now I need only one more."

He went to a river and found a big, fierce alligator sound asleep, his ugly teeth sticking out of the sides of his huge mouth. Everybody was afraid of him.

"I know Tío Alligator is fierce and everyone is afraid of him, but I must get him just the same."

He raised a big stick and hit Tío Alligator a few times on his thick hide. Tío Alligator awoke, opened his terribly big mouth wide, and lashed out with his tail toward Tío Rabbit. But Tío Rabbit was quick and he leaped away and ran off into the woods. He needed a little time to think about this.

While Tío Alligator went back to sleep, Tío Rabbit was thinking. He decided to go back and see if he would have better luck. Tío Alligator was wide awake now, and his little eyes were gleaming, full of fight.

Tío Rabbit went to the river to drink, as if nothing had happened.

"So there you are, villain! You beat me with a stick, and now you dare to come back here. I'll teach you how to act! I'll—"

"You say I hit you, Tío Alligator? I'm just a little fellow. I wouldn't dare hit a big ten-foot alligator like you. I'm your friend. It must have been another rabbit that looked like me."

"It was you, you rascal! I know you when I see you."

"Ah, now I know! It was my brother. He looks exactly like me. He is a mean fellow. Everyone knows I'm always getting blamed for the bad things he does."

"Well, if it was your brother, he's a very ugly fellow, and when I catch him I'll tear him to pieces. He tried to kill me with a big stick like the one you are carrying. Ha! Ha! Ha!"

"I'm sorry to hear that. He *is* mean. But why do you laugh?"

"Because he's a fool, trying to kill me by beating my skin. He could beat me all day and all night and could not do me any harm."

"He really couldn't?"

"Never. There is only one place he could harm me. Right there!" And he pointed to his eyeball.

"I never knew that. It is great not to be hurt anyplace except in one little spot. Since we are friends, I'm going to give you some fine monkey meat I have tied up in my bag. Take as much of it as you like."

Tío Alligator went up to the bag and began to untie the string. While he was untying it with his teeth, Tío Rabbit took his stick and rammed it into Tío Alligator's eyeball. That finished Tío Alligator.

Tío Rabbit quickly took off Tío Alligator's skin, put it into his bag, and ran as fast as he could to Papa Dios. He was out of breath when he got there.

"Papa Dios," he said, "you told me to bring you the skins of a tiger, a monkey, and an alligator. Here they are."

"What?" cried Papa Dios. "You got the skins of these three animals in one day?"

"That I did, in just one day. The skins are here in this bag."

"How is this possible? A little animal like you can't get the skins of three such big animals in one day. You really must be very bad to be able to do this so quickly."

"Not bad—just smart, very smart. Now will you make me as big as a horse?"

"I will not! If you do such terrible things in one day when you are so little, what will you do when you are as big as a horse? No, I'll not make you any bigger than you are!"

"But you promised, Papa Dios. You promised!"

"Yes, I did, Tío Rabbit, and I'll keep my promise. Come here."

Tío Rabbit came close to Papa Dios.

"I'll make you bigger, Tío Rabbit."

Papa Dios took hold of Tío Rabbit's little ears and began to pull them. He pulled and he pulled, and Tío Rabbit's ears got longer and longer.

"Now you are bigger," said Papa Dios. "You have the longest ears of anyone."

Yes, nobody has ears longer than those of Tío Rabbit.

The King of the Leaves

Tío Conejo—Uncle Rabbit, or Br'er Rabbit, as we call him—has a very bad reputation in Nicaragua. He is famous for being a clever rascal and a shameless rogue. And because he is always making trouble for everybody, the people are tired of him. But he always says he doesn't care what people think or say about him, and he never changes his bad habits.

One day the king of the land said, "We must do something about that troublemaker." The king and his advisers talked it over for a long time, and finally the king said, "Tío Conejo has given us trouble for many years. We must get rid of him. Go out, all of you, and catch him and bring him back to me, dead or alive!"

They all went out, giving suggestions to one another on the best way to catch Tío Conejo. Finally some said, "Let

us go to the water hole, where all the animals come to
drink, and hide. Rabbit will get thirsty and come there.
Then we'll catch him and take him back to the king. Or
maybe if he sees us and is thirsty and can't get any water,
he'll go away to another land." They did not know that
Rabbit was right behind the bushes, listening to them talk.

"I will drink all the water I want, and I'll not go away
to another land," he said, laughing to himself.

He went to another village and passed by a shoe shop.
The shoemaker had beside him a fine pair of shoes for the
princess.

"*Buenos días*, Señor; good morning, sir," Rabbit said
cheerily to the shoemaker. "It's a hot day."

"It is a very hot day," replied the shoemaker.

"You should sit inside, where it's cool and the sun won't
burn you. At least you should have a drink of cold water.
It will do you good."

"That's a good idea," said the shoemaker. "I am thirsty.
I'll go into the house and have a drink of cool water from
my clay jar."

As soon as he had gone into the house, Tío Conejo took
the pretty shoes and away he went—lippety-lop. He came
to a highway and followed it—lippety-lop, lippety-lop,
lippety-lop.

Far down the road he saw a man coming toward him.
The man was walking with his head bent forward and a
big gourd on his back.

"Hah! That man is carrying a heavy gourd full of sweet
honey. Now, that is something I like," said Rabbit, and he
quickly dropped one of the shoes he was carrying in the
middle of the road, and hid behind some nearby bushes.

As Rabbit had thought, the man was a honey merchant,
and on his back was a big gourd full of sweet, golden
honey, which he was carrying to market to sell.

He saw the shoe in the road and stopped. "What a pretty shoe!" he said. "But where is the other one?"

He looked around everywhere, but he could not find the other shoe. "Well," he said, "one shoe is not worth taking. One must have two to make a pair." So he left the shoe in the road and walked on.

Tío Conejo knew what he was doing. He ran ahead as fast as he could, and when he came to a turn in the road he threw the other shoe down and again hid in the bushes.

Soon the honey man came along and saw the other shoe.

"Ah! There is that other shoe. I'll run back and pick up the first shoe and then I'll have the pair. I'll just put this heavy gourd of honey right here beside the road, behind this bush, where no one will see it, so I won't have to carry it all the way back."

He ran back down the road. As soon as he was gone Tío Conejo jumped out, picked up the gourd, and scampered off with it through the woods. He didn't stop until he came to an open place covered with dead leaves.

There he sat down and ate and ate honey until he was so full he could not swallow another bit. Then he poured the rest of the honey over himself, over his head and long ears, all over his furry body, and over his soft feet and bushy tail. Then he lay down and rolled over and over, until dead leaves had stuck to all parts of his body. Never in this world has anyone ever seen an animal like that. He looked like a great pile of leaves on the move.

Back to the village he went, lippety-lop, lippety-lop. Everybody stared at him. No one had ever seen anything like that before. Many were afraid to come near him.

He went to the water hole where the king's men were waiting to catch him, but no one recognized him. No one came near him. He put his mouth into the water and drank and drank until he was full and could not drink another drop.

"Who are you?" they asked him.

"I'm the King of the Leaves," he answered, and then he walked away slowly.

This was exactly the way Tío Conejo had said it would be. He came up boldly, drank all the water he wanted, and did not leave the village!

PANAMA

The Spanish Donkey and the Indians

The Spaniards were coming to the New World in swarms, like locusts. Many of them came to that narrowest strip of land connecting the American continents, which is now called Panama. Everywhere they went they kept looking for gold and silver and precious stones. Often they found gold, although many of them died from disease or from the poisoned arrows of the Indians whom they tried to destroy.

Among those who came from Spain was one named Gaspar de Espinosa. He went to the region now called Panama when he heard that it had more gold and jewels than any other part of the new-found lands. He was a lawyer and a very smart man.

"I hope to get much gold," he said. "There are many ways to catch flies, but the best way is with honey. No armor, no swords, no killing for me. I'll find a simpler way." That's what he told himself and his friends.

For a long time he studied the matter, thinking about the different ways in which he might get gold from the Indians peacefully.

He saw that the Indians were a simple people who loved many of the same things the Spaniards loved. In some ways the Indians were just like the white invaders—they were fond of new things; they marveled at new sights; and, like all people, they were curious.

One day a brilliant idea came to Gaspar de Espinosa. The Indians had never seen a donkey and might pay to see one and to hear him "speak."

He bought a donkey that had come over from Spain in one of the ships. For many days he fed the animal well, until it was sleek and shiny. Then he put a fine saddle on it, mounted his Master Longears, and began traveling through the Indian villages, far away from the ports, where the Indians knew very little about the Spaniards.

When he came to a village, the Indians gathered around him and looked with awe and surprise at him and his donkey, as though he might be a god with mighty magic.

Now, Espinosa had learned enough of the Indian language to talk with them in simple words, and when he did not know the proper words he used sign language. He told the Indians that his donkey was a magic animal and could speak.

The simple Indians were amazed and wanted to hear the donkey speak.

"I'll have him talk for you," Espinosa told them, smiling. "Of course, he speaks only Spanish, so I'll have to translate what he says for you."

The Indians said they would not mind that. All they wanted was to hear the donkey speak.

"I'll have the donkey speak for you," Espinosa said to the Indians.

Well, wily Espinosa bent over Mr. Donkey, spoke to him, prodded him hard, and pulled his ear, as if to tell him that the people wanted to hear him talk. The donkey did not like the prodding and ear-pulling, so he began to bray: "A-ee, a-ee, a-ee!" Espinosa kept poking him and shouting in Spanish, and the donkey kept on braying. Finally Espinosa stopped, and Mr. Donkey was silent.

"What did the magic beast say?" the Indians asked.

"He said he would very much like to have some of your yellow metal and shiny stones," answered Espinosa— meaning, of course, gold and jewels.

The Indians, wiser than the Spaniards, used gold and jewels only for ornaments to adorn themselves. They did not put great value on these things, as the white people did. They were so pleased to hear the donkey speak that they gladly gave the scheming Spaniard what he asked for.

On through the jungle Espinosa traveled, from one village to another, with his "magic" donkey whose fame spread far and wide, and all the Indians wanted to hear him. Wherever he went the Indians gladly gave gold and jewels to hear him speak, for they had gold and jewels all the time, but only once in a lifetime could they hear a donkey speak.

PARAGUAY

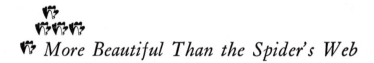

More Beautiful Than the Spider's Web

Ñandutí is a Guaraní Indian word in Paraguay that refers to a type of white spider and its beautiful gleaming white web that glistens in the early-morning dew of the jungle. They tell a lovely story about this spider and its web.

Once there lived a beautiful young Guaraní couple. The girl was graceful as a bird; the boy was tall and as strong as a young tree. The boy hunted and brought food while the girl worked in the hut, prepared the food, and wove delicate fabrics for their clothing. When the day's work was done they danced and sang with their friends, and so these two lived in happiness.

But one day their happiness came to an end. War came to their tribe, which had lived for so many years in peace. A neighboring tribe declared war, and the men gathered to defend themselves, their homes, and their families. The young man who was so happy was brave as well; he was one of the chief warriors of his village. He went off with the other men, leaving behind the old people, the women, and the children.

The men fought in the woods and the women worked in the fields, all hoping and wishing for the war to end. The beautiful young bride wished even more than the others that the war would end and that her husband would come back to her.

Many months passed. They seemed like years. One night the beautiful bride had a sad dream; she dreamed that the warriors came back to the village, but that her beloved husband was not among them. From that time on she was even sadder than before.

Soon news came that the men were winning the war,

One day war came to their tribe, and the young warrior went off.

but still she was sad. One morning runners came to bring the news that the war had been won and the men were on their way home. Everyone was happy except the young bride. Soon there were shouts and cries as the warriors appeared. Women looked for their husbands; children searched for their fathers. Parents gazed anxiously for a sight of their sons. The young bride looked and looked for her husband, but he was not there. Her sad dream had come true: He had been killed fighting fearlessly, and his body had not been brought back.

From that day on the girl was silent. She did not speak to anyone. Neither did she join in the dances or take part in the fiestas. She was always thinking of her loved one whom she had lost. Nothing could make her smile.

One night she could not sleep, and in the half-light of the coming dawn she walked out into the jungle forest. Soon the sky was red as gold on fire. As she looked up through the dim green she saw the most beautiful lace she had ever seen. It was silvery white, and it hung gracefully from the branches of a tree. And in that lace she saw . . . the image of the face of her beloved!

The full sun rose and she knew that what she had thought was lace was really a spider's web hanging from the tree. What she had thought was the face of her beloved was only the reflection of leaves and twigs!

But why couldn't it be lace? Why couldn't it be a beautiful lacy shroud, like the spider's web, to cover the body of the one she loved most—if she could find it!

"I must make lace like the spider's web and have it ready when I find him," she cried.

She went to her hut, got needles and thread, and came again into the jungle early in the morning when the beautiful webs hung glistening in the morning sun. She sat on the ground and began to make lace just like the spider's web, but it was even more beautiful, for she wove into it designs of flowers and leaves and butterflies. In the center she put the design of the guava flower, and around the edges that of the passion flower.

When she finished, she had created the most beautiful lace that had ever been seen in Paraguay, for it had in it not only the beauty of the spider's web, but all the beauty of her love and sorrow.

The story does not tell whether the lovely bride ever found the body of her beloved, but it does say that songs and poems have been written about the *ñandutí* lace, as it is called in Paraguay. And since then all women of Paraguay have woven *ñandutí* lace like that first woven by the young bride.

The lovely lace became famous throughout Latin America and all over the world. If you ever go to Paraguay you'll see women still making *ñandutí* lace, the lace more beautiful than the spider's web.

The Blue Virgin

In a valley of Paraguay there is a little town called Caacupé. In that town there is an image of the Holy Virgin called the Blue Virgin, who is famous through all Paraguay because she has performed many miracles and cures. She is called the Blue Virgin because the color of her clothing is blue.

All the people of Paraguay will tell you eagerly about their wonderful Virgin, and they also like to tell you how the Blue Virgin came to their town. Here is how it happened.

The Indians who lived in that part of the land had a little church, but they had no statue of the Virgin in it. They all wanted one, both to love and also because every other church had one. And they wanted a very, very beautiful Virgin.

One day some of the Indians from the valley saw a very beautiful Virgin, dressed all in blue, in a church near Asunción, the capital city of Paraguay.

"This is just the right Virgin for us!" said one.

"We must have that Virgin!" said another.

"This church has many Virgins; surely they can give us one."

So they came to the church in the middle of the night, when all the people were asleep. They took the beautiful Blue Virgin, wrapped her carefully in a blanket, put her on a mule, and began to travel homeward.

The next day, after a long trip, they came to the valley in which they lived. The mule that carried the holy burden ambled along for a while and then stopped. The Indians prodded and coaxed and begged the mule to go on. They even beat it, but nothing would make it go.

"I wonder what has gotten into that beast," said the young men.

"Perhaps the Virgin wants to stay here," said an old man.

"That's it!" they all said. "She wants to stay in this very place."

The men stopped and got all their friends and relatives together, and there they began to build a church for their Virgin.

Finally the church was finished. The holy image was piously placed in the church, and from that day on, the Virgin brought good luck to the people. East and west, north and south, from one end of the land to the other, word spread of the marvelous cures and miracles performed by the Blue Virgin. Soon a town grew up around the church. It was the town of Caacupé.

There the holy statue has been, and there it still is. Thousands of people come there on the eighth of December, which is her feast day, to celebrate, to worship, to pray, and to plead for help in their problems and ills; and there she has been, listening to them and helping them, except for one time. . . .

Now, in the dark, dark days of the Chaco War, when the people of Paraguay were fighting fiercely against great odds for their lands, money was needed for the army and the people. So the jewels that had been brought to the Blue Virgin in thanksgiving by endless faithful worshipers were sold, and this money kept the army and the people going. But the war grew worse, and Paraguay was in heartbreaking need of help.

One day those who came to the church to pray found the Blue Virgin gone from her accustomed place. They searched and they searched and they searched everywhere, but she could not be found. . . . But on the battlefield the Paraguayans were now winning.

In the midst of the fiercest fighting, where help was needed most, the figure of the Blue Virgin was seen fighting fiercely beside the men of Paraguay. She encouraged them. She begged them to keep up their spirits and not to give up. The men became stronger at the sound of her voice, and they were no longer afraid of the numbers of their enemy. . . . And the war was won.

Then, one morning when the people came to her church to pray—there was the Blue Virgin where she had always been! Her robes were torn to pieces, and a snake from the jungle was twined around her ankle.

The people were overjoyed at this sight, and they loved her and worshiped her even more than before. And so it has been ever since.

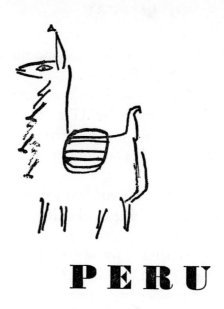

PERU

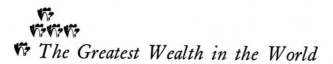

The Greatest Wealth in the World

When the first Spaniards surged through Peru, there, in the Inca capital of Cuzco, was a great temple dedicated to the sun that gave warmth, light, and power.

The proud temple stood high in the clouds, and its walls were lined on all sides with plates of pure gold. The gardens around it had trees and flowers, birds and butterflies designed in gold. Even work tools, such as spades and hoes, were made of gold.

But the great marvel of all was the giant solid gold disk behind the altar. A face was graven on it, and a thousand rays ran out from the face, adorned with precious gems. It was so brilliant, so dazzling, that one could not look directly at it, as one cannot look directly at the sun.

The Spaniards, lusting for gold and still more gold,

destroyed the Indians, and the divine emblem of the sun fell to a soldier named Mancio Serra de Laguicano.

"Now you'll have enough to gamble and drink for years to come," said Pizarro to Mancio. Mancio was a cruel fellow and was known as an ugly, hard gambler who wouldn't hesitate to put up as a stake all that was dearest to him.

The divine emblem worshiped by the great Inca nation meant nothing to him. It was only gold for gambling and drinking.

When the bloody work of conquest was over, and the booty divided, the men turned to their favorite pastimes of drinking, gambling, and abuse.

Mancio was no different than the rest, and gambling was his passion. Of course, he joined the others, but that day was not a lucky day for him. For hours he gambled with a wild crowd of his comrades, losing on every throw of the dice. One by one he lost the gold ornaments and vessels that had been his share of the loot.

"Luck is not on my side," he growled.

"You can afford to lose. You still have that gold disk, which is worth more than all the gold here."

Mancio's eyes were red with anger. His face was set.

"Maybe those devil priests set a curse on you, Mancio," said one of his companions. "You have the image of their god. They worship the sun, and the Devil may be in it."

"I don't believe in devils. It's only a plate of gold, just like the others," Mancio roared. "I know how to play, and I can beat any of you at any game."

"Beat us with what? You wouldn't dare gamble with that sun disk," they taunted him.

Mancio sat staring at the stone wall before him. They were playing in one of the temples.

"You wouldn't dare to gamble with that idol," he heard

one of his comrades say again. "It's your unlucky day. Or have you lost your clever hand at throwing dice?" This taunting came to him like something far away.

Suddenly he roared out, "Put up all your gold against my gold sun disk. I'll try my luck on a single throw. I'll show you that luck is on my side!"

There was silence in the big stone chamber. These men who were not afraid of the Devil had gambled for much, but never for such high stakes. Finally one said slowly, "Do you mean what you say, Mancio?"

"You heard me!" His eyes gleamed like fiery coals.

Each man put his gold in the middle of the room. Mancio took the marvelous gleaming gold disk and put it on the top of it all.

"I'll throw the dice," he said with set teeth.

He took the dice in his hand, closed his hand like a cup, then shook and shook the dice. Then he opened his fingers and threw the marked little squares across the stone floor. They rolled and rolled, and then stopped.

Mancio's face, brown and wrinkled by the sun and winds, turned pale. The men were silent. They just looked. Mancio had lost the golden sun!

He got up and walked away without saying a word. . . .

Mancio did not speak much from that day on. He acted differently than he had before; he was even different to the Indians. Something seemed to have happened inside him. People have many words for what happened in Mancio's mind and heart, but they all mean the same thing. He had a change of heart. He saw that he had done wrong and wanted to undo the evil he had done.

He stopped gambling and drinking, and he was kind to the Indians. He tried to stop others from being brutal.

Then he married the daughter of an Inca and spent his

days helping the Indians and trying to repair the tragic wrongs he and other Spaniards had done. He had found a nobler task in life than that of helping to conquer lands and rob people of their possessions. He had found the greatest wealth there is: the happy work of doing good and helping others.

✂ Tale of the Good, Gay Lady

In the great city of Lima, capital of Peru, there are many tales about a gay and mischievous lady, who was called La Perrichol.

La Perrichol was an actress and very beautiful. She loved the Spanish viceroy of Peru and he loved her. Half of the people of Lima said she was a dreadful person, and the other half said she was a saint. I'll tell you now a tale told by the second half.

One cold, damp night, when a sharp wind was blowing, La Perrichol was driving from the theater in her gilded carriage.

"Make the horses go fast," she said to the driver. "It will keep them warm and get us home quickly."

The horses trotted briskly over the wet cobblestones. Soon La Perrichol and the driver saw a lantern swaying in the dark, and as they came closer they could make out a figure in a long cowl trying bravely to walk steadily in the wind. They came up to him.

"Stop the carriage," said the lady to her driver. "Where are you going, Father?" she asked, leaning out of her carriage window. "Where are you going on this wild night?"

"I'm going to a poor, dying man, to give him the last sacrament, if the Lord so wills."

"Does he live far from here?" she asked kindly.

"Yes, he does."

"In which direction does he live?"

He pointed in the direction from which she had just come. Though dressed in her silks and satins, La Perrichol jumped out of her carriage. The wind almost swept her off her feet.

"You take the carriage, Father," she said. "My driver will take you wherever you wish to go."

"And you, noble lady?"

"I'll find my way home, never fear. I'm not afraid of a little wind, and I know no one will harm me."

She was a spirited woman of great courage.

"Sister," said the priest, "you are doing a deed that, in the eyes of the Lord, is sweeter than the songs of angels."

"Thank you, Father," she said gaily. "Get into my carriage. My driver will take you to the man who needs you, and I'll go to my home."

"May the Lord bless you now and always!" said the priest.

He climbed into the carriage. The driver called to his horses to start, and they were off in a gallop.

The lovely lady turned homeward on the cobblestone streets of Lima. The wind blew her silken skirts in high waves about her, as if in applause of her lovely deed.

Now, wouldn't you say that those who thought she was an angel were right?

⚓ Evil Rocks and the Evil Spirit of Peru

High in the Andes Mountains of Peru an Indian woman and her daughter were looking for one of their goats that was lost. They walked and they walked, over stubble and stones, looking for the goat, until they were a long distance from their home.

"Mother, I'm tired," said the little girl.

"You stay here and play while I look a little farther," the mother said. "This is a safe place. Stay here until I come back."

But it was *not* safe. It was a fearful place that "swallowed" people. Two tall rocks stood side by side, and when anyone came near them, they would open wide, draw the unlucky person in, and close up again. That was the end. Everyone had heard of this place, and so had the mother, but she had never actually seen it. She did not know that it was *right there*.

The little Indian girl stayed behind happily playing with stones. Suddenly a dark, jagged cloud came up in the sky, hovered, and came down. In that cloud was *la vieja Capusa*, as everyone in those parts called her. She was the Devil.

She could change into any form she pleased, but there was one part of herself she could not change: her feet. They were always black vulture's feet with sharp claws.

Capusa came down to the earth and changed herself into the little girl's mother. The poor girl thought it really was her mother and ran to her. Capusa took the girl by the hand and led her to the two rocks, which she had changed to look just like the little girl's home.

"Come in, daughter," Capusa said with a honeyed voice, and the girl followed her willingly. The outside of the house now changed into rocks again, and the poor little girl was imprisoned deep down in the earth.

Her real mother did not find the lost goat, but it was getting late so she came back to get her daughter. She looked all around, but there was no child there. Where was she? The mother looked and looked, and called and called, but no answer. Finally night came, and the poor mother went home crying.

The next day she and the little girl's father and the people of the village went back to look again. They hunted everywhere, but it did no good. The sun went down and it grew so dark they couldn't look any more, so again they went home full of sorrow.

Months passed by and they gave up all hope of ever finding the little girl. She must be dead, they thought.

One day the girl's father went out to hunt partridges and approached the rocks where his daughter had disappeared. He was constantly passing near those rocks—just hoping against hope. When he was some distance from them, he saw a great partridge fly up and then land beside the rocks. He crept up slowly, then stopped. The rocks were wide open now, and right beside them was his daugher, playing with little colored stones. She would hold a few in her hands and then throw them into the air.

The father had heard of the magic power of the rocks and was afraid to go close to them. He hoped his daughter might wander a little distance from them, near to where he was hiding. Instead, she suddenly ran into the opening between them, and in a second the rocks closed. The father waited there for a long time, hoping they might open and his daughter would come out again, but nothing happened.

He returned home but didn't tell anyone except his closest friends what he had seen. They promised to go with him the next day to see if they could help him rescue his daughter.

The next morning, very early, they all went up from the high valley to the place of the evil, magic rocks. Hiding all around, they watched and waited.

After a time the rocks opened and the little girl came out playing with her stones, running here and there. Her father and his friends waited for her to get a short distance away from the evil rocks. Suddenly she came near the men. Quickly her father threw a big stone into the opening between those two monster rocks, and they closed.

The little girl looked around, frightened, and began to cry. "Mother! Mother!" she called.

Her father and his friends rushed out, picked her up, and ran home quickly. All the way home she kept crying for her mother. When they got home, and her real mother took her in her arms, she did not recognize her. She didn't know any of the people who had been her neighbors all her life, and she would not speak to anyone. She just sat in silence, all day long, day after day.

Her father and mother didn't know what to do, so they called a witch doctor. He came and took some yellow and white corn, said a few words, and rubbed the little girl all over. The Incas believed that yellow and white corn brought people back to their senses. The magic helped the little girl, too.

Before long she was her old self again, and she told her family the whole story of what had happened to her—how a woman who seemed to be her mother had come, and how they had lived in a place that looked like her home.

The witch doctor and everyone else knew at once that it was Capusa who had taken her deep, deep down into the earth and kept her there and made her think she was in her own home.

But the little girl was not really well again. As time went on she became worse, and no witch doctor could help her. Then she left this earth.

From then on Indian mothers teach their children that when they see a dark, raggedy cloud or anything with vulture feet, it might be Capusa, and they must cross themselves quickly and say, "Jesus, Joseph, and Mary!" And if Capusa appears even after they say the holy names, they must ask her quickly to show them her vulture's feet. Then Capusa knows she has been discovered and cannot do any harm, and she runs away.

PUERTO RICO

🐦 The Story of the Smart Parrot

There lived a man in Puerto Rico who had a wonderful parrot. There was not another like him. He was smart, and he could say anything in Spanish as clearly as any Puerto Rican. But there was just one word he could *not* say—the name of the town in which he was born: Cataño. The master of the parrot tried everything to teach the bird that word, but all his trying was of no use. The parrot just couldn't say it.

One day a man from San Juan saw and heard the parrot and tried to buy him. Since the owner of the bird needed money very badly at the time, he sold him the bird for a good sum. But he told the man about the one word the parrot could not say.

242

"I'll buy your bird anyway," said the man. "I'll teach him to say 'Cataño.' You can take my word for that."

He took the parrot home with him to San Juan and immediately set about trying to teach the bird to say "Cataño." He tried and he tried and he tried, but it was no use; the parrot simply would not say the word. After a while, the man began to lose his patience and became angry.

"You stupid bird! What's the matter with you? Why can't you learn that one word, when you can say so many others? You say 'Cataño' or I'll kill you!"

But the parrot still would not say it, although the man spent hours trying to teach it to him. Finally the man became so angry that he screamed and ranted at the bird. "You say 'Cataño' or I'll kill you!" he repeated. But he might as well have been speaking to a stone wall.

One day, after trying again for hours to make the parrot say the word, the man became very, very angry. He picked up the bird and threw him into an old chicken house in which he kept the fowl to be eaten.

"You are more stupid than the chickens, and soon I'll finish you as I finish them."

In the chicken house were four old chickens that were to be eaten the following Sunday.

The next morning the master came into the chicken house to get the parrot and the chickens. He opened the door and stopped, astounded at the sight he saw.

There were three chickens lying dead, and the parrot was standing in front of the fourth one, screaming over and over again, "Say 'Cataño' or I'll kill you! Say 'Cataño' or I'll kill you!" The other chickens had not been able to say "Cataño," so the parrot had killed them.

The man looked and looked, then he began to laugh. "This is one time I was fooled by a parrot," he said.

He prepared the fourth chicken for dinner and had a fine meal. He never called that parrot a fool again, for a wise master knows a smart servant.

It's Better to Be Smart Than Strong

Long ago all of the animals of Puerto Rico lived together in the woods under their king, the lion. The woods were full of them, all the way from Aguadilla to Humacao. There were roosters and hens, dogs and donkeys, horses and cats, sheep and goats, rabbits and turtles, and every other kind of animal you can think of. Each lived according to its nature. Those that liked meat ate meat. Those that liked fruit or vegetables ate fruit or vegetables.

One day something happened and there was no meat for the animals that liked meat. Most of all, there was no meat for the lions. All the animals were worried about this and looked at one another, but they didn't speak about it.

One day King and Queen Lion were talking to each other.

"I'm not going to eat carrots like a rabbit!" said the king of the woods.

"I don't like carrots or greens, either," said Queen Lioness.

"I'm hungry," growled King Lion.

"And I'm hungry, too," said his wife. "What shall we do?"

"I'm thinking about it. I'll find a way."

King Lion thought a long time, and an idea came to him.

"I've found a way!" he growled to his wife in a low voice. "I'll tell you what we'll do. It is written that the big animals shall eat the small animals. We are the biggest and the strongest, so it is right that we should eat the smaller ones. The goat is a small animal, and I like goat meat."

"But how can we get good, juicy goat meat? I'd love to have a piece right now." And the lioness licked her chops with her long, rough tongue.

"It's very easy, dear wife," the lion said, "very easy. This is how we'll do it. We'll invite all the animals to a great dance in front of our house. It will be at night, and we'll have a big fire so people can see. We'll invite every animal in the woods, including Mr. and Mrs. Goat. When the music is playing and everyone is dancing, you and I will dance near Mr. and Mrs. Goat. We'll dance nearer and nearer to them, and when we are very close we'll push them into the fire. Everybody will be frightened and run away, and you and I will be left alone. The goats will roast nice and brown, and we will have a fine meal."

Queen Lioness thought this was a fine idea, and they both began to work on it at once. They ran through the woods, inviting every animal they saw to come that night to their home for the dance, and they asked everyone to spread the word.

Night came, and so did all the animals, to the home of King and Queen Lion. A great fire was burning to light up the place. Every animal was there. King and Queen Lion gave them all a friendly greeting and asked some to help with the music.

They asked Horse, Donkey, Rooster, Dog, Ox, Cow, and Cat to make the music, because they were all fine singers.

Then they began. Dog barked, Horse neighed, Donkey brayed, Ox bellowed, Rooster crowed, and Cat meowed. All the animals began to dance to that fine music.

Now, Dog and Goat were good friends. But Dog was very smart and he was a little suspicious about that dance. Soon he stopped barking and went over to Goat, who was sitting alone. He had not brought his wife. She had refused to come because she didn't have a new dress to wear.

"Good friend Goat," said Dog in a low voice, "I don't trust our King Lion. I smell trouble."

"So do I," answered Goat.

"He'll try to eat one of us. I know he's hungry for meat."

"I agree with you, friend Dog. What will we do?"

"We'll do this: you and I will run away. It's lucky we didn't bring our wives. Now, let the two of us dance together, around the edge of the crowd. I can see from the corner of my eye that King Lion is watching us. We'll watch our chance, and when his back is turned we'll run away."

"Very well. That's a good idea," agreed Goat.

So Dog and Goat danced together, and when both King and Queen Lion had their heads turned in another direction they saw their chance and dashed off into the woods. They ran and ran until they came to a river.

Soon Lion turned around and saw that Dog and Goat were gone. He looked all around among the animals, but he couldn't find them anywhere.

"Wife," he whispered, "Dog and Goat have gone! Let's dance over to the side of the crowd, where no one will

All the animals began to dance to the fine music.

notice us, and I'll go out into the woods and look for them. When I catch them, we'll roast them both." So the lions began to dance and move slowly toward the shadows.

Meantime, Dog and Goat stood beside the river. It was swollen from the recent rains. Dog could swim, but Goat could not. Dog jumped into the water and swam across, but Goat just stood there, trying to figure out what to do. They both heard King Lion's angry roar in the distance.

When Lion went into the woods, he saw neither Dog nor Goat, but he found their tracks and followed them. Soon he came near the animals, who heard his roar becoming ever louder.

Goat looked around and saw a pile of straw lying near the river bank. He crawled into it and covered himself completely, except for his tail. In those days goats had fine, long tails.

Lion came up roaring. Dog saw him from across the river and barked loudly.

"Ho there, King Lion! You thought you'd make a

meal of me. Why don't you swim across and get me?"

Lion roared with fury, for he couldn't swim. He just stood there roaring.

Now, I told you Dog was very smart. He knew that his friend Goat was hiding in the straw. He knew he'd have to get him across the river before Lion caught his scent and made an end of his poor friend. Suddenly Dog had a good idea. He began to bark loudly.

"Ho there, King Lion! You think you're strong. I don't think so. There, look at that pile of straw with the thick branch sticking out," and he pointed to the pile of straw where Goat was hiding with his tail sticking out. "I bet you're not strong enough to throw that branch across the river."

"You stupid Dog! Wait till I catch you. I'll show you how strong I am. I'll show you right now how strong I am. I'll just throw that branch and straw across the river."

He took hold of the branch-tail with his mouth, picked up the pile of straw with the goat inside with his paws, and flung them across the river. But he was so angry that he forgot himself and bit off the branch—that is, the tail—and held it between his teeth.

Goat jumped out of the straw. He was so happy to be alive that he forgot the pain of having his tail bitten off.

"Thank you, King," Goat shouted across the river. "Thank you, King Lion, for helping me across."

Then Dog and Goat ran happily home to their wives. But Lion turned back in fury, tearing Goat's tail to pieces as he went. Ever since that time goats have very short tails.

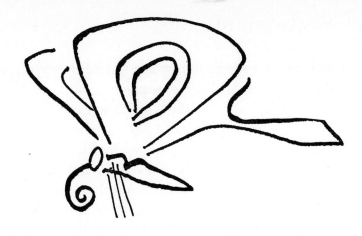

TRINIDAD

The Legend of Pitch Lake

In the cities, towns, and villages of Trinidad, folks will tell
you about Pitch Lake, the black lake on which you can
walk, and from which, for years and years, thick, black
pitch has been taken to top streets and roads all over the
world. No matter how much pitch is taken out of this
lake, more always comes up from the bottom. There is
not another lake like it in all the world.

These are things the world knows about Pitch Lake.
But the black folk of Trinidad tell a great tale about the
lake that goes back for thousands of years, to the time
when there were no white men in Trinidad, and no black
folks either, but only red people: the Indians.

The Carib Indians told this story to the black men who
were brought against their will from Africa to Trinidad as
slaves.

249

It happened in the days when Trinidad was called by the Indians *Ïère*, which means hummingbird, the loveliest of all the birds, sacred to the Great Power of Life.

In those ancient days the Chayma Indians lived in the beautiful rich valley, the valley where Pitch Lake now is. This valley was as lovely as Paradise, rich in fruits and flowers, birds and butterflies. Everything to satisfy men and animals grew there, but loveliest of all were the hummingbirds, protected by the Great Spirit because they were the souls of people who had gone from this world.

One day the Chayma Indians went to war with a neighboring tribe. They won the war and came home with rich booty, shouting war songs and dancing war dances. They were so proud of their victory that they forgot the Great Spirit and what was due him. They forgot that the hummingbirds were the souls of people gone from this life, and that they were loved and favored by the Great Spirit of the World. Wild with the joy of their victory, they shot these innocent birds with their arrows, day after day. They slaughtered so many of them that there was enough meat to feed the whole tribe.

The Indians used hummingbird feathers as ornaments on their spears, bows, and bodies. They broke the ancient laws of the Great Spirit and the priests.

The Great Spirit looked down on the needless killing and sacrilege in deep anger. "I will punish these people who have no kindness or respect!" he said.

But the Chayma Indians, drunk with power and victory, did not hear him or even think about him. They kept on killing the beautiful birds and bedecking themselves with their feathers.

Then the Great Spirit's anger rose like a black cloud before a storm, and a terrible thing happened in that rich valley. It opened wide, wide, and swallowed up all the

Wild with joy, the Indians shot the innocent birds.

Chayma tribe. It swallowed up their homes and their possessions. It swallowed up the trees and everything that grew in the valley.

And over the valley spread a great lake of ugly, black, thick pitch. Higher and higher it rose; it covered the valley almost to its top, leaving only a fringe of green around it. And deep down under the black pitch were the Indians who had slaughtered for pleasure and committed wrong against the Great Spirit.

The pitch lake has been there ever since that time, and underneath it lie the Indian tribe and its village. Once a tree came up from that under-land, alive and growing. It grew to be about ten feet high. It looked at the black folk working and heard their sad songs. Then it sank back down again into its own black world.

Sometimes bones are found by those cutting pitch out of the lake where the lovely valley once was. These bones show that the story told by the Caribs to the black slaves from Africa is true. And now the free men who live there tell it as we have told it to you.

URUGUAY

A Sad Tale of a Silly Fellow

Once there lived a man in Uruguay who had a fine house and a big garden. And though he liked to have everything in order, he did not have much sense in his head. He was that kind of man.

One day he saw a branch on one of his trees growing in the wrong direction, over and around two other branches.

"That branch must be cut away, and I'll do it myself," he said.

So he took a saw and climbed slowly up the tree. When he got to the branch he wanted to cut, he sat down on it and got ready to saw it off.

Then he began to saw it, close to the trunk. See-saw,

see-saw, see-saw, went his saw, back and forth. He was getting along fine. It was a nice day. The sun was shining and the birds were singing and flying about.

A man passing by heard the noise of the sawing and stopped and looked up to see where it was coming from. There he saw the man, sitting on the limb of the tree and sawing it at the same time.

"Holy Father!" he said to himself. "Ho there, my friend!" he called. "What are you doing? You're sawing the limb on which you're sitting! You'll fall down."

"What did you say?" asked the man in the tree, stopping his work.

"I said you're sawing the limb on which you're sitting! You're a very foolish man."

"Why am I foolish?"

"Because you'll fall down and maybe you'll break your neck."

"My dear fellow," said the man in the tree, "it is you who are foolish, sticking your nose into other people's business. This is not the first time in my life I've cut a branch off a tree. This is my big garden, and I keep it in good condition. Just look at it. Go your way, man, and let me do my work."

The man went away, shaking his head and mumbling to himself, "Born a fool, stays a fool."

The man in the tree kept on sawing away at his branch. Pretty soon he had cut over halfway through it, and it began to bend from its weight and that of the man. *Plump!* As sure as fishes swim in rivers, down went the man until the ground stopped his fall. It was a good thing the branch was not very high and he didn't fall very far, so he was not badly hurt.

"That man was a good fortuneteller," he cried. "He is a very smart man. I must talk to him."

He jumped up, ran after the man, and caught up with him.

"Ho, there, fortuneteller!" he called. "Ho, there! I fell down, just as you said I would. Can you foretell everything?"

"Oh, yes, I can foretell everything about you."

"You can?"

"Yes, I can. I can tell you that you will die. I can even tell you when you'll die."

"You really can tell that?"

"Yes, I can."

"You can tell when I'll die?"

"That's what I said," said the man.

"Then tell me!"

"You will die when you ride on a horse and the horse drinks three times on the road."

"Now that you've told me, I'll watch out and be careful. Thanks for telling me."

Then each went his way, and time went by. Each day went along, only to be overtaken by the next day.

One time it happened that our silly man had to go on a journey to a faraway place. He got on his horse and set out. Trot, trot, trot, he rode along the road.

It was a hot day. The red sun burned in the sky so brightly the man could not look at it. He and his horse came to a creek. The horse stopped and drank for a long time. Then they continued their journey. The sun rose higher and higher in the sky, and the higher it rose, the hotter it became. They came to another wide creek, and once more the horse stopped to drink. After a long drink they went on, but before coming out of the creek the horse stopped to drink again. His third drink! The man saw it, and quickly remembered what the fortuneteller had told him.

"Oh, I'm going to die!" he cried. He fainted and fell off his horse. He fell into the creek and the cold water revived him, but he was so frightened he could not get up. He almost died of fright. But luckily for him two men came along with an oxcart.

"What's the trouble with you?" they asked him. "What's happened to you? Why don't you get out of the water?"

"Oh, I'm going to die!" the man wailed. "I'm going to die!"

"Why are you going to die?" they asked. "Are you sick?"

"I'm going to die because the fortuneteller said so."

Then he told them about sawing off the branch, and how the fortuneteller had told him he'd fall and he did, and how he had then predicted his death.

"Come with us in our cart, and then we'll take you home," they said. "Maybe the fortuneteller was wrong this time."

They helped him into the cart and tied his horse behind it. Then they continued their journey and soon came to a river. It had been raining in the mountains, and just as they were crossing the river they saw a great flood of water racing down it. There was no time to reach the river bank; the water rose and flowed into the cart.

The man lying in the cart had either fallen asleep or fainted again, but the water splashing over him woke him. He didn't know where he was, and he couldn't remember how he got there. All he could remember was that his horse had taken a drink three times, and that the fortuneteller had said he would then die. He really thought he was dead. He sat up and looked at the water rushing all around him.

"When I was alive," he shouted, "I crossed a small

creek and my horse took a drink. Then I crossed a wider creek, and my horse took a second and then a third drink. Now I'm in a big, swollen river, and I'm dead!"

When the two men in the oxcart heard this, they became frightened. They thought they had a ghost in their cart. They were scared to death and raised their sticks to defend themselves against the ghost. They thought the ghost would bring death to them, so they hit it first.

They hit and they hit until the foolish ghost was no more.

So you see that what the fortuneteller foretold really did happen.

Oversmart Is Bad Luck

Señor Rooster was a fine bird, and he lived in a village in Uruguay. He was smart, too, and he liked to take walks beyond the village to see the world.

One day he took a long walk and wandered deep into the forest. He came to a tall tree and decided to fly high up into the branches and look at the whole world from there. So he flew up into the tree, branch after branch, until he got high, high up.

Now Señor Fox came walking through the woods. As he passed under the tree he heard Señor Rooster flapping his wings in the branches, and he looked up. He saw the feathers of Señor Rooster and his fat body, and he thought what a fine dinner he would make. But Señor Fox had no wings and could not fly up into the tree. Nor could he climb. Well, he remembered that good words often pave good roads.

"My dear, dear friend, Señor Rooster!" he cried. "How are you today? I see you are all alone up there. It seems very strange for a famous gentleman like you to be all alone. I'm sure all the fine fat hens in the henhouse are worried about you, wondering where you have gone, and are anxious to see you."

"Good Señor Fox," replied Señor Rooster, "just let them wait. The longer they wait, the happier they will be to see me when I return."

"You're a smart gentleman, Señor Rooster, and very wise. But I wouldn't let the poor hens wait too long. Come down and we'll walk together to the henhouse. I'm going that way."

"Ha, ha, ha!" laughed the rooster. "What sweet and honeyed words you use to catch me! Do you really think I'll come down so you can make a good dinner of me? Sweet words catch fools."

"Don't say that, Señor Rooster. Maybe in my former days of sin I was guilty of such things, but no more . . . no more. . . . I've reformed completely. Besides, haven't you heard the news? Don't you know about the new decree now in force in our forest? No animal can eat another; all are to be friends. That's the new law. Anyone who breaks it will be punished severely. I'm surprised you haven't heard about it. Everyone knows it."

"Well, that's news to me, Señor Fox."

"I wouldn't dare to eat you now, even if I were starving to death, my good friend. Honestly. On my honor."

"Do you think I'll come down and let you eat me?" laughed the rooster.

"Well, it must be so, when you talk like that."

"It's the absolute truth, Señor Rooster. So you see, you can come down now."

"Really!" said Señor Rooster, but still he did not come down. Instead, he looked around in all directions. Suddenly he saw a hunter approaching with his dogs. That gave him an idea. He began to count slowly: "One . . . two . . . three . . . four . . ."

"What are you counting, good friend Rooster?"

"Five . . . six . . ."

"What *are* you counting? Tell me, friend."

Señor Rooster pretended he hadn't heard, and said, "Six fine big hunting dogs running this way, and a man with a gun behind them!"

"Dogs! What dogs? Coming this way? With a hunter?"

"Yes, Señor Fox, all coming this way!"

"From which direction are they coming? Please tell me quickly! From where?"

"They're coming from over that way," and he pointed with his wing in exactly the opposite direction from which he saw them.

"I'd better run along now," cried Señor Fox. "I'm in a hurry." And off he ran, as fast as his legs would carry him.

"Señor Fox! Señor Fox!" called Señor Rooster. "Don't run away! Don't go! You can tell the dogs and the hunter about the new decree among the animals in the forest."

Señor Fox ran into the dogs, and Señor Rooster sat in the tree.

If you dig a pit to catch someone innocent, you often fall into it yourself. Oversmart is bad luck.

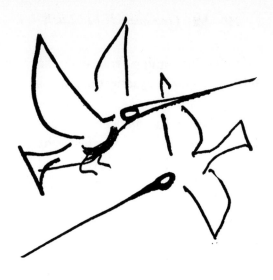

VENEZUELA

🐦 Poor Little Girl, Rich Little Girl

In a village of Venezuela, two little girls lived across the street from each other. One was poor, but she was kind to people and to animals. She was humble and quiet and did her work every day without asking questions or complaining.

The other was rich, and she lived in a fine big house with a beautiful patio and a lovely garden. She was harsh and bitter with people and with animals. She was proud, envious of everyone who had anything she liked, and she wouldn't wet her hands in water because she said she was too delicate.

The poor little girl was one of the breadwinners of her home, and so she went out every day to look for any kind of work she could find. She had to walk a long way to the big town to find work.

One day she walked over the mountains and came to a valley, where she saw two bulls fighting. Their heads were lowered and they butted each other fiercely.

The poor little girl was frightened, but she did not become panicky. She crossed herself and prayed to the Virgin to let her pass the bulls without being hurt. The bulls suddenly stopped fighting and she went on her way quietly.

She walked on the soft green grass and came to a rushing stream. She looked up and down the stream, but she could see no bridge.

"What shall I do? How can I cross this stream? I must cross it to get to town," she said anxiously. "The only thing I can do is to pray to our Holy Virgin. She will let me pass those bulls and help me over this stream."

So she prayed to the Virgin to help her. Slowly the stream stopped flowing, then it stood still. And directly in front of her was a dry path. She walked across without so much as wetting her ankles.

She walked on and on. Suddenly she saw a castle she had never seen before. "Maybe I can find work in that castle," she said. She went up to its big gate, and there stood a nice old lady.

"*Por favor, Señora*—please, lady—is there any work I can do in your castle?" she asked. "We are very poor, and I must help my parents earn our daily bread."

"Yes," answered the kind old lady, "there is enough work here for you. Come right in, and you can start at once."

They both went into the kitchen, and there stood a tub, full of earthenware dishes.

"These dishes must be washed so clean that you can see

your face in them as if they were mirrors," said the old lady.

The tub was huge and the earthenware dishes were caked with dirt. But the poor little girl never said a word. She just smiled and said, *"Muchas gracias, Señora*—thank you, lady—I'll finish as quickly as I can." Smiling, she went to work, and in no time at all the dishes were all mirror-clean.

The kind old lady was pleased. "That's fine!" she said. "Now there's one thing more I'd like you to do. Some insects bit my back, and it itches terribly. A little scratching would make me feel better. Scratch my back a little."

The poor little girl smiled sympathetically and said she would.

The old lady bared her back, and the poor little girl noticed it was covered with small pieces of broken glass. But she didn't say a word. She just began to scratch, and although her fingertips were cut to shreds by the broken glass, she never complained one bit. She simply went on scratching.

When the old lady saw that the little girl did not complain, she said, "Now you've done enough for one day's work. I'll pay you. Come with me."

The girl followed the lady into a large room filled with barrels of all sizes.

"Take any barrel you like," said the woman. "That will be your pay. I'm sure you'll be satisfied."

The poor little girl looked around until she saw the smallest barrel in the room. She put it on her back, thanked the old lady, and left the castle.

When she came to the stream, there was the clear path across it again. When she came to the bulls, they were grazing quietly.

Finally she got home, told her parents about her day's

work, and they opened the barrel. It was filled with gold coins. You can imagine how happy the poor family was. Now they were not poor any more. They could have all the food and clothes and comforts of life they wanted.

The rich little girl across the street heard about the poor little girl's good fortune, for such news always travels quickly, you know. The poor little girl told the rich little girl the whole story from beginning to end—how she had passed the bulls and the river, where the castle was, what the old lady made her do, and how she had rewarded her.

The rich little girl was greedy. Though she really had everything a little girl could want, she wanted more. So she decided she'd go and get a barrel of gold, too.

She walked over the mountains until she came to the valley and the bulls. They were fighting and butting each other. But she didn't pray humbly to the Virgin—she took a rock and threw it at the bulls. They ran away and she went on.

She came to the raging stream. But she didn't pray to the Virgin. Instead, she scolded the waters and screamed at them to dry up. They did, and she crossed the stream.

She came to the castle, and there was the old lady standing by the gate. "Good morning, little girl," the old lady said pleasantly.

"Good morning, old woman. I'm poor and hungry and I want work. Do you have any?"

"Yes, I have plenty, if you want to work. Come right in."

The old woman led the little girl into the kitchen. There was the huge tubful of terribly dirty dishes.

"Wash these, and I'll pay you for it."

"I never saw such dirty dishes in all my life!" cried the girl crossly. But she thought about the barrel of gold, so she went to work without any further complaint.

She was grumbling to herself all the time and broke many of the dishes. It seemed to her that she'd never finish, but at last she did.

"Now I've washed all those dirty dishes," she said.

"Good," said the old lady, "but there's one more little thing I'd like to have you do. My back is all bitten by mosquitoes, and a little scratching would make me feel better. Please scratch it for me."

"I've never scratched anybody's back before, and I won't scratch yours! Pay me for what I've done. I'm going home!"

"*Muy bien*—very well," said the old lady, with no sign of impatience at these bad manners. "Come with me."

She led the girl into the room packed with barrels. As you can guess, the rich little girl grabbed the biggest barrel she could find. Out she went, as fast as she could go, without a "thank you" or "good-by." She dragged the barrel along after her—and it wasn't easy work.

On the way back, the river was dry and the bulls were quiet, and finally she reached her home.

She dragged the barrel up to her room, for she didn't want to share her gold with anyone. Then she opened it and looked in eagerly. But there was no shining gold inside. The barrel was full of insects and snakes!

She tried to run away, but she had locked the door and all the windows and she couldn't get out.

You can imagine what happened to her. Just the thing that happens to anyone who is envious and greedy and who wants more than he needs. Those insects and snakes taught her the right lesson.

👑 The Secret of the Hidden Treasure

One day the abbot of the Capuchin monastery on the Caroni River in Venezuela was standing before a large company of priests, guards, and Indians with mules. There stood thirty-two mules laden with enough gold and silver to buy a kingdom, along with eighteen priests, a few Spanish soldiers, and a great many Indians. The abbot was speaking to them.

"The ungodly rebels, enemies of our Church, will try to steal the gold and silver we took from our mines and minted. They will try to destroy us, but they will fail in all their efforts, for the Lord is with us.

"I learned from our friends that General Manuel Piar will try to capture us and our treasure, and even our mines, which we have sealed well. Only we know exactly where the entrance is, and we are sworn not to tell. Anyone who betrays our secret will be cursed by God and the Church and will die a terrible death, and the curse will follow his family for generations to come.

"Now we must get to the coast, where Their Majesties' ships are waiting to take us to Spain. The Lord is on our side, and we will reach the coast safely. But the enemies of the Church and the king will be cursed and will perish.

"We must get our gold and silver and sacred vessels to the ships before General Piar can lay hands on them. Let us begin our journey with courage and faith. Ten Indians will go first, to see that the way is clear. The rest of us will follow. At the slightest suspicion of the presence of the enemy, give us warning."

The Indians started off. The long cavalcade followed.

At this very moment, General Manuel Piar, one of the leaders in Venezuela's fight for freedom from the tyranny of Spain, was speaking to his company of soldiers.

"Soldiers, we are battling to throw off the yoke of oppression. We need gold to feed our people. I have learned that the Capuchin monks, who own the greatest of our mines, are fleeing to the coast with a great treasure of gold and jewels. Ships are waiting there to take them to Spain. We must get that treasure back. It came from this land of ours and belongs to us, and we need it. They already have plenty. They are on their way to the coast. Let our loyal Indian scouts go first and try to locate where they are now. We will do the rest."

The general's Indian scouts set out, followed by his soldiers.

Thus it was that the abbot's men and the general's men were hacking their way through the jungle at the same time, the former fleeing and the latter pursuing them.

The abbot's Indians sighted their enemy first and rushed back to tell him of their discovery.

"Let us separate into four groups, each taking eight mules with treasure. This move will mislead Piar. If he finds one group, he will lose time, and the rest of us will be able to get to the ships. We must reach them. The accursed traitor must not and will not find us. God is on our side.

"And remember, we are the only people who know how

One group was fleeing, the other pursuing.

to get into our mines. We must never reveal this secret to anyone, no matter what happens. We must be silent. The one who betrays our secret will be cursed forever—him, his children, and his children's children, through all generations to come.

"Remember, *quédense callados*, keep silent! If you don't, the black curse will fall upon you.

"Let the first company start. The others will follow me. I'll give the signal when the next group should separate from us."

The first group went off quickly.

But the general and his followers were also moving swiftly. Soon the general's Indian scouts reported that they had seen the fleeing group. It did not take long before the first group with the mules was sighted. After a short struggle, only one of the Indian treasure guards remained. General Piar captured thousands of ounces of gold, worth millions of dollars. But that was only one-fourth of the treasure. General Piar never got the rest of it.

He questioned the one surviving Indian for hours, but the Indian would not speak. He remembered the abbot's warning: "*Quédense callados*, keep silent!" He remembered the abbot's curse.

Nobody ever found the rest of the treasure or the rich mine from which it had been taken.

As the abbot and the others fled toward the coast, their scouts warned them that there was no escape, so they stopped and buried their vast treasure, the richest in all Venezuela, in two places.

Where did they bury it? No one knows. The abbot's words had filled the Indians with such mortal fear that they never spoke. They kept silent and carried their secret to the grave with them.

The priests carved a statue of a monk on a rock to indicate the spot where the treasure was buried. Indeed, this statue points to the spot. But the arms of the stone monk are crossed, and his ten fingers point in ten different directions. The "Monk on the Rock" is still there, but no one has ever found the exact spot where the treasure is buried.

Another part of the treasure was buried in a cave on a very steep, high cliff that is almost impossible to climb. On the side of the cliff can be seen the spikes the monks used to climb to the cave.

But no one has ever found this part of the treasure, either. Nor has anyone ever found the entrance to the rich mine. Many have tried, but the curse of the abbot stops them. And the Indians never speak. They, too, are afraid of that curse. They do exactly what the abbot said: *quédense callados*, keep silent!

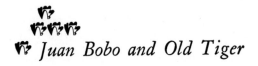

Juan Bobo and Old Tiger

Juan Bobo—silly John—lived in a hut in the woods of Venezuela all alone with his old burro. This burro had been his faithful friend for many years, helping him in his daily work.

Juan was happy, and so was everyone else who lived there, until an old tiger settled nearby. That tiger was a terrible beast. He killed chickens and hogs; he killed everything that came near him. Men and animals alike were afraid of him.

One morning Juan Bobo woke early. He was going to take some cassava roots to sell in the village. He went out to the place where his old burro always grazed, but no burro was to be seen anywhere.

He looked here, there, and everywhere. He looked around the little garden and in the woods. No burro in sight.

He ran deeper into the woods, and there, at the foot of a tree, he found what was left of his burro—just some skin and bones, and tiger's footprints!

"Oh, that terrible beast! That fierce tiger!" cried silly John. "He has eaten my burro." He cried and he stamped his foot. But that did not give him back his burro.

A great anger came over him, and he said, "I'll teach that tiger a lesson he'll never forget."

He picked up a big thick branch that had fallen from a tree and set out to look for the tiger.

He walked and he walked through the dark jungle. He saw all kinds of animals: foxes, tapirs, and snakes, but he did not see that awful old beast, the tiger.

He met a little vine, lying along his path.

"Good morning to you, Juan Bobo," said Little Vine.

"It is *not* a good morning," answered Juan Bobo.

"It *is* a good morning," said Little Vine. "Why do you say it is *not* a good morning? What has happened to you, Juan Bobo?"

"Old Tiger ate my good burro. I'm looking for him. When I find that cruel thief, I'll destroy him."

"Ah, that's too bad! I knew your fine old burro. He was a faithful and patient animal. You are right. That thief should be punished. Take me along, I'll help you."

"You are very small, Little Vine, but perhaps you can help me. Who knows? So come along with me."

Little Vine and Juan Bobo went on through the deep jungle. Finally they met Little Onion.

"Good morning, Juan Bobo and Little Vine."

"Good morning, Little Onion. May God bless you!" said Little Vine. Juan Bobo just grumbled.

"Where are you two going?"

"I'm going to kill that old beast Tiger who ate my burro. He's a thief and a murderer, and everyone is afraid of him. His crimes must be stopped!" said angry Juan Bobo.

"You are right, Juan Bobo!" said Little Onion. "I know Tiger, and I know what he has done. Even the trees are afraid of him. We must get rid of him. Take me with you, Juan Bobo. Maybe I can help you, even though I am little. Remember that big, fat stick in your hand came from a little seed."

"You are right, Little Onion! Come along with us. It may be that you can help."

On and on they went, until they came to the deep, dark cave of Tiger. They didn't hear a sound, so they went in. In the middle of the cave a fire was burning. Over it hung a big iron kettle. And inside the kettle a meat stew with vegetables was cooking.

"Let's decide what we'll do when Tiger comes," said Little Vine.

"I'll jump in the stew and keep watch," said Little Onion.

"I'll lie near the mouth of the cave and look for him," said Little Vine.

"I'll wait behind the woodpile and hold my club all ready," said Juan Bobo.

Little Onion jumped into the stew; Little Vine lay down near the opening of the cave; and Juan went behind the woodpile holding his club tightly.

"Grrrr! Grrrr!" came a growling at the entrance to the cave, and Old Tiger stalked in, lashing his tail right and left. He was angry. Hunting had not been good and he was hungry.

"At least there is that stew I can eat. But I'd like raw, red meat better!"

Little Onion in the soup began to sing and gurgle.

"*Glglglgl glp! glglgl glp!* Oh-oh-oh!"

"Quiet, you silly stew. I'll swallow you soon enough."

"*Glglglgl glp; glglgl glp.* Oh-oh-oh!" Little Onion sang.

"Quiet!" roared Tiger, "or I'll throw you out to the ants."

But Little Onion just kept on stewing, *glp, glp, glp.* "We've come to kill mean old Tiger. We've come to kill mean old Tiger."

That made Tiger angrier than he had ever been. With a mighty blow of his huge paw he knocked the kettle of stew off the fire, and it splattered all over the cave. Little Onion hit a rock and bounced back, right in Tiger's eye! It blinded him and Tiger started to run out of the cave. But when he got as far as the mouth of the cave, Little Vine, lying there, entangled his feet, and he fell to the ground.

Then Juan Bobo jumped out and began to beat Tiger with his big stick until Tiger was very, very quiet.

"Now you won't eat any more good, honest, hard-working burros, you thief, you murderer!" cried Juan Bobo.

"Now nobody in the jungle need worry about him any more," said Little Vine.

"You see, Juan Bobo," said Little Onion, "even a little onion can help to do a big thing."

NOTES

𝕎 ARGENTINA

Don't Make a Bargain With a Fox

The animal tale of the fox and the viscachas is a standard folk theme adapted to a particular country. This type tale is found everywhere, and is the kind of story told young people in schools.

The Eternal Wanderer of the Pampas

Gaucho stories are as popular and as much loved in Argentina as cowboy stories are in the United States. There are hero stories of gauchos, and innumerable gaucho stories of every type and plot. Spanish books are full of such tales.

The gaucho ghost story told here—"The Eternal Wanderer of the Pampas"—is just one sample of the variety that could be told if space permitted.

The eternal wanderer who expiates sins he has committed is a widespread theme the world over, and this particular tale is known throughout the pampas. It was told by an Argentine theatrical manager we met in Haiti and who went with us as far as Havana. He said it was the kind of story told by a fire at night.

The Girl and the Puma

"The Girl and the Puma" is certainly influenced by Spanish lore. There really is a city called Maldonado, founded by settlers who went originally to Buenos Aires. Some parts of the story are supposed to have happened when the settlement was first established, and doubtless there is some substance of reality in it, clothed with the glamour of legend.

🦇 BAHAMAS

Nassau is one of the Bahama Islands, of which there are more than three thousand. They are as colorful and as beautiful as the marvelous fish found in the water nearby. Nassau is lively and exciting, as are all large West Indian cities, and we spent many hours talking to people and occasionally buying a basket or some lovely figurine made of delicately colored seashells. Sometimes we walked in the streets, where one finds natives and others, living, working, singing, and dancing. The better the people knew us, the more songs and tales we heard.

Here are two told by James Ward, an old man who sells baskets. The introductory and concluding verse, we were told, is always used to open and close stories.

Jack Who Could Do Anything

The Jack tale, like most of the folk narratives of the Bahamas, are doubtless chiefly of European tradition, perhaps with a little African admixture.

Smart Working Man, Foolish Boss Man

We do not recall having previously encountered this story. It is undoubtedly a local tale, but it follows the general pattern of the folk jest.

🌱 BARBADOS

The House That Strong Boy Built

Barbados, like the other Caribbean Islands, is gay and sunny, and its folk tales are often amusing and full of simple, pleasant humor. "The House That Strong Boy Built" is a commonly known tale, and you will hear it when you ask for local stories "nicely." Thus we heard it.

🌱 BOLIVIA

If you keep your eyes on the ground, you will find money. I live in New York city, and one evening as I was on my way to visit a friend, I stopped before a large lighted window to look at the endless rows of deep-colored bottles of wine. Next to me stood two young men, discussing in Spanish the merits of different kinds of wine, and I told them I knew of a Portuguese wine that was reasonably priced and excellent.

One word led to another. I asked if they were Puerto Ricans, and they said no. One came from Argentina, and the other from Bolivia. Then I told them I was trying to find Latin-American folk stories, and soon we were sitting at a table telling tales. It was there I heard the Bolivian stories.

The King of the Mountains

This is a purely traditional Indian story, well known in schools and among the young people of Bolivia. I am sure it has been told many times before, although I have not seen it.

Greed in Heaven, Grave on Earth and *The Hero in the Village*

Both of these may be local stories. They have an Indian character and flavor. The former may be a modern anecdotal survival of an ancient Indian myth, in which the fox was the culture hero who brought plant foods to his people.

☝ BRAZIL

So Say the Little Monkeys

"So Say the Little Monkeys" is a well-known expression used by people along the Rio Negro in Brazil when speaking of anyone who puts off doing things. This tale may well have grown up locally on Brazilian soil. João Barbosa Rodrigues has it in his splendid collection, *Poranduba amazonense*, which first appeared in Rio de Janeiro in 1890.

Clever Little Turtle

Tales of turtles are very common along the Amazon River in South America, where they are found in great abundance. Generally the turtle outwits other animals, and human beings as well, as we see in "Clever Little Turtle," which shows Indian, or perhaps African, influence and has many parallels, as most folk stories do. These and similar tales were collected by José Vieira Couto de Magalhães in *O selvagem*, Rio de Janeiro, 1876.

The Boy Who Was Lost

"Don't shoot bacurau birds or you'll be left on the other side of the stream," is an expression much used along the great river in the northeastern part of Brazil. The theme of hiding in the crop of a heron or other animal is widespread; so is that of turning into a certain animal by putting on the skin of the animal. "The Boy Who Was Lost" combines all these motifs in one story, though it never makes clear why the boy liked the Pig People so well.

☝ CHILE

Lion and Man

Folk stories of the type of "Lion and Man" are very ancient. This is a primitive expression of man's superiority over animals.

The Fox Who Was Not So Smart

Races between small and large, or notably fast and slow, or stupid and clever animals or people is a common type of tale all over the world. Hiding in the tail of the obviously superior animal is also well known. The ending of our story is somewhat different from the usual form.

The Good Man and the Kind Mouse

This is a well-known type of European folk tale, and has been extensively annotated in European collections and classifications.

Both *Lion and Man* and *The Fox Who Was Not So Smart* were published originally by Rudolf Lenz in his *Araukanische Märchen und Erzählungen*, Valparaíso, 1896.

ᐯ COLOMBIA

Rosita García from Colombia has worked in my house for nearly twenty-five years. When she came, she could speak no English. Today she can speak English well, has become accustomed to life in America, and has no desire to return to the place where she was born. She says she is half Indian. She is very intelligent, and it was she who told me these Colombia stories, which we have tried to keep as close to her own words as possible.

The Lord Said, This Is My House

The legend of the Christ painting in Cartagena, Colombia, which insisted on staying in its place—"The Lord Said, This Is My House"—is a variant of a well-known type of story. Here the picture gets bigger. Often it is a statue that gets heavier the farther it is carried from the place it desires to remain in, until finally it is almost too heavy to be carried any farther. And it becomes lighter as it is taken back to its place. This has been called the "miracle of ponderosity." It is only one of several ways in which a holy image manifests its will. The painting in this story is still in the Santo Domingo church in Cartagena.

The Great Flood

The flood myth is one of the most widely known of all folk-lore narratives, being found in the majority of world cultures over the past four thousand years. This is the Chibcha version, with the local characteristics one expects to find in folklore.

The Mysterious Lake

The story of the enchanted Indian princess in "The Mysterious Lake" is an excellent example of an Indian narrative with a typical European theme, for the enchanted ducklings is quite a common theme throughout Europe. It is interesting to note the introduction of the element of El Dorado, or the Golden One, and treasure in the lake, which was such a powerful lure to early adventurers of all nations.

🖋 COSTA RICA

Costa Rica is a fine country because it has more teachers than policemen.

In San José, the capital city, there are many bookstores, and many of the people who sell books in these stores have read what is in the books they sell. They are very well-read people, and they are friendly. I told one of them we were looking for stories of Costa Rica, and here is one he told us.

Juan in Heaven

This is obviously a European tale that has been transplanted to Costa Rica. It is interesting to see how these European stories are made to fit into their new setting in the New World. Dream tales are found among some of the oldest stocks of world folk tales.

🎵 CUBA

The Silly Owls and the Silly Hens

We heard this Cuban tale under unusual circumstances—in a dance hall in New York City where a Latin-American dance contest was being held. Again and again couples would come on the floor, imitating the strutting of roosters and hens in their dancing.

Our Cuban and Puerto Rican companions told us this was a favorite pantomime dance in those islands—and then we heard the tale of the courtship of the owls and the hens.

Some time later, in Havana, we had the pleasure of meeting Miss Lydia Cabrera, who is undoubtedly the foremost Cuban folklorist and collector of Cuban folk tales. She presented us with some of her printed works. In going through the one on Negro folk tales we found this one among them. The version we had first heard varied in some small details from hers.

This is an Afro-Cuban tale, a typical product of its environment. It is a lively reflection of the life and outlook of the large colored population of Cuba. These people feel close to, and in harmony with, the natural environment that surrounds them. Their attitudes are well expressed here through their use of the symbolism of nature. Miss Cabrera's contribution to Cuban folklore deserves high praise, and it is regrettable that we do not have more of her writing available in English.

🎵 THE DOMINICAN REPUBLIC

Who Rules the Roost?

This story and the next were told us by Tijides Garrido, a native of the Dominican Republic and mother of Edna Garrido de Boggs, author of "*Folklore infantil de Santo Domingo*, published in Madrid, Spain, by Cultura Hispanica in 1955, a 661-page volume of Dominican children's folklore.

The Haitians in the Dominican Republic

This is an old folktale theme, long popular in Europe. It thrives best where people speaking quite different languages live close to each other and frequently visit each other's country. Although Dominican Spanish does show some dialect features, it is quite close to standard Spanish and is easily understood by anyone who knows Spanish. Well-educated Haitians speak pure French, for many of them have been educated in France, but the large majority of country people in Haiti, like the Haitians of our tale, speak a dialect that has French as its basis. It is difficult for an outsider to understand it, even though he knows standard French perfectly. Although Haiti and the Dominican Republic have a common border, few Dominicans have ever been to Haiti.

🐚 ECUADOR

The two Ecuadorian stories told here are the common heritage of that land. Everyone, young and old, in every part of the country, knows them. Wherever we asked for stories, when we were there, these were the first two told, and they are probably the best known among common folk and the highly educated as well.

Faithful To Death

This is purely an Indian story, even though it has many parallels in European traditions. Probably European influence helped to mold it into the form in which it is known.

The Head of the Inca

This story is a blending of history and legend, and to this day a subject of popular discussion among the Indians and even in the schools.

🖎 EL SALVADOR

In El Salvador one notices the absence of Indians. Alvarado and his Spaniards destroyed them, but he could not destroy their tales, many of which still live in the memory of the people. Indigenous and European tradition mingled there to produce a national heritage of folk culture. The two tales given were heard in a hotel in the capital.

One of the highlights of our visit was the very pleasant time spent with María Baratta, probably the most important collector of folklore in that country. Her two large volumes on Cuscatlán constitute the most formidable storehouse of the folk culture of El Salvador available in print.

How Much You Remind Me of My Husband!

This is a charming local tale to bring a smile to your face. It has a little double meaning and is often told among friends to illustrate a point.

Pedro Alvarado and the Indian Girl

The footprints in stone, found in the legend of "Pedro Alvarado and the Indian Girl," is a very common type of legend found anywhere. Any particular aspect of natural formation that attracts attention is apt to inspire a legend. Near the old town of Bath on the North Carolina coast, for example, there is a curious little sinkhole to which a legend has become attached, explaining that it is the hoofprint of a horse. To make it more intriguing, natives assure visitors that if they fill up the depression with dirt, making it level with the ground around it, the depression will mysteriously reappear.

🖎 GUATEMALA

A strap on my valise was broken in Chichicastenango in Guatemala and we were directed to a shoemaker to have it fixed. He lived down a steep cobblestone street.

In his big, cool, low workroom, hides, shoes, and scrap leather used for fertilizer were arranged neatly.

Yes, he could cut me a strap, but he asked why we were there when there was no fiesta.

"To hear stories of your land and your people."

"What kind of stories?"

"About gods and people."

"There are many."

"Do you know any?"

"Some."

"Would you mind telling me some?"

He told five in that noon hour and four that evening. We have used three of them here.

The Great Blessing of the Land

Corn is one of the most important sources of food for the Indian, and there are many stories associated with it. This is one we heard in Guatemala. Teosinte is derived from a Nahuatl word *teocintli*, composed of the two words: *teotl*, "god, divinity"; and *tzintli*, "corn." Its flower looks like the flower of corn, and the plants are often confused when they are young. Pilpil Indians have a tale of the princess who married the king of the bats. When famine came to her people, she went out to seek corn for them. Finally she sowed her own teeth, from which corn grew.

There are many other legends about the origin of corn in Latin America and elsewhere over the world.

The Little, Little Fellow With the Big, Big Hat

"The Little, Little Fellow With the Big, Big Hat" is well known in Antigua and other places. This and "Golden Goodness" were related by a young Guatemalan of French origin who is an oculist in Guatemala City and who took us in his car from there to Antigua. This story shows considerable European influence.

The Sweetest Song in the Woods

The *chirimía* or oboe can be heard everywhere in Guatemala. This story, which tells the legend of its origin, is well known. We heard the instrument played in Chichicastenango, in the Mayan Hotel.

Golden Goodness

"Golden Goodness" is one of the most humane and best-known tales of Guatemala.

🐾 THE GUIANAS

The Guianas, on the north coast of South America, are divided into three parts: British, French, and Dutch. The same Indian tribes are found throughout most of the territory of all three and are much intermingled. The folk stories found among these Indians are common throughout the territory, and for that reason have not been separated here, for the three divisions are political rather than cultural. All the stories are retold from older collectors.

Many parts of the Guianas are swampy and humid, and so the frog plays an important part in the life there.

Bahmoo Rides the Wrong Frog

This amusing tale was collected by H. Brett around 1870-1880.

Who's Strong?

This is a story that well illustrates animism, for it makes a person of lightning. To give human attributes and form to the forces of nature is common among primitive peoples.

The jaguar is often described as a silly, boasting animal, and in this story, collected by Koch-Greenberg, he is regarded as a proper warning against boasting.

Smart Dai-adalla

This story, collected by Walter E. Roth, illustrates very well superstitions of Guiana Indians and also gives a moral lesson in obedience.

A Promise Made Should Be Kept

Honey is an important food among the South American Indians, as is shown by this story. Like the other Guiana stories, it seems to be purely Indian. It was collected by Roth.

When a Man Is Foolish

This story shows the South American Indian concept of noodle-head behavior and belongs to the world-wide category of "fool tale." It, too, comes from the Roth collection.

✍ HAITI

In a hotel in Port-au-Prince, the capital of Haiti, our table was served by a sweet, quiet, elderly man named Joseph. Acquaintance and friendship with simple and kindly people are made easily, and before long Joseph was not only our friend but also a source for many tales, including this one.

No tales are better known or more popular in Haiti than those of Uncle Bouqui and Little Malice. They abound and seem to be growing, like the lush plant of a tropical forest. Whenever a Haitian invents a new trick, it is promptly attributed to Bouqui and Malice, just as we attach stories to the names of our folk heroes, especially stories that suit their particular personalities.

Uncle Bouqui and Little Malice

Bouqui and Malice are relatives—Malice the nephew and Bouqui his uncle. Stories about them are said to have been brought to Haiti by the first slaves. It is only to be expected, therefore, that Malice sometimes should have the face of a rabbit—classic symbol of the trickster in African folklore—and that Bouqui sometimes should have the face of a donkey, which savors more of the symbolism of the French, former masters of Haiti.

So well known is Bouqui that in the Dominican Republic a glutton is called a bouqui, and in French Louisiana a bouqui is a stupid and selfish person.

Friendship between trickster and fool is quite commonplace in world folklore. In Romania these two prototypes are named Tandala and Pakala.* In Spanish America they are often called Juan Bobo and Pedro Animal, the latter epitomizing stupidity, and the former, despite his name—"John Fool"—frequently turning out to be surprisingly clever. Tales about them usually appear in general collections of folk tales from most parts of Spanish America and also from Spain.

The introductory formula is a well-established device in folk tales. This particular one is used by the French and was borrowed from them by the Haitians.

✌ HONDURAS

At the University of Miami, Florida, there are many students from all parts of Latin America who know stories of their countries and are pleased to tell them. Miss Carolina Banegas from Honduras was particularly helpful about stories from that area.

How the Caribs First Came to Honduras

This story refers to the Caribs and Carib black folk. Various groups of Indians were found in Honduras before the Spaniards came, none of whom were Caribs, strictly speaking, for the Caribs were found along the coast of Venezuela, spread out through the islands, and are really a people of the eastern Caribbean area, though the early explorers applied the term somewhat loosely to a variety of tribes.

Even today the term "Caribs" is used loosely and really means an admixture of many strains of people. They are the descendants of Negroes who were brought in slave ships and of the Mesquito Indians. They intermarried and their descendants are the "Black Indians." Then there are the true Caribs who lived in the eastern part of the Caribbean and who also intermarried with Negroes, producing a large population of more black Caribs. All of these, together with Spaniards and English, came to the northern coast of Honduras from the sixteenth to the eighteenth centuries.

* See *Noodlehead Stories Around the World*, by M. A. Jagendorf. New York: The Vanguard Press, Inc.

The Virgin of Honduras

Up in the mountains, not far from Tegucigalpa, the capital city of Honduras, stands the little village of Suyapa, with its church housing the image of "The Virgin of Honduras," patron of Honduras. Pilgrimages and festivals in her honor are centered in Suyapa, to which people come from far and wide. She is to Honduras what the Virgin of Guadalupe is to Mexico. In both cases, legends have evolved, telling of a miraculous visitation of her image, which indicated the spot upon which her temple was to be built.

When Boquerón Spoke

Eruptions of volcanoes and the consequent destruction of cities have often been associated in the folk mind with the punishment of the inhabitants because of their sins. In truth, people often see the hand of divine justice in a variety of catastrophes caused by natural phenomena. The modern department of Olancho, in Honduras, founded in 1825, took its name from the old town of Olancho, at the foot of the volcano Boquerón, which erupted in 1611 and destroyed the town. The town has never been rebuilt, but some of its ruins still remain.

🕷 JAMAICA

In rich-green Jamaica lives Anansi. He must have come from far Africa many years ago. Sometimes in the stories he is a spider with long legs, crawling on ceilings and trees. Sometimes he has the face of a man, and the rest of him is a spider dressed in man's clothing. Sometimes he is entirely a man, old and hairy.

But whatever he is, he is very smart, always playing tricks, always making people laugh or making them angry at his tricky ways.

We heard many Anansi stories in the Caribbean islands—in Trinidad, Jamaica, Haiti, and elsewhere.

Anansi is spelled many different ways. I chose "Anansi" because this is the way it is pronounced by the storytellers I heard.

Anansi Play With Fire, Anansi Get Burned

I heard this tale from a woman who cleaned our room, a Mrs. Robinson. She was middle-aged and knew many other tales. One of the waiters who helped me with the Jamaican dialect also knew the story.

"Jack Madoora, that's all," or "Jack Madoora (or Mondory) me no choose none," is a typical form for concluding a tale. An elderly man in Old Spanish Town, who told me the story of "The Gold Table" used it all the time.

The intermixture of old and new in the ancient tale is interesting. Nearly all the Anansi stories I heard had something of the present in them, proving once again that folk tales change to conform with their tellers' life and times.

The Gold Table

This is a well-known legendary tale in Jamaica. We heard it from Mrs. Robinson, and again from our helpful waiter in the hotel where we stayed.

💥 MEXICO

The Hotel de Cortés in Mexico City is a paradise for folklorists. It is an ancient, many-hued, terra-cotta-colored building where the stones tell tales and where old customs are still observed. This is particularly true at Christmastime. The fountain in the patio is then filled with *flores de Navidad* (Christmas flowers), red, greens, yellows, in a luminous holiday color-song. The balcony around the patio is trelissed with clusters of colorful *geranios*, *hortensias*, and *rosas*, and across the full length of the patio are strung marvelous forms of paper birds and beasts in gay colors. In the center hangs a large *piñata* in the form of a green bird, filled with flavored sweets that will be enjoyed at the end of the *posadas* (a series of fiestas on the nine nights preceding Christmas). Then there is a grand game of a kind of blindman's buff that goes on until one of the blindfolded merrymakers, groping about the area cleared under the *piñata* and blindly batting the air with a stick, strikes the bird and breaks the pottery jar that the paper form conceals. Then the sweets come tumbling down and everyone joins in the mad scramble to get them, in a great spirit of fun.

Many come to Mexico during the Christmas festival to join in the joyous spirit. As we sat together with Mexican friends in the patio during the sunny afternoons and mild evenings of Christmastide, and told them we had come to hear the stories of their beautiful land, they overwhelmed us with one of the richest stocks of folklore to be found anywhere. Everyone told stories. We heard enough to fill a volume, but, alas! we can tell only a few of them here, for in this book we must visit many lands of the Americas. Four exceptionally good storytellers we had the pleasure of meeting were Tomás López, Rómulo Prados, Alberto Romero, and Angelina Huerta. They were people much like you and me, and they wanted us, and you through us, to know something of the rich heritage of the traditional culture of their land.

The Love of a Mexican Prince and Princess

In a high mountain valley in the heart of Mexico, before the Spaniards came, one of the greatest indigenous New World civilizations flourished in the ancient Indian capital called Teotihuacán, now called Mexico City. From the city, when the sky is clear, off eastward one sees rising majestically two of the highest peaks. Their snow line rises and falls with the temperature. but most of the year they are covered with snow and stand out gleaming white in the tropical sun against the deep blue sky. The taller peak, a rather sharply defined volcanic cone, is called Popocatépetl. The longer, lower one, whose ridge resembles the outline of a woman lying on her back, is called Ixtaccíhuatl—"The Sleeping Lady." North Americans often call them Popo and Ixta for short.

One of the best-known legends of the Valley of Mexico is "The Love of a Mexican Prince and Princess," which explains how the two lovers became converted into these two famous peaks. Like all folklore, it has many variants. We offer here the one we like best, and we hope our readers enjoy it as much as we did.

Coyote Rings the Wrong Bell

Animal tales are found all over the world, and they abound in Mexico. This story sounds very much like the animal tales told in our own country, as well as in many others. These animal stories are world travelers.

The Sacred Drum of Tepozteco

This story is part of the great narrative cycle of the gods and culture heroes of Mexico. Despite the profound influence of modern European and Christian civilization, these idols, and many other cultural patterns of the past, have not yet entirely disappeared from the Indian mind. A striking parallel to the Tepozteco story appears in Italy, where it is told of a "noodlehead." *

The Holes of Lagos

This story belongs to that most popular type of folk jest, anecdotes of stupidity, a type found in Mexico and everywhere else in the world. The standard hero of this type has acquired the obvious name, in Spanish, of Juan Bobo (John Fool). Most collections of folk tales from Spanish-speaking countries include a large section of Juan Bobo tales.

The Miracle of Our Lady of Guadalupe

"The Miracle of Our Lady of Guadalupe" is the best-known legend of Mexico. This Virgin is the patron of Mexico, and her shrine is a beautiful basilica on the edge of Mexico City, whose location was determined by her miraculous appearance on that spot, as narrated in the legend. In this basilica one can still see the portrait of the Virgin that miraculously appeared on Juan Diego's *tilma*. This was a common garment worn by all poor Indians of that time, woven from ixtle or maguey fiber. It was woven in two pieces and then sewed together down the middle. The figure on it is about three feet high. The events of the legend supposedly occurred from Saturday, December 9, to Tuesday, December 12, 1531, the latter being the date of the annual celebration of the Virgin's festival. Presumably an Indian, Antonio Valeriano, who lived at the time the miracle occurred, wrote it down in Nahuatl,

* See *Noodlehead Stories Around the World*, by M. A. Jagendorf. New York: The Vanguard Press, Inc.

but the earliest available text of this account does not appear until over a hundred years later, in its Spanish translation by Luis Lasso de la Vega, published in Mexico City in 1649.

Juan Diego was a native of the village of Cuautitlán, about nineteen miles north of the center of Mexico City, which still exists. The bishop to whom Juan brought his message was Juan de Zumárraga, a Basque Franciscan, who was named Bishop of Mexico by Charles I in 1528.

Pancho Villa and the Devil

One of the greatest folk heroes of Mexico is Pancho Villa. Stories about him still live in the minds of the Mexican people, many of them tales similar to the narrative patterns about our own folk heroes. The story we have told has a European flavor, probably due to Spanish influence.

🦋 NICARAGUA

Some persons have called Nicaragua the land of fiestas. In a way, this is a true and lovely description of the country.

In Nicaragua, saints' days are always gay days, when there is as much playing as there is praying. The people adore their saints and rejoice that they are there to help them.

All over Latin America people look upon saints in a personal manner, hence personal stories are told about them. Saints have all the characteristics of ordinary mortals, as we see in the story entitled "A Promise Made Should Be a Promise Kept."

Uncle Rabbit Flies to Heaven

Rabbit tales are as popular in South America and the Caribbean as they are in North America. Such animal tales may have come to America with the slaves brought by the Spaniards from Africa in colonial times, but it is difficult to trace the family tree of a type of tale so widely popular throughout the world.

These animal stories have parallels through the Caribbean area and elsewhere. The tale of the animal carried into the sky by a bird is an ancient and widespread motif in folk literature. Anyone wishing to trace such themes further should consult, first, Stith Thompson's Index.

A Sacred Pledge Should Not Be Broken

The holy days for Santo Domingo de Guzmán are celebrated with particular gaiety, for he is one of the most popular and favorite saints of the land.

Ha! Tío Rabbit Is Bigger

This is another amusing "why" tale known throughout the world, as well as in Latin America.

The King of the Leaves

To give an idea of how widespread some of these themes are, let us cite that of leaving first one shoe and then the other in the road, found in this story. It is found in the West Indies, among Negroes in the United States, in the French settlements of Missouri, among the Flemish in Europe, and also in Russia, Sicily, Norway, among the Finns, Lapps, Estonians, and in India.

We heard many Nicaraguan tales while visiting there, and we heard many in New York City, that storehouse of the folk tales of the world. We chose the ones in this book as good examples of what we heard.

Pablo Antonio Cuadra's fine little book of stories entitled *Tío Coyote y Tío Conejo* was of great help, as was listening to him.

🦋 PANAMA

The Spanish Donkey and the Indians

The tricking of the Indians by a Spaniard is frequently told as a jest or an anecdote to this day. Spaniards themselves often became disgusted with the greed of their fellow countrymen, and they probably invented this anecdote, "The Spanish Donkey and the Indian," to ridicule those who could think of nothing but looking for gold. In Spain the burro or donkey is the symbol of stubbornness and stupidity, thus giving the anecdote the flavor of satire it is intended to have.

Teaching a donkey to speak was often the plot of medieval stories.*

⚑ PARAGUAY

More Beautiful Than the Spider's Web

The two stories from Paraguay are among the most popular and best known in that land. You are apt to hear them there whenever you mention the word "story."

So many Indians still live in Paraguay today that almost everyone there still speaks Guaraní as well as Spanish. In Guaraní the word *ñandutí* means "white spider."

The Blue Virgin

About a thousand miles up the Paraná River lies the capital of Paraguay, Asunción—the Spanish word for "Assumption"—so named for a fort founded there in 1536 on the Day of the Assumption. Caacupé is a town of about six thousand people in Los Altos mountain range, not far to the east of Asunción, and is famed as a sanctuary of the Virgin. People come from all around to this shrine on her saint day, December 8. Paraguay is famed for its exquisitely fine *ñandutí* lace, delicate as a spider's web, which all visitors buy who visit there.

These stories obviously are deeply rooted in local tradition. We are not aware of any parallels elsewhere of the story about the lace, "More Beautiful Than a Spider's Web." However, Virgins and saints helping their people in battle, as in "The Blue Virgin," are common in saints' legends, and have been since the Middle Ages.

* See *Tyll Ulenspiegel's Merry Pranks*, by M. A. Jagendorf. New York: The Vanguard Press, Inc.

🎋 PERU

With the great Inca capital of Cuzco and the Spanish colonial capital of Lima, Peru has proved a rich storehouse of both indigenous and Spanish culture, and the folklorist who looks there can find a wealth of material.

The Greatest Wealth in the World

The story of gambling away the gold disk of the sun is known throughout the Inca country. It is as well known there as are stories of Washington and Lincoln in the United States.

Tale of the Good, Gay Lady

Almost every gentleman of Lima knows the story of La Perrichola, the gay, good-bad actress who, in the past century, set that capital agog with her antics. Both these stories can be heard anywhere, even as we heard them in our travels through Latin America.

Evil Rocks and the Evil Spirit of Peru

The Indian legend of Capusa shares with European tradition the closing up of rocks over mortals, and death or eternal disappearance of a victim, a common theme in legend and literature.

🎋 PUERTO RICO

There are many Puerto Ricans in our neighborhood, and they have told us many stories, which they say they heard from their parents and their grandparents. And, of course, that is true. We also traveled through the island of Puerto Rico and heard stories there.

The Story of the Smart Parrot and *It's Better To Be Smart Than Strong*

These two tales, which are among many we heard, are popular not only among the folk of the island of Puerto Rico but among those who have come from there to live in the United States. There are similar stories in Africa and other lands. They may have been brought to the land of the "Rich Port" from those countries, or the native wit and genius of the people of Puerto Rico may have invented them. However that may be, they are a part of the culture of that lovely island and the people who live there.

🖤 TRINIDAD

The Legend of Pitch Lake

Not far from La Brea Point in Trinidad (*brea* means pitch, tar, asphalt, in Spanish) is the famous Pitch Lake, known to every visitor to Trinidad. So is the Indian legend told here. Its pattern is similar to that of legends of sunken cities found in the folklore of Europe and Asia. We heard the tale from the driver who took us on a tour of the Island.

🖤 URUGUAY

A Sad Tale of a Silly Fellow and *Oversmart Is Bad Luck*

Both Uruguayan stories included here appear to have been imported from Europe. Such tales are common not only in Spain but also elsewhere in Europe, Africa, and Asia, as well as in North America.

We heard both from Uruguayans at the United Nations in New York City, where you can find men from nearly every part of the world.

✌ VENEZUELA

We were in Port-of-Spain, Trinidad, waiting for a plane to Caracas, Venezuela, when news came that landing would be difficult. There was a revolution afoot.

Among those waiting was a Venezuelan with whom we had become acquainted and who knew why we were going to Venezuela. He was deeply disturbed about conditions in his country. When we sat down together in the evening, we began to tell him some amusing folk stories from the United States to take his mind off his worries. This stimulated him to tell us some stories from his country, and he told us the three we have included here.

Poor Little Girl, Rich Little Girl

This story is typical of European folktale tradition, from which it was probably transplanted to Venezuela, where it has acquired some local color. Its moral and didactic tone, obviously adapted to child education here, has something of the flavor of the exempla, so popular in medieval Europe.

The Secret of the Hidden Treasure

This is a local legend, told around the Caroni River region. At some distance from the river is a town called El Callao (folk pronunciation of the Spanish word *callado*, meaning "silent"). Buried-treasure legends, of course, abound everywhere, but this one has considerable local color. Likewise, lost and hidden mines have always appealed to the folk imagination and have inspired a multitude of local tales. The curse is typically associated with such themes, and is well known in modern folklore as the curse that pursues the owner of a fabulous diamond, for example.

Juan Bobo and the Old Tiger

Juan Bobo and the Old Tiger is part of an enormous cycle of folk tales about Juan Bobo, or Silly John, many of which are found wherever Spanish is spoken in the world. However, the stories are not peculiarly Spanish, but simply the Spanish versions of that huge international stock of folk tales that tell of the incredibly stupid antics of a fool—who sometimes turns out to be not so stupid. His apparent stupidity may, in the end, show that he is uncannily clever, or perhaps he was simply fortunate enough to have good luck on his side. Sometimes it is difficult to distinguish between Silly John and Clever John.

GLOSSARY

This is a small guide to help you pronounce the Spanish, Portuguese and Indian words in this book. The phonetic spelling is not according to scientific rules but rather according to everyday sounds in English. The accent marks indicate where the words are stressed.

ay: long *a* as in *day*

ah: as in *ah;* the *a* commonly found in Spanish. The short *a* (as in *cat* in English) does not occur

ee: long *e* as in *feet*

ī: long *i* as in *ice*

o: long *o* as in *note*

oo: as in *boot*

y: as in *yacht*

A

Adiós: Ah-dyós
   (Good-by)
Aguadilla: Ah-gwah-deé-yah
   (Town in Puerto Rico)

Aire: I-ray (*i* as in *ice*)
    (Air)
Ajusto: Ah-hoós-to
    (A mountain range)
Alcalde: Ahl-káhl-day
    (Mayor, Justice of the Peace)
Amanhã: Ah-mahn-yáh
    (Port., tomorrow)
Amigo: Ah-meé-go
    (Friend)
Asunción: Ah-soon-syón
    (Paraguayan capital)
Atahualpa: Ah-tah-wáhl-pah
    (Inca ruler destroyed by the Spaniards at the time of the Conquest)

B

Bacurau: Bah-koo-ráhoo (final *au* is like *ow* in *cow*)
    (Brazilian bird)
Bahmoo: Bah-moó
    (Guiana Indian name)
Bitol: Bee-tól
    (Father of the gods in Guatemala)
Bobo: Bo-bo
    (Fool, dunce)
Bochica: Bo-cheé-kah
    (Colombian Indian name)
Boleadoras: Bo-lay-ah-dó-rahs
    (Three *bolas*—balls, mostly stones worn smooth and covered with rawhide. They are tied to three twisted rawhide thongs which are tied together. The gaucho holds one ball in his hand and swings the other two around and around. Then he lets them fly through the air aiming them at an animal or person and so entangles the legs)
Boquerón: Bo-kay-rón
    (A volcano in Honduras)
Bouqui: Boo-keé
    (Famous Haitian character)

Brea: Bráy-ah
    (Pitch, tar)
Brujo: Broó-ho
    (A conjuror, wise man, witch doctor)
Bueno: Bwáy-no
    (Good)
Buenos días: Bwáy-nos deé-ahs
    (Good day)

C

Caacupé: Kah-koo-páy
    (A Paraguayan town)
Cabeza: Kah-báy-sah
    (Head)
Cacique: Kah-seé-kay
    (Chief)
Calabash: also English word
    (gourd, or a utensil made from a gourd)
Callados: Kah-yáh-dos
    (Be silent!)
Capitaleños: Kah-pee-tah-láyn-yos
    (People who live in a capital city)
Capusa: Kah-poó-sah
    (Name of Peruvian mean old woman or witch)
Casa: Káh-sah
    (House)
Casita: Kah-seé-tah
    (Little house)
Cassava: Kah-sáh-vah
    (Tapioca)
Cataña: Kah-táhn-yah
    (A town in Puerto Rico)
Chaco: Cháh-ko
    (Paraguayan tribe)
Charque: Cháhr-kay
    (Dried meat)
Chayma: Chí-mah (*i* as in *ice*)
    (Name of Trinidad Indian tribe)

Chichimec: Chee-chee-mék
    (Name of a Mexican tribe)
Chiltota: Cheel-tó-tah
    (Ecuadorean bird)
Chirimía: Chee-ree-meé-ah
    (A Guatemalan wind instrument similar to an oboe)
Compadre: Kom-páh-dray
    (Friend, godfather, protector)
Conejo: Ko-náy-ho
    (Rabbit)
Conquistador: Kon-kees-tah-dór
    (Conqueror)
Corial: Ko-ryáhl
    (A Guiana boat)
Cortadera: Kor-tah-dáy-rah
    (A plant with sharp leaves that grows in the Andes)
Cotopaxi: Ko-to-páhk-see
    (A volcano in Ecuador)
Cuzco: Koós-ko
    (City in Peru, formerly the Inca capital)

D

De: Day
    (Of)
Del: Del
    (of the)
Día: Deé-ah
    (Day)
Dios: Dyós, as in Adiós
    (Lord, God)
Don: Don
    (Sir, sire)

E

El: El
    (Masculine article *the*)

F

Fiesta: Fyáys-tah
    (Feast, festivity)
Flores: Fló-rays (final syllable is pronounced *race*)
    (Flowers)

G

Gaucho: Gów-cho
    (Herdsman, cowboy, especially in Argentina)
Geranio: Hay-ráh-nyo
    (Geranium)
Gracias: Gráh-syahs
    (Thank you)
Guadalupe: Gwah-dah-loó-pay
    (A common place and person name)
Guaraní: Gwah-rah-neé
    (Paraguayan tribe)

H

Hermano: Ayr-máh-no
    (Brother)
Hortensia: Ohr-táyn-syah
    (Hydrangea)
Houngan: Oo-gáh (nasalized vowels)
    (Witch doctor)
Hoy: Oy (as in *boy*)
    (Today)
Humancas: Oo-máhn-kahs
    (Place name in Puerto Rico)

I

Iëre Ee-áy-ray
    (Hummingbird; ancient name for Trinidad)
Ilayacapan: Ee-lī-yah-káh-pahn
    (A kingdom in Mexico)

Ixtaccíhuatl: Ees-tahk-seé-wahtl
    (Mountain in Mexico)
Ixtli: Eést-lee
    (Maguey fiber; the century plant)

J

Janarí: Jah-nah-reé
    (Brazilian palm)
Jorge: Hór-hay
    (Spanish name for George)
Juan Bobo: Hwáhn bó-bo
    (Silly John)
Juez: Hwáys
    (Judge)

K

Kashiri: Kah-shee-reé
    (A strong drink made of honey by Guiana Indians)

L

La: Lah
    (Feminine article *the*)
Ladino: Lah-deé-no
    (A person of mixed European and Indian parentage)

M

Maba: Mah-bah
    (Guiana Indian name for the Mother Spirit of honey)
Madre: Máh-dray
    (Mother)
Maguey: Mah-gáy
    (The century plant, which yields fiber and from which a strong drink is made)

Ma-ix: Mah-eés
    (Name of a Guatemalan princess)
Maiz: Mah-eés
    (Corn)
Malice: Mah-leés
    (Famous Haitian character)
Managua: Mah-náh-gwah
    (The capital of Nicaragua)
Mañana: Mahn-yáh-nah
    (Tomorrow)
Manioc or *Mandioca:* Mahn-yók or Mahn-dyó-kah
    (Brazilian names for cassava root, used in making tapioca)
Montaña: Mon-táhn-yah
    (Mountain)
Muchas: Moó-chahs
    (Much, many)

N

Nahual: Nah-wáhl
    (Quechua Indian name of a bird)
Nahuatl: Náh-wahtl
    (The language of the Aztecs prior to the Conquest)
Ñandutí: Nyahn-doo-teé
    (Guaraní Indian name of a kind of white spider)
Navidad: Nah-vee-dáhd
    (Day of Nativity; Christmas)
Negro: Náy-gro
    (Black)
Nima-cux: Nee-mah-coóks or coósh
    (Name of Guatemalan princess)
Noche: Nó-chay
    (Night)
Nonc: Nonk (nasalized *n* as in *long*)
    (Haitian word for *uncle*)

O

Olancho: O-láhn-cho
    (A town in Honduras)

Olla: Ó-yah
  (Round earthen cooking pot)

P

Padre: Páh-dray
  (Father)
Pampa: Páhm-pah
  (A very large plain, especially in Argentina)
Papachiuchi: Pah-pah-chyoó-chee
  (A small Bolivian bird)
Paraná: Pah-rah-náh
  (A great South American river, running through Brazil and
  Argentina and forming part of the Paraguayan border)
Patio: Páht-yo
  (Courtyard)
Payaguá: Pah-yah-gwáh
  (Powerful warlike tribe in Paraguay before the Spanish Con-
  quest)
Perrichola: Pay-ree-chó-lah
  (The name of a woman in Peru)
Piñata: Peen-yáh-tah
  (Clay jar filled with toys and sweets covered with papier-
  mâché and broken by a blindfolded person during the Christ-
  mas festivals)
Poncho: Pón-cho
  (A man's jacket, made of a square piece of cloth of varied
  designs and colors with a slit in the middle through which the
  head is put. The sides fall over the shoulders, front, and back)
Popocatepetl: Po-po-kah-táy-paytl
  (A Mexican volcano)
Por favor: Por fah-vór
  (Please)
Posadas: Po-sáh-dahs
  (Lodgings; also, a series of Christmas parties, December 16-24,
  dramatizing Joseph's and Mary's journey to Bethlehem and
  asking for lodgings)
Puma: Poó-mah
  (South and Central American lion)

Q

Quédense callados: Káy-dayn-say kahl-yáh-dos
  (Keep quiet! Don't say a word!)
Querandí: Kay-rahn-deé
  (An Indian tribe in Argentina)
Quetzal: Kayt-sáhl
  (A Central American bird with brilliant plumage and a very
  long tail. The bird is the national emblem of Guatemala, since
  it cannot live in captivity and is regarded as the symbol for
  freedom. The quetzal is also the Guatemalan unit of cur-
  rency.)
Quinoa: Keén-wah
  (A kind of grain found in Bolivia and other Andean coun-
  tries)

R

Río: Reé-o
  (River)
Rosas: Ró-sahs
  (Roses)

S

San: Sahn
  (Saint)
Santo: Sáhn-to
  (Saint)
Señor: Sayn-yór
  (Mr.)
Señora: Sayn-yó-rah
  (Mrs.)
Sí: See
  (Yes)
Socorro: So-kór-ro
  (Help)
Sombrero: Som-bráy-ro
  (Hat)

Sombrerón: Som-bray-rón
    (Big hat)
Suyapa: Soo-yáh-pah
    (Town in Honduras where that country's famous shrine of
    the Virgin is located)

T

Tarde: Táhr-day
    (Afternoon)
Teosinte: Tay-o-seén-tay
    (A Guatemalan name)
Teotihuacán: Tay-o-tee-wah-káhn
    (A city in Mexico)
Tepeyac: Tay-pay-yáhk
    (A hill not far from Mexico City)
Teponaztli: Tay-po-náhst-lee
    (The drum on which the coming of the Tepozteco is an-
    nounced)
Tepozteco: Tay-pos-táy-ko
    (Ruler of the valley of Tepoztlán)
Tepoztlán: Tay-post-láhn
    (A rich valley in Mexico)
Tilma: Teél-mah
    (Poncho)
Tlaltelolco: Tlahl-tay-lól-ko
    (A district of Mexico City)
Tío: Teé-o
    (Uncle)
Toltecs: Tol-téks
    (A Mexican Indian tribe)
Tonantzin: To-náhnt-seen
    (Mexican goddess of earth and corn)
Tequendama: Tay-kayn-dáh-mah
    (A waterfall in Colombia)
Tortilla: Tor-teé-yah
    (Mexican and Central American pancakes made of finely
    mashed hominy, which in turn is made from dried corn
    soaked in lye to remove the hard covering)

Trog: Trog
    (Guiana Indian name for *barrel*)
Tzakol: Tzah-kól
    (Guatamalan name of Mother God)

V

Vieja: Vyáy-hah
    (Old)
Villa (*Pancho*)   Veé-ya (Páhn-cho)
    (The word *villa* means town; Pancho Villa was a great Mexican hero)
Viscacha: Vees-káh-chah
    (A small rodent about the size of a hare)
Viva: Veé-vah
    (Hurrah!)

Y

Yucca: Yoó-kah
    (Spanish dagger or Spanish bayonet, seen frequently in southwestern United States growing wild on the hills. The root may be eaten like a potato.)

Z

Zancudo: Sahn-koó-do
    (A small wading bird with long, thin legs)